Putt for Show

Marj Charlier

DEDICATION

To my husband and to Carly
for their patience
and love

Table of Contents

1 INCOMPETENCE 1
2 SEARCH 15
3 KURT 30
4 PRACTICE..48
5 RYNE...62
6 TRIAL 75
7 CALIFORNIA...91
8 KIM..102
9 OPENER 118
10 TERRY...133
11 QUALIFYING 150
12 GEORGIA...160
13 TOURNAMENT 172
14 AWARDS 180
15 WALLA WALLA 190
16 AUTUMN..200
THANKS...215
ABOUT THE AUTHOR 216

PUTT FOR SHOW

1 INCOMPETENCE

Lena pulled her driver out of her golf bag and walked the slight incline to the 16th tee with a stiff, humid breeze in her face. The wind blew her short hair around her visor and into her face. Otherwise, it didn't bother her.

In fact, she felt at home swinging into wind. Whenever it rained in Seattle, which was most of October through June, the wind howled out of the northwest on her home course at Suncadia on the east side of the Cascades. This Georgia golf course, home of her first USGA tournament, had been too still and hot for her taste over the past week, especially given the humidity. A little wind might cool things down a bit and drive away the pesky gnats in the air.

While her opponent, Jan, was cursing the wind behind her, Lena was more disturbed by the growl in her stomach. She was hungry. As she stepped up to the tee box, she promised herself she could have the banana she had stuffed in her golf bag if she hit a good drive.

Food? she wondered. After all she had learned about food and hunger over the past 20 years of trying to control her weight, why did she still set up food as a reward? But, struggling with the exhaustion of a tenth round of golf in six days, she needed something for motivation. With Jan up 5 to 4 with three holes left, Lena needed to take at least two of the final three holes to win the tournament. If a little banana helped, she'd take it.

Lena stuck a tee in the ground and tried to shift her focus from her stomach to the fairway ahead. In spite of the small crowd gathered around the tee box and a few onlookers scattered along the edges of the fairway, she wasn't nervous. She'd always enjoyed a gallery, even back when she was just a beginner teeing off in front of a gaggle of golfers stacked up at a tee box in the plodding pace of weekend play. Having people watch reminded her to finish pretty – the "camera finish," a former instructor called it.

But, today, she was reaching the limits of her ability to concentrate. After two days of practice rounds, two days of stroke play, and now her sixth round of match play, she was generally tired, but especially tired of playing golf. She stared down the fairway and tried to focus on a target.

Jan losing her cool didn't help. The day before, Jan had grounded her club in a bunker, and her opponent called the official's attention to it. When she was assessed the two-shot penalty, Jan lost her composure. She barely managed to hang onto her lead, and won her semi-final match on the 18th hole. Today, she had played well in the first nine holes in her match against Lena – scrambling to turn in sandy pars on two holes and reaching the rest of the greens in regulation. But, Lena could tell that she was reaching the end of her psychological reserves. Mumbling about the wind was just one of the clues.

Lena put Jan's troubles out of her mind as she lined up her target. Stepping up to her ball, she didn't take a practice swing. This late in the round, she needed to conserve energy.

Her drive was her best of the day, putting Lena within reach of the green with a short iron. She'd heard that professional players – even the most highly ranked players in the world – think they only hit two or three perfect shots a day. She'd had one other today – an approach shot to the fourth hole that rocketed crisply off of the club face and stuck six inches from the hole for a tap-in birdie. But the timing of this perfect drive couldn't have been better. It was a needed shot of confidence.

Lena had established a psychological advantage over Jan by walking with a caddie rather than riding in a cart. It had never occurred to Lena to take a cart at the event. Preparing for the tournament, she walked whenever she could. When Jan found herself in the final match with a walker, she decided to walk too, and had asked for a volunteer caddie from the country club where the tournament was played – a stranger, which wasn't ideal. Lena and her caddie, Kim, had been playing together for more than a year, and he'd caddied for her a dozen times before the tournament started.

As Lena retreated to her bag to retrieve her banana, Jan set up for her shot and, after a quick pre-shot routine, swung harder and faster than she had all day. It must have been because of the wind, Lena thought, watching the result. The extra effort had pulled Jan out of her rhythm, and her drive sliced abruptly into the rough about 180 yards down the fairway, robbing her of at least 30 yards and leaving her with a bevy of nasty pot bunkers to carry to the green.

Lena peeled her banana and headed down the fairway, pausing after a few yards to let Kim catch up with her bag on his shoulder.

"That's a nice opening for you," he said, barely speaking above a whisper so Jan wouldn't hear.

"Yeah. I hate to take advantage of a big mistake like that," Lena nodded, grinning conspiratorially. She looked sideways at Kim.

"No, you don't!" he laughed and reached over to tousle her hair above her visor.

Lena ducked away from his reach and took the last bite of her banana. "Don't mess up my hair!" she complained with her mouth full, pretending to be irritated. "What if I win this thing? My hair will look horrible in the photos!"

"It's already a mop."

"Hey, thanks, big boy. I'll remember you said that when you're asking for my autograph later."

She handed her banana peel to her caddie and scanned the sides of the fairway for her friend Terry. More than 30 spectators – mostly USGA staffers and volunteers – had followed them all day, but in the past hour, the small crowd had grown to about 50, as morning golfers finished their early rounds on other courses and joined the gallery. Other than Terry, Lena had never met any of her audience before coming to the tournament. Now she knew some of the marshals and the rules officials by name, but Terry and her caddie were her only fans.

Terry was standing under a big cypress tree to the left of the fairway holding a beverage can, her wild red hair blowing around in the wind. When Lena caught her eye, she waved with her free hand. Was she drinking a beer? Lena wondered. She fought the urge to run over and steal a swig. Instead she waved back, and Terry shouted something at her that got lost in the wind.

It was Terry who had talked her into taking some time off from the career treadmill to see how far she could go in amateur golf. Lena knew there were times that Terry had regretted it, especially when Lena was struggling with her game. But, reaching the final match in this tournament was as much a vindication of Terry's faith in her as it was of her own perseverance. And coming across the country to the tournament with Lena gave Terry a chance to escape her own romantic troubles for a few days.

Jan reached her ball, and Lena stayed discreetly behind her and waited. The rough was thick and still damp from the early morning irrigation. A shot from there called for strong forearms and wrists if Jan had any chance of reaching the green 150 yards away with an iron. Lena had seen her opponent's mastery of many tricky finesse shots in their round, but Jan's power didn't impress her. Lena was by far the bigger hitter.

Taking a solid stance and keeping her body steady, Jan gave the shot all she had. The ball flew smartly off of the face of her 8 iron, indicating she'd managed to make good contact in spite of the rugged Bermuda grass, but it landed in the rough, a foot from the edge of the bunker closest to the green. Lena and Jan both knew that a good chip out of this rough was no sure thing. Still, it only seemed polite to say "Good shot," and Lena did. Jan shot her a frown that said, "You and I both know it wasn't."

Lena eyed her own 65-yard shot to the pin. Now, she wished she had left herself a longer shot. A 100-yard full swing with her lob wedge would have been easier than a long chip over the uneven rough. She either had to try a long flop shot or take a chance that her bump-and-run would stay straight in spite of the thick grass.

"What do you think?" she asked Kim. She didn't really need his help with strategy on the course, but she asked his opinion anyway. It seemed like the right thing to do, as long as he'd come all this way to help her. Kim was a good player, but his strength was more in his Ernie-Els-like smooth swing than his touch around the greens. He wasn't a smart strategist playing his own game, either.

He went for long shots even when he didn't need to, and could let a bad shot on one hole ruin his attitude for the rest of a round.

"Go for it," he said, unhelpfully. She turned to him and grimaced. He was grinning at his meaningless advice, and it made her laugh.

But, he was right in a way. She had momentum and now was the time to play to win, not just to tie a hole. Lena pulled her lob wedge and took a practice swing, focusing on a executing a big arching approach shot – a lazy backswing, a sharp descent on the ball to produce spin and a high finish. She stepped up to the ball and let her mind go blank. When she looked up, the ball was arching high and lazily toward the pin. It landed with a dull thud two feet beyond the pin and rolled slowly back to about eight inches from the cup. "Yes!" she yelled, pumping her fist at her side. Birdies were rare and sweet, and she had likely just caught one. Terry was clapping and jumping up and down just beyond the fringe on the other side of the green.

Jan flashed Terry an irritated frown for bad spectator etiquette before she passed her ball and walked up on the green. She crouched behind the pin to study her line, walked back to her ball and took a few practice swings to get the feel of her chip. It seemed like an eternity before she stepped up to the ball and with a final glance at the pin, stubbed her club into the thick turf. The ball jumped forward a couple of inches. Disgusted, Jan picked it up. "Yours is good," she nodded to Lena and slammed her club into the bag her caddie was holding.

Lena picked up her ball and tossed it to Kim for cleaning, trying to hide her smile. Winning this tournament was now a real possibility. Sitting even with Jan at 5 and 5, she just needed to stay calm and execute solid shots. Winning one of the last two holes and tying the other was all it would take.

Terry met her as she walked off the green and patted her on the back.

"Did you see the stink eye Jan gave me?" she giggled.

"You should behave," Lena chided, giving her a quick hug before catching up with Kim and climbing up to the tee box on the 17th. But her stomach had suddenly turned from hungry to queasy, and Lena wished she could have chugged Terry's beer.

Lena wasn't used to this kind of pressure. The qualifying round she had played two weeks before was the first USGA amateur event she had played in her life. The daily USGA blog that reported on the six-day competition ignored her until the last two days of match play, which wasn't surprising. The USGA bloggers wrote about former amateur winners and LPGA or Futures Tour winners who had given up their professional status to return to families or careers, but still enjoyed competition. Jan was one who was mentioned early and often, having won the mid-amateur twice in the past 10 years. Like Lena, she had just turned 50 and was now eligible to play in the senior amateur.

But unlike Jan, Lena hadn't taken up golf in high school or college. In fact, she'd started to play in her early 40s, making her one of the rare tournament rookies to qualify for the tournament and one of the longest shots to win. Even she couldn't have imagined she'd be here in the final round.

Lena didn't take up competitive golf because she loved competition. She hated the sick feeling she got when she felt that too much was on the line. She'd taken it up because she loved to play golf and she loved her friends who played it. And no less importantly, at the point when Terry convinced her to try competing, she didn't have a lot of other appealing options. She needed something to work at. And golf was there just when she needed it most.

THE DAY after she lost her job at TrueWeb – was it only 16 months ago? – Lena woke with a hangover. The impromptu party her co-workers – suddenly, former co-workers – had thrown for her the night before, after she was escorted out of the office with her boxes of personal possessions on a cart pushed by a security guard, was gracious and generous. Lena didn't pay for a single drink, didn't pay for the cab ride home, and probably hadn't even found her keys, unlocked her door or undressed herself. Her office friend Sarah had probably helped her. She couldn't remember for sure.

There was nothing new discussed at that party. The office-mates waxed endlessly about her talents and guts. They regurgitated the gripes they had shared over the past six months about their new boss, Connie. They laughed condescendingly about management's narrow-mindedness and insecurities. Lena knew they would all go back to work the next day and put up with the same inane corporate behavior they were complaining about, and she was relieved that she wouldn't. A paycheck isn't always worth what you have to do for it.

She knew she had set the course to her own firing two weeks before it happened. That Friday, Lena had returned to the office mid-day, threw her computer bag and oversized purse on her desk and collapsed into her desk chair. She'd flown back to town after four days on the road with the CEO, visiting some of their biggest clients and industry competitors, and as usual, the trip had sapped all of her energy. The cross-country travel was more exhausting every year, but adding to the discomfort of being away from home was the growing hassle of flying. TSA pat-downs and x-ray screenings were one thing; her fellow passengers were even worse. On her flight home the night before, she was forced to share her narrow coach seat with someone who wasn't successfully accommodated by his own seat, to put it nicely. It was the second time in a week she had less than a full coach seat – what, 12 inches of space? – to herself.

It hadn't been a particularly satisfying business trip anyway. The first day in New York, she and the CEO met with a number of the company's clients, not to seal any particular deals, but to help cement relationships. She didn't expect to be more than a bystander in those meetings, and indeed, she was mostly ignored.

But over the next three days of meetings with business partners, she grew more and more perturbed at the role she played. The company and its partners were forming a public-relations and lobbying alliance to counter negative publicity about recent privacy breaches that were giving companies in their little internet niche a black eye and threatened to provoke expensive regulation. She had spearheaded the industry initiative, engaged the interested companies, created the scope for the alliance, written the white paper providing the argument for creating it, and prepared the agenda and potential action plans for the meetings. She'd written the script and follow-up Q&A her CEO used in leading the meetings, and had prepared him for the face-to-face negotiations planned for the week.

Even in these meetings, however, she realized how irrelevant others saw her to be. In most cases, she wasn't even introduced to the other CEOs and lobbyists gathered. She was assigned to a seat away from the board tables where the discussions took place. At times, she struggled even to hear the conversation. Her own CEO ignored her, and even when he couldn't answer their questions or articulate the company's position, he didn't acknowledge her presence, let alone ask for her help.

Why should she have expected anything different? It was always this way. The men in the meetings – and other than she, they were only men – were only interested in dealing with the CEO who could make decisions. She was powerless and invisible.

She was so irritated leaving the last meeting that when the CEO turned to her to report, cheerfully, "that went very well, I thought," she had no response. She was sure he thought her reaction was inappropriately cold, when in reality she was seethingly hot. She used the excuse of catching up on e-mails on her mobile phone in the limousine that took them to the airport to avoid talking to him, and when they reached the terminal, she curtly waved him toward his first-class line and abruptly got in line for coach. From her seat in the back of the plane, she successfully avoided him all of the way back to Seattle.

Lena had the nagging feeling that a more professional businesswoman would have done a better job of asserting herself in the meeting, would have found a way to retain a role in the conversation, and would have improved her status in her boss's eyes while doing so. It reminded her of the way some of her colleagues at her old newspaper job and others in her present company – people with no more knowledge or skills than she had – were able to get promotions and fit into the corporate culture with ease. She didn't have the knack. Was this how she was going to end her professional career? As a well-functioning lackey at the bottom of the management rung at the most mediocre company in America?

Looking out the window of the plane from her seat next to the bathrooms at the rear of the plane, Lena steamed. Even after all of these years, she still lacked a basic understanding of how to comport herself in the corporate world. Without exception, the successful and neatly professional women she had watched slither up the ranks had come from upper-middle-class, management-class homes, and either graduated from Ivy League schools or small, elite business colleges. Certainly there were others like her – small town kids from blue-collar families – who had mastered the manners and finesse needed to secure a rung high on the corporate ladder, but she didn't know any.

She didn't feel any better when she opened a two-month-old copy of The Economist to read an analysis of what had taken place at the World Economic Forum gathering in January in Davos. What would it be like to have been invited to attend? Perhaps to present a paper or lead a discussion? It was so far out of her league, she was embarrassed for thinking that it ever could have been a possibility. Could it have? What if she'd majored in engineering or international finance instead of journalism? What if she'd tried harder to get a coveted internship at a classy think tank or Congressman's office? What if she'd not been so eager to get out of school and pay back those student loans that haunted her back when she graduated? What if she'd figured out how to get a scholarship at an Ivy League school? What if she'd ingratiated herself with the faculty at Creighton instead of working part-time at the Dairy Queen to cut down on the amount of money she had to borrow to stay in school? Obviously, she'd had the wrong priorities and the wrong instincts early on. There was no way to fix that all now.

Returning to the view out of the plane window, she acknowledged that some people would think she was successful. She had a VP title in corporate America – and not even at a bank, where everyone had VP titles – took frequent trips with the top brass at the company, garnered a very nice salary, and had a decent severance agreement, however measly it was compared with those of her bosses, and a comfortable personal life.

But it didn't seem all that successful to her. At the same time, she hated the chip she carried on her shoulder from her lower-class background. She wanted to get over it, but reading the New York Times Business section over the past five years, she saw more and more stories about women her age and younger who were CEOs, CFOs and executive vice presidents with real power. And not just in corporate life. Successful women were starting non-profit agencies, making significant inroads into the male-dominated power elite in Washington, D.C., succeeding as avant garde artists, authors and Hollywood directors. Some had gone to Davos.

Abandoning her magazine and closing her eyes in hopes of a quick nap before they landed in Seattle, Lena tried to focus on more positive thoughts. At least she wasn't living in Nebraska anymore. At least she wasn't married to Kurt anymore. And at least she had taken up golf – an endeavor where she was rewarded for her own successes. A good shot was hers and no one else's. A great round was recorded on her scorecard, and no one else could claim credit for it. And, in spite of her late start, she was surprisingly good at it.

ON HER RETURN TO THE OFFICE that Friday, the phone message light blinked a steady beat, and a week's worth of mail threatened to slip off of top of the piles of files she had been working on before she left on her trip. As she stared at the mess on the desk in front of her, she questioned whether she had the energy to dig into it today. Maybe she'd go home, crawl back into bed and wait for the jetlag to work its way out of her system before coming back. Of course, that was impossible. She simply had too much to do.

Lena pushed her shoulder-length brown hair behind her ears and set to work. She unpacked her laptop and snapped it into the docking system on her desk while accepting drive-by greetings from her office neighbors. A few dropped by to roll their eyes and tell her the latest inscrutable thing Connie had done while she was gone. The woman had been busy, it seemed, interfering with projects that had been proceeding apace just fine without her input. Of course, her input improved nothing; it just added detours and extra work, but she apparently needed to interfere to prove her worth. After six months, no one in the department could figure out why she had been hired in place of the former VP of communications, who was fired to make room for her. She couldn't write an e-mail without calling a consultant. She knew nothing about the company's financial results, and couldn't read an income statement. She didn't seem to have a strategic bone in her body, and wasn't a good public speaker. What was it that the CEO had seen in her?

Lena clicked on the computer and, while it booted up, picked up her coffee cup and headed for the lunch room down the hall, nearly running over Tahi Svengh as she turned out of her doorway.

"Connie wants to know if you noticed the appointment she put on your calendar for 3 o'clock this afternoon," Tahi said in a near whisper, fairly cowering against the hallway wall after their near collision.

"Yes, I accepted it yesterday on my Blackberry. Didn't that come through?" Lena asked, striding past the small Asian man. She hated this habit of Connie's. The woman would send an e-mail and then run over to Lena's office to announce that she'd just sent her an e-mail. Or she would schedule a staff meeting on Outlook and then send Tahi around to tell everyone about it. Who had time for all of this redundancy?

Lena ran into three more co-workers between her office and the coffee pot, which ate up another 20 minutes, so that by the time she returned to her desk she'd lost a half hour of her afternoon to greetings and small talk. Lena knew this kind of interaction was important to keep a team together. But she didn't like to spend any more time in the office than she had to, and if she could focus efficiently on the tasks at hand, she could keep her in-office time to eight hours, and have more time for the rest of her life. The less she schmoozed with office mates, the more time she had for real friends, golf and enjoying her home in Suncadia.

Still, Sarah, her next-door colleague, tweaked her sympathy. Sarah had been married to the love of her life, a good-looking but lazy drinker who worked a job that prized his ability to play softball more than his ability to work spreadsheets or close deals. Sarah wanted children, and her husband didn't, and finally after eight years of suffering with a bad marriage and dashed hopes, she'd divorced him, married a man of few admirable qualities, had the children she wanted so desperately, and then ended up as a single mother.

Whenever Sarah wanted to chat, Lena found time for her, even if it meant working an hour late in the day to get a script written. Lena thought of it as a way of giving back to the mothers of the world, who did their part in creating the next generation, while she avoided it. And, she sincerely liked Sarah, even though the woman had sabotaged advancement in her career for the sake of breeding a couple of fast-food workers of the future. She couldn't help but recall the line from the movie, Caddyshack – "the world needs ditch diggers, too" – when Sarah despaired over the low ambitions her now-teenaged children displayed.

Still, many years ago, Lena had learned that people like you if they believe you like them, so she had worked on being friendlier, less curt and, well, less Type A in the office, and not just to Sarah. She tried to take an interest in her co-workers' hobbies, pets and families. She assiduously remembered birthdays and anniversaries and took the time to deliver cards and flowers personally, not just leaving them on desks to be discovered. Like with Sarah, she found it a bit harder to discuss their children, which never held much fascination for her, but she enjoyed talking about books or movies. As long as the conversations were short.

Before attacking her e-mail inbox, Lena scrolled through the online Wall Street Journal and New York Times. There was a chance that her meeting with Connie in the next half hour would involve some financial news that Connie needed her to explain so that she could feel comfortable talking about it with the CFO or other executives. Lena had read very few newspapers over the past week, barely finding time to attend all the meetings they scheduled in New York, sitting through late-night dinners with customers and briefing the CEO on the agendas and attendees prior to all of their meetings.

But a quick scan of the news websites revealed nothing earth shattering happening in the business world.

Lena listened to a dozen phone messages to fill her time before her meeting with her boss. As usual, about half of the messages were from vendors, selling consulting services that ranged from industry analysis to language translation. She quickly deleted those. The other half were from people inside the company who wanted help with something, writing business proposals, writing the overview for the 10K and answering media questions – the latter was something Connie should have been handling, but refused, stating it was below her station.

Lena's Outlook pinged. It was time to meet with her boss. She was just starting to push back her chair when Connie walked in and stood in her doorway.

"Are we meeting in here?" Lena asked.

Connie nodded, looking anxious. She was underweight from obsessive and manic workouts in the gym, and her thin face was lined with stress that added 10 or 15 years to her age. Lena guessed that she was probably only about 40, but side-by-side, strangers usually guessed that Connie was the elder of the two. Maybe it was because she was the boss, but Lena surmised it was really due to Connie's lack of collagen. Staying skinny isn't necessarily the best way to age and watching Connie from afar in the office cafeteria or in meetings always made Lena feel better about her excess weight.

"Do you want to close the door?" Lena stood up so she wouldn't have to tilt her neck to look up at the woman. Connie habitually walked into people's offices and stood above them in a kind of control-by-body-English that irritated Lena.

"No. I wanted to talk to you about letting me know when and where you're going from now on before you leave," Connie said. "I had no idea where you were the past few days." Lena assumed the open door served Connie's purpose of broadcasting the same message to the rest of her staff as her voice carried down the hallway. And, it demonstrated to her direct reports that she was the boss of Lena.

"I'm responsible for this department's travel budget, and you need to get approval from me before traveling," Connie continued. "And I need to know who you are traveling with and what the purpose is of the trip."

Lena's close relationship with the CEO had always been an undercurrent in the rocky dynamic between the two women. Lena spent more time with all of the C-level executives than Connie did because she needed to know what was on their mind and catch their syntax so she could replicate it for them in their speeches and conference call scripts. While Connie reported directly to the CEO, it was Lena who travelled with him, sat in on the strategy sessions and played golf with him. Before Connie had come to the company, Lena had managed her own schedule, traveled when she needed to and took vacation days when the work demands allowed her to. She wasn't accustomed to asking permission, and she wasn't interested in beginning to do it now. On the other hand, if it meant getting Connie out of her office sooner, she could at least pretend to concede.

"Sure," she nodded, glancing back at her computer screen, which had just beeped to let her know she was overdue for her meeting with Connie. "I'll be sure you know my schedule from now on," carefully skipping the subject of pre-approval.

Connie didn't move from her pose in the doorway. Clearly, there was more.

"What else?" Lena asked, turning away to hide her irritation.

Connie paused for a minute, as if she were building up courage to continue. "I also wanted to talk because I don't think things are going very well between us," Connie said.

Lena sighed and dropped into her desk chair in exasperation. She really disliked this woman and was in no mood to placate or humor her more. She stared at her desk and took three deep breaths. Then, looking Connie directly in the eye, she stated in a steady voice — one that they both knew would carry down the hallway to her co-workers — "That's because I think you're incompetent."

Immediately, Lena knew that she'd just said something that was going to get her fired, but saying it felt so right. She remembered something from a philosophy class in existentialism she had taken as an undergraduate. She couldn't remember what philosopher they were studying, but he had said that the way to happiness was to live your life as if you would have to live the very same life over and over and over again throughout eternity. If she had to work for this woman through eternity, she'd prefer an early mortality.

Connie stood with her mouth open. She didn't ask for details or an explanation. She didn't argue. She stood in the doorway and her face turned from shocked to angry, her jaw taking on a hard, angular edge. She turned and stomped away. Lena heard her door slam shut down the hallway. She also heard Sarah next door snickering.

It took only two weeks for HR to help Connie come up with a "going in a new direction" excuse for letting her go — an excuse that would relieve her boss of developing a "performance improvement plan" and going through the sham of a process that was used to make firings withstand lawsuits, not really to help an employee "improve." Lena was so relieved to be finished with the woman and collect her severance that she didn't even consider appealing her case to the CEO.

2 SEARCH

THE MORNING AFTER she was fired, Lena pulled back the covers to feel the cool May marine layer that Seattle TV weather personalities called "nature's air conditioning." The queasy feeling in her stomach was mostly from the hangover, but she also recognized a bit of anxiety. What to do? She didn't have to get up. She didn't have to do anything. It had been years since she hadn't worked. She'd never even quit a job before without having another one to start within a couple of weeks.

She lay still, accepting the anxiety and assuring herself there was no reason to panic. Even in the harsh light of the day-after, she wasn't worried about money; she had saved a good share of her bonuses over the past four years. Much of what she had put away was locked up in her 401(k), untouchable until she was nearly 60, but she had enough in liquid savings to get by for some months. Even if she was still not working next May, she could borrow from her brokerage firm, using the 401(k) as collateral. But, she resolved on the spot that she wouldn't touch her retirement savings. Since she had entered the full-time workforce at 22, she'd been repeatedly, subtly brainwashed by the sales reps for the retirement fund managers – Smith Barney, UBS, Fidelity – into believing that Social Security wouldn't be solvent by the time she retired. If she didn't want to die on the streets or in a shabby, subsidized nursing home, she had better never touch that precious 401(k).

Her anxiety in check, Lena rose, slipped on a robe and slippers and went down the stairs of her loft to her tiny kitchen. She put a teapot on the stove to heat water for her French press – an affectation her friends teased her about ("What's wrong with drip?") – sliced a bagel and dropped it into the toaster. She opened her condo door and retrieved the New York Times – another affectation, her friends said ("What's wrong with the Seattle Times?"). A few minutes later, she poured a cup of coffee, spread peanut butter on the bagel and arranged them and the Times at the kitchen counter bar. It was her morning routine, and it seemed unnecessary to let a little thing like losing her job ruin her favorite part of the day.

She started with the international stories, which had once been her favorite part of the newspaper – at least until the Iraq war and subsequent Middle East rebellions shifted more than half of the coverage to that part of the world. She preferred stories about Latin America – they seemed so much more relevant, so much closer to home. Skipping over the bad news about the war, she found a story about Quechua ki'pus – mysterious knotted strings that were used as a form of writing or accounting by ancient Peruvians. She should have been an archeologist like she had hoped to become when she first applied for college admission, she mused for the millionth time in her adult life. Sure the pay would suck. But if she never had become accustomed to an upper-middle class salary, would she miss it?

What had attracted her at to archeology was a fear – more like panic – at the idea of being normal. Average, normal, boring. That's how it felt growing up in what she thought of as normal, boring, conventional, conservative small-town Nebraska. Like a life sentence. And while "normal" was her greatest fear, there was little she could do as a child or teenager to escape it. Her family's resources left no allowance for eccentricity. Certainly, she couldn't express herself through fashion, about which she was nearly unaware, as were most of the kids who went to school with her. Nor was she a political or social rebel. Her father didn't abide political conversation that veered from the standard Republican fare, and his authority was complete. Her opinions were neither sought nor tolerated if they did not align with his.

She read magazines and books at the school library that gave her plenty of access to ideas she didn't encounter in her classrooms or at home. But she learned to censor herself, and even after her parents were gone, she retained a shy, restrained style of personal expression that she didn't shed until well after college.

When she graduated from high school, pragmatism outweighed romance, and a journalism major replaced her study in archeology. In some ways, she thought, journalism is anthropology – just contemporary and domestic, not ancient and foreign. And, journalism gave her the opportunity to be different in a subtle way – as an outsider, not an insider. She never had to clap at political speeches or grovel before CEOs. She could stand back from the crowd, and she didn't have to join any organization or church or political party.

She really hadn't changed much from the outsider perspective over the past 30 years. Being from rural Nebraska, it was pretty easy to feel like she was outside-looking-in at the hip, clued-in, sophisticated world. When she left journalism and Denver for a corporate job in Seattle, it wasn't to switch to a more normal, insider's life, it was to avoid the spotlight that her marriage to Kurt had thrust on her.

Finished with the paper and her bagel, Lena stood and put her plate in the sink and refilled her coffee. She shuffled 10 feet into the living room and sat down in her robe, looking out over the warehouse roofs that stretched out in front of her. What would she do with her day? Unemployment didn't feel quite real yet – it felt more like a day off. She should probably be wondering what she was going to do with the month or months or year or years it might take to find a new job, but she couldn't tolerate pushing her thoughts any further out into the future.

She'd felt this way in the aftermath of Kurt's arrest seven years earlier. She wallowed for months in uncertainty, unable to make a decision or change any aspect of her life. Awaiting trail, he sat in jail, ineligible for bail. She stayed in the same bungalow she had bought before their marriage, she held on stubbornly to a job she had grown to hate, she didn't buy new clothes. She lived day to day and found it impossible to think about the future. Once the trial was over, though, and Kurt was sentenced to life in prison, she had forced herself to make radical moves – divorce, quitting her job, selling the house and moving to a new city. Combined with his long sentence, the physical move to the Northwest, she was convinced, would put enough distance between Kurt and her that she'd never have to deal with him again.

Once she had moved to Seattle and started the speechwriting job at TrueWeb, though, she settled into a day-to-day, anonymous, mediocre corporate existence. She became horribly normal – except for one thing: she never thought much about her future. Planning for the future was for people with kids – people who had to support a family, pay for a new TV-room addition, save for college and, eventually, beg for grandchildren. But, for Lena, the future just looked like more of the same. The exciting, adult life she had once imagined had not materialized, and somehow she had settled for mediocrity. The mediocrity might have gone on for much longer at work, but then Connie had arrived, and Lena had begun to think about moving on. The latest trip to New York with the CEO only added to her discontent with how things had turned out.

Now, she'd done herself a favor, getting herself fired. Shaking things up was no longer an option – it had happened.

Lena sat on the couch, stared out the window at Capitol Hill in the distance and let her mind wander. The phone startled her out of her reverie, and she glanced at the display. It was the CEO. She didn't want to talk to him. She didn't want him to try to convince her to come back, or to try to explain why he supported Connie's decision. She really didn't want to know what he wanted. Instead, she felt much like she had when Kurt had been jailed – a relief that her only rational option now was radical change. The corporate, mainstream life had betrayed who she had always thought she was – someone different, someone not so "normal."

Now, she should she get started on the rest of her life. Did she need to find another job that paid as well, or could she finally take the plunge into the non-profit world where she could be more of an eccentric? She tried to do some quick math in her head to figure out how long her retirement savings would last, but decided she could worry about that later. This was her first day "off" and she was going to play.

In one quick hour, she showered, got dressed, packed a small overnight bag and retrieved her golf clubs out of her storage unit. She drove over the mountains to Walla Walla, found a bed and breakfast, and spent three days touring wineries, playing golf, reading and drinking wine late into the night. The rest of her life had begun, and if it was this much fun, that would be more than fine with her.

FOR TWO WEEKS, Lena managed to put off focusing on her future or looking for a job. She shopped for new golf clothes, cooked some time-consuming recipes, played golf at Suncadia, had her hair colored, bought some new rugs for her Suncadia Lodge condo and cleaned out the closets and storeroom in her loft in Seattle. It was refreshing to finally get a chance to do – at a leisurely pace – all of the errands she used to have to squeeze into the evenings after work or to discipline herself to do on weekends when she'd rather have been playing golf or traveling.

But after two weeks, she grew impatient with the nagging feeling that she needed to figure some things out – like exactly how far her current savings would take her. How long could she extend this time off, if she had to, by selling her Lodge unit at Suncadia? By giving up her golf membership at Suncadia? By cutting how much she spent on wine and food at the grocery store, or how many books she bought for her Kindle?

Finally, on a rainy Saturday morning in Seattle, she sat down at her computer and created two spreadsheets. What, she wondered, did people do before Excel? Perhaps her head worked less well than other people's in juggling multiple options and complex data. But, she loved the control and clarity she achieved by putting big questions to a spreadsheet.

The first spreadsheet she started on was a budget that would help her see how long her savings would last without taking harsh measures, and then how much more time a few harsh measures would buy her. It took about an hour to finish, as she toggled back and forth between her online brokerage and bank statements and the new spreadsheet. At the end of the hour, she figured that if she decided to, she could stay unemployed for at least two years without worrying about making her payments or selling either of her condos. Any more time off would require cutting back on her lifestyle and golf – or borrowing against her 401(k).

With that figured out, she started a second spreadsheet that listed the pros and cons of different kinds of jobs, going back to school, or taking on a volunteer position for a while. It was crude, but she needed to organize her thoughts and a little objective structure helped. She set up four rows titled "Financial," "Fun,"

"Future," and "Difficulty." Then, she made five columns for "Non-Profit," "New job – same profession," "New job – different profession," "Retire," and "Take a year off."

She spent two hours estimating whether the financial impact of each decision deserved a plus-2, a minus-2 or something in between, and then estimated the same values for whether the choice would be fun, set her up for a better or worse future, and how hard it would be to pull off. Then she added up the numbers in each column.

She frowned. Not only was she proving to herself what a nerd she was by creating a spreadsheet to make a decision, she didn't like the result. While it registered fairly low on the "fun" parameter, it was clear that finding a new job – whether in the same profession or a different one – was the overall best choice – especially at her age. Another job would make her retirement more certain, cover health insurance costs for at least a couple of years, hold more doors open for the future and wouldn't be as difficult as trying to move into the non-profit world where hiring managers often looked down on people who had spent their lives in "corporate America." Even if returning to a corporate job meant returning to a "normal" life, it would only be for a few years. Then, more financially secure, she could veer off the straight and narrow and do something different.

The next morning, she drove up I-90 to Suncadia from Seattle in the rain. It was rare, even in Seattle, for rain to last a full two days this late in the spring, and Lena was eager to get over the pass and on the sunny side of the Cascades for the first time in a week. She called Terry from her cell phone as she crossed over the pass, and in spite of the fact it was almost 11 a.m., the call woke her friend up. Terry agreed to get out of bed and hustle fast enough to meet Lena at the Brick in Roslyn for lunch in a half-hour.

They ordered burgers and fries and a pitcher of beer before Lena told her about her plans to look for a new job.

"Whatever would you want to do that for?" Terry was clearly surprised. Lena had told her just a week earlier that she was thinking of taking the rest of the summer off to travel, relax and play golf. Terry was a big fan of Lena's better-than-average golf game and, unlike Lena, she was constantly struggling financially. If she'd had Lena's resources, she'd not only avoid employment, but she'd be a lot more grateful for the ability to be a lady of leisure.

Terry had quit her job after a divorce that soured her not only on her husband's hometown of Seattle, but also for all lawyers in the world – including those she was working for as a paralegal. She used the money she got from her half of the house she and her ex-husband had built in Seattle to buy a tiny miner's cabin and a small storefront in Roslyn. She moved up to the little town with her golden retriever, Rex, five years earlier.

Roslyn was once a coal mining town. At the end of the 19th Century, hundreds of immigrants from dozens of European and African countries blasted and shoveled underground tunnels and filled the taverns of the mountain town, turning it into a bustling, dirty, disheveled jumble of cabins and shops. The mines declined in quality and profitability by the 1930s, and although the final operation didn't shut down until 1963, the town had already declined in population and stagnated as a shabby but not charmless small town.

The filming of the exterior shots for the TV series Northern Exposure in the early 1990s brought some prosperity to Roslyn, but it was short lived, and did nothing to upgrade the long-term prospects for the town. Then, ten years later, a group of developers outlasted the state's outspoken and powerful environmental groups and got permits to start building Suncadia, a golf resort catering to sun-starved Seattle residents just outside of town. Up went a huge lodge, a smaller inn, a family recreation center and winding trails that wove in and around huge log cabins, woodsy mansions and three golf courses. Terry watched it happen, and believed that prosperity for Roslyn was just around the corner. It would be a great place to start a small business. And, an extra benefit: there wasn't much up on that side of the Cascades to remind her of Seattle.

Lena had met Terry on Prospector, the first public golf course at Suncadia, two years after Lena had moved to Seattle and months after she started playing golf with some friends from work. Lena bought a unit in the Lodge at Suncadia shortly after that and after prices had tumbled with the recession. She'd probably still paid too much for it, given that the real estate market continued to fall and the developer was planning a fire-sale auction of its unsold units, but she was willing to take the financial hit without a grudge because she could afford it, because she craved the sun on the

Suncadia side of the Cascades, and because she fell in love with the golf course.

The course was pretty hard for beginners and for high-handicappers like Lena or Terry. But that first day they played together, it didn't bother them. They laughed and trash-talked their way through the trees and sand traps, becoming fast friends before finishing the front nine. After the round, they moved from the course to the bar by the pro shop and finally to the Brick in Roslyn as the day turned into night.

Terry, meanwhile, had opened a shop in the commercial building she bought in Roslyn, selling pottery, hand-knitted garments, quilts and turned wooden bowls made by herself and other local artists. In the past year, she had started selling wines from the Columbia Valley in the eastern part of the state, and business had been better than she expected. She could carry many wines from small wineries that didn't distribute in Seattle or Portland, and yet had a loyal following among wine connoisseurs, including the new, wealthy homeowners at Suncadia.

Still, there wasn't a time when Lena and Terry got together that Terry wasn't on the verge of declaring bankruptcy and having to give up her small-town mountain life. She worked as many hours as possible, keeping the store open six days a week and from 10 a.m. to 9 p.m. on weekends, and if she had a group that lingered past 9 at the wine tasting bar, she'd stay open until they sauntered out. But she barely broke even and hadn't saved any money for retirement since she'd moved out of the city.

Of course, it didn't help that she loved to go out drinking with friends, and always had to have the latest in fashion.

"I really think you should take some time off and spend the rest of the summer up here," Terry said. "You've never met most of my friends here in Roslyn, and I'd love to have a little help at the wine shop on weekends. You could play golf all week and help me out on Friday and Saturday nights."

Terry was nearly whining, and Lena crossed her index fingers in front of her friend's face. "Down, witch!" she said, mockingly. "You try to trick me into taking time off so I can work for you for nothing!"

"Yeah, well, you don't have to help out. I just thought it would be fun," Terry laughed, recognizing how selfish she had sounded.

"Oh, I'd love to, don't get me wrong. I'd love to live more like you do," Lena said, pouring their first glasses of beer from the pitcher the waitress had finally delivered to their spots at the bar. "I'd love to have a job without a boss like you, but if I did, I would be living in your cabin and not in my condo."

"What's wrong with my cabin? Is it that bad?" Terry looked hurt.

"No, of course not. It's not that. It's that I have none of your nesting instincts or Bohemian aesthetics. I'm a house snob. I'll admit it. And, I like playing golf every weekend and vacationing in Palm Springs in the winter. You have a lot of friends and a very full life here. It's just different."

The two women sat at the antique bar with their beers for a few minutes in silence. How had they become friends, anyway? Sometimes Lena was reminded of how little they had in common, really. Terry was far more gregarious and had at least a dozen close friends that she saw at least once a week somewhere in Roslyn. She was more creative, too, and had an eye for art that made her little gallery a community treasure. And while Lena had saved money for retirement and had an easier time paying her bills, Terry didn't fret about her likely end-of-life financial disaster. She simply refused to think that far ahead.

Lena believed one of the reasons they had become such fast friends was that they both lacked any significant family connections or obligations. None of their parents had survived their 30s, and while Lena was an only child, Terry was nearly so. Her two brothers were so much older than she was that she never grew close to them. She had four nieces whom she barely knew and who seemed to get along fine without knowing her. In the three years she had known Terry, Lena had never met any of her family, and it was never a topic of conversation for Terry.

Other than that similarity, Lena concluded that there was no way to know why they got along so well. But, she knew from her own experience that if two people could have long conversations and relax together, they could be friends. It didn't matter if they lived differently, voted differently or read different books. As long as they spoke the same language and shared a sense of humor, they could share what was going on in their heads in a compassionate way. If they shared some politics, some hobbies, some favorite movie directors or authors, so much the better.

"So what do you think you're going to do? Where're you going to look?" Terry asked, turning toward Lena and resting her head on her beer-free hand. Her elbow knocked her bar coaster off of the bar and it landed in the flowing spittoon at their feet. Long just a historical artifact, the spittoon hadn't been used for its original purpose for years, but neither woman was interested in retrieving the cardboard circle anyway.

"I don't know yet. And I don't really want to think about it yet," Lena said. She changed the subject. "How's Rick?"

"Arghh…." Terry hid her face in both hands and shook her head, elbows still resting on the bar. Finally she turned back to Lena and told her how the latest romantic interest – a ski instructor at Snoqualmie Pass and a part-time postman at the Roslyn Post Office – had ended.

Not much different from her other short-lived romantic forays, it had collapsed over the weekend in a high-decibel argument over how much the man drank and how much she despised drinking and driving. The fact that it happened out on the street in front of her cabin at 2 in the morning added to the drama, but otherwise it didn't vary much from the endings of most of Terry's other relationships.

"Why do you try?" Lena asked. Lena couldn't empathize with the drive to pair-up that kept Terry trying out boyfriends. Early on in their friendship, Terry had nixed Lena's theory that Terry would be uncomfortable with a constant companion in her house because she had grown up as a de-facto only child. "Why not just live alone?"

"I do live alone, except for Rex. I don't like it," Terry said. "I don't know how you do it. I don't like not having sex. I don't like eating all of my meals alone. I don't want to grow old alone."

"You eat out with friends almost every night," Lena countered. "Don't tell me you eat alone."

"You know what I mean. I want to sit down at my own dining room table and have dinner and talk about the icky boss – his, of course – and retire to the living room to watch the evening news like everyone else," Terry said. They'd talked about it dozens of times. And, as usual, Lena countered, "Everyone else doesn't do that."

"I know, I know." Terry whined. "But it's what I want. I just can't seem to find it."

"Well, it does limit the possibilities when you live in a place like this," Lena said, and the two of them simultaneously rotated their heads to survey the other patrons in the bar. It was Sunday afternoon, and without any football on the bar TVs, the place was deserted but for a couple of aging hippies playing pool and two middle-aged Suncadia couples slumming with burgers and beers at the town joint.

"Yeah, I know," sighed Terry. "But I do love it here. And eventually the right guy has to move to town. I did. Why not my soul-mate?"

LENA STAYED in her condo at Suncadia Sunday night, and drove back into Seattle with the rush hour traffic on Monday morning. Starting the next day, she did what the second spreadsheet recommended and started to look for a job that she hoped would last for at least a couple of years.

At first, it was exhilarating, considering all the different paths she could take in the next iteration of a career. She'd been a writer all of her life, but she thought that marketing and sales would give her a chance to stretch her skill set. She liked traveling and meeting new people. She was good at weaving a tale and making convincing arguments, both which she thought would be useful in selling 401(k) plans to employers or business insurance to companies.

Or perhaps a job in a venture capital firm helping to evaluate potential acquisitions and investments. She'd been writing about corporate M&A either as a reporter or for the internet company for at least 15 years. She had pulled all-nighters with company executives many times in the past five years, looking at deals and comparing investments in product development to acquisitions of new businesses. She had a skill for articulating and simplifying synergies, and a nose for underserved market niches that turned out to be great opportunities. She'd never even considered how much her last job had strayed beyond speech writing until she looked back and started to write her resume.

The first two days of her job search, she cruised the job sites of the companies she thought she might enjoy: Nordstrom, REI, Starbucks, Amazon, Expedia, Russell Investments, the Bill and Melinda Gates Foundation. She steered clear of Microsoft; she didn't want to suffer the hour-plus commute across the lake to Redmond, and she had enough unhappy acquaintances at the software giant who were buried under the pile of bureaucratic detritus that seems to collect at huge companies and squelch innovation and energy. And the culture had a reputation as rapacious.

At the same time that she searched, she worked on her resume, stealing ideas from the job postings she was reading, and beefing up some of the descriptions of her former jobs to highlight the strategic nature of her work and the concrete results employers were seeking. But when she sat down to write the "cover" letters – they would all be electronic these days, of course – she realized that each of the job descriptions was amazingly specific: You MUST have five years of experience in evaluating business acquisition targets in a private equity firm. You MUST have a Series 21 license and at least two years in sales and marketing at a Fortune 500 financial firm. You MUST have a BA in economics, mathematics or accounting and 10 years' experience in business analysis for a biotech company.

How did anyone qualify for these jobs? she wondered. Was there no room for career change anymore? If we all have to work until we're 70, how can we pick the one thing we'll do for the rest of our lives when we're 22?

Then she started to notice another trend: More than half of what looked like decent mid-level jobs were being advertised as "internships" – which she took to mean "don't expect to get paid well, if at all" and "old people need not apply." Lena didn't like it, but the reason was obvious: Why should companies pay good salaries to experienced, well-rounded, mature adults when they can harvest the energy and willingness of the freshly minted MBAs to work for nothing more than experience and a job listing on their resumes?

Frustrated, Lena started reading blogs from recruiters and others who claimed to offer advice about changing careers or finding jobs when you're more "seasoned" (read: older) and therefore less marketable. Networking was the key, they all said, and so she began making a list of friends and business associates and their phone numbers. Calling them over the next two weeks, however, turned out to be depressing. It was as if they were afraid that unemployment was a disease they might catch by talking to her.

"Hi I'm really busy right now," more than one of her network "friends" said, not even pausing between the salutation and the excuse for the quick dismissal.

"Sure," Lena answered. "I'm just doing some networking to see what opportunities there might be out there for me and who you might suggest I talk with."

"I'll call you back in a couple of days when things settle down," her "network" would tell her. Of course, they never did. And except for those who were also looking for jobs, all of her LinkedIn contacts responded to her e-mails the same way – with silence. If everyone was so busy, how could there be so many unemployed people in America? she wondered. It appeared as if corporate America should have been hiring like crazy and giving these folks a little time to take a phone call now and then.

After a while, Lena began to wonder where the idea came from that "networking" was the best way to find a new job. Perhaps it only worked if you started it long before you lost your job – keeping lines of communication open with ex-colleagues and former employers even when there didn't seem to be any practical reason for it. But she had made friends with many former employees at her last company, and it occurred to her that fellow employees who had been let go in the company's frequent management changes might be good targets for networking as well. Wouldn't they be happy to help a fellow aggrieved party? she thought.

She culled through her old contacts from work; she'd kept a copy at home as a spreadsheet for weekend crises. Her eye stopped on the entry for a former business analyst who had landed a job at Starbucks, and since then had met with some of her colleagues who had lost their jobs in layoffs over the past year. Riley had been let go in a very early round of layoffs, way back at the beginning of the recession. Lena called a couple of friends and got her new number. Riley was glad to sit down with her over coffee, she said, and discuss opportunities at Starbucks.

Lena dressed casually in straight pants and a tunic for their appointment, not wanting to look too eager or desperate by wearing a suit. They met at the Starbucks in the first floor of Riley's new building first thing in the morning.

Riley had always been a talker when they worked together. She'd stop by Lena's office and stand in the doorway with her hands behind her back, leaning on the door jamb as if she had all the time in the world and didn't realize Lena might actually have work to do. But the day of their meeting at Starbucks, she was a different person.

"I've only got a couple of minutes," Riley announced when she approached Lena's table at a near-run.

"Can I buy you a cup of coffee or a latte?" Lena asked, standing up to take Riley's strangely formal handshake.

"No, thanks. I've really got to get back upstairs pretty quickly."

Lena sat back down across from her and, taking Riley's cue, skipped the small talk. "Did you look at my resume?" she asked, pulling a hard copy out of her bag and handing it to Riley.

"Yes, I looked at it and I passed it along to our recruiters. But, I have to be honest. I don't see a lot of opportunity here for you," she said, bluntly, pushing the resume back across the table. "We tend to only hire people who have been doing exactly the same jobs as we're looking to fill. I don't see any speech-writing jobs on the horizon here. Our management team doesn't do a lot of public speaking."

Hum, Lena thought. She was certain she had seen news coverage of a number of Howard Schultz appearances lately, but now was not the time to argue that point. "But, I have many skills beyond speech writing, as you know," she argued instead. "I've worked on strategy, I've done a lot of marketing and due diligence on acquisitions, although perhaps that isn't clear enough on my resume," Lena said, glancing down at the copy in front of her. "And you're doing a different job here than you had before," she pointed out, hoping that she didn't sound confrontational or argumentative.

"Not really," Riley countered, tossing her long blonde hair behind her shoulder. "You only knew me in my latest role, but I've managed operations at a number of companies before. I have some pretty valuable experience," she sniffed as she looked at her watch.

Lena didn't know what to say. It suddenly occurred to her that Riley really wasn't eager to help Lena – nor maybe her other unemployed former colleagues, either. She was eager to gloat. She'd been one of the first to be let go in the downsizing and management changes at TrueWeb, and she seemed to relish the fact that others had lost their jobs now, too. Maybe she felt that Lena should have lost hers long before she did.

Lena replaced her resume in a file in her bag and stood up, ready to end the charade. Her chair squealed on the tile as she pushed it back, startling the couple at the table next to them.

"Well, thanks for meeting with me, although I don't really know why you agreed to do this when you don't think I have a chance here," she said, straightening her tunic and gulping down the dregs of her latte.

"Oh, I'm always happy to try to help," Riley said disingenuously, moving toward the escalator so quickly that she had to reach back toward Lena to take her handshake. And with a little wave, she was gone.

Asshole, thought Lena. She hoped Riley got enough joy out of that one-upmanship to justify the five minutes she took away from her work that morning.

3 KURT

Lena's quest for a job continued uninterrupted over the next month, but her exasperation with the lack of prospects and constant rejections turned May into one of the most humiliating months of her life. It was far worse than reading about successful Davos participants; she was now likely to have to step down far, far below her already mediocre career.

The hardest part was accepting the fact that she'd gone from merely normal – bad enough – to being one of the millions of unemployed, decently skilled, overly ambitious, jobless, middle-aged corporate rejects seeking to extend their employment long enough so that they could limp into retirement without whittling down their retirement funds too early.

She considered returning to journalism as an option. But long before she left the newspaper in Denver after Kurt's messy trial, she had grown to hate reporting. On the one hand, her stories were supposed to come off as unbiased. She wasn't supposed to favor one side of the story over the other. Readers constantly complained about the "liberal" media – except those who complained about the "conservative" media. But while she was expected to look unbiased, she was also supposed to have a new theory – a point of view, one editor called it – on every news item or feature story she wrote.

The struggle between not taking sides and clearly expressing a particular point of view was a balancing act she found untenable, and she knew she wasn't pulling it off very well. She knew that every story she wrote naturally leaned one way or the other, and the stress of having to face the recriminations of the unfavored party the day of publication kept her awake at night. She was tired of trying to pretend like every subject in a story was equally laudable and legitimate, and she was sick of trying to pretend that she'd discovered some new, deep truth every time she wrote about a debate on the Senate floor or the joint-committee wrangling over a bill.

Besides, the current state of the newspaper industry was worse than bleak. Most of her former journalism friends had been laid off and were scrambling for any kind of work, including the jobs she was looking at. What friends she still had in the media were spending their days editing videos of their interviews and posting either extemporaneous superficial blathering or pseudo-intellectual theories on blogs two or three times a day to meet the demands of their employers who now required them to be "multi-media specialists," not just reporters anymore. Their work was reduced to little more than "point of view" – all style and opinion, and no substance.

June started with a Tuesday morning of fruitless networking calls and two new rejection e-mails from employers who hadn't even taken the time to call her for a phone interview, let alone a real meeting. She was looking forward to a four-day weekend in Suncadia, where the chances of sunshine were better. Even if the course was crowded, she planned to play four rounds in four days at Prospector, spend evenings carousing the small-town bars with Terry and hanging out at the wine tasting bar with Terry's other friends and customers. If she made a serious effort to find a job the first three days of the month, she would feel less like a slacker and less guilty for taking the long weekend off.

But after a depressing four-hour search on the internet, Lena's resolve waned. She changed into a pair of golf shorts and polo shirt, packed her rain pants and jacket in a bag with a lunch sandwich, pulled her clubs out of her storage unit and headed up I-90 to Mount Si – a municipal course just a couple of miles off of exit 31, just beyond North Bend. She'd played it many times when she'd first started playing golf. It was relatively easy, straight and mostly flat. After weeks of job-hunting, she needed a confidence booster like a good round of golf, even if it didn't prove anything about her employability.

"Hi, Bob," she greeted the pro-shop manager she had come to know over the past couple of years as she was learning the game. "Can I get on this afternoon? I don't care who I play with."

"Sure Lena. I've got another single at 2. I'll put the two of you out together. I think your games are pretty similar."

"Man or woman?"

"A guy. He works in Woodinville, although not too hard, I think. We see him up here fairly frequently. Name's Greg."

"You're not trying to set me up, are you Bob?" Lena laughed. She had never shown Bob anything to indicate she had the slightest interest in romance. But, she had to figure he was either wondering if she was gay or just didn't like men, as she'd never shown up with a male companion in all of the time she'd played the course.

"Would that be such a bad thing?" Bob asked, turning to announce the four-some ahead of her over the loud speaker outside above the first tee, his voice carrying all of the way to the small dining shack down the cart path to the left.

"Oh, I suppose not," Lena conceded as he turned back to her to hand her the credit card receipt to sign for her round. "But, I'm afraid I don't have much to offer anyone right now. I've been out of work for a month."

"Maybe you can find a guy who can support you and you can just play golf for a while," Bob said. He winked and nodded toward the door. Greg had just entered.

"I don't think so," Lena whispered, furrowing her brow at the suggestion that she needed someone to support her. Bob couldn't know that she could survive on her savings just fine without a job, but it always irritated her when someone made the assumption that she would be better off with a husband – or at least a steady boyfriend.

She'd had enough of marriage with Kurt. Long after she had left the Midwest town where she grew up, long after she got her degree in journalism from a small liberal arts school in Omaha, and five years after she'd begun working as a newspaper reporter in Denver, she'd fallen for Kurt's entreaties that she should settle down with someone before too much more time passed or she'd end up with no one to share her life's memories.

She was already 41 by then, and when people asked her why she'd never been married, she never had a good answer. It just didn't seem to be one of her priorities, and up to then, it seemed to her that only people who set a goal to get married actually did. Also, up to then, she'd only met one man who wanted to get married enough to try to talk her into it.

Lena met Kurt in an apartment complex where she had arranged to interview the manager about a proposed city ordinance that would affect multi-family dwellings. Kurt was sitting behind the manager's desk when she entered the office, and at first she thought he was her interviewee.

"I'm Lena Bettencourt," she announced to the tall, square-jawed man, her outstretched hand leading her across the room to initiate a handshake.

Kurt looked up at her with a slight smirk on his face and kept his hands on the table, leaving Lena standing with her hand suspended half-way across the desk, dangling in mid-air. "And why should I care?" he asked, returning her steady gaze – the straight-on, look-them-in-the-eye visual contact she'd groomed over years of being a small, female reporter who was, by sight anyway, unlikely to otherwise intimidate any recalcitrant interview subject.

The clumsy scene was interrupted by the slam of the office door behind her, and Lena turned to meet the real apartment manager.

"Are you Lena?" the short and stout manager asked. He stood with his hands in his pockets, but flashed her a pleasant smile. "I'm Ted. And I guess you've already met Kurt, our maintenance manager," he said, nodding toward the lanky man still relaxing behind the desk. "Get up Kurt and leave us alone. I'll come and find you about that furnace problem in an hour."

"I'll come by at four," Kurt answered, rising to tower over the two of them. "Maybe I'll get a chance to chat with Lena, too." He winked and waved a confident dismissal to his boss.

The four-o'clock return of Kurt ended the interview with the manager, and true to his word, he asked Lena for a chance to "fill her in on all the real dirt around here" at the bar down the street at a corner on edge of Washington Park.

Lena could see no reason to refuse – she had no deadline that afternoon, and rarely turned down a chance to get another – especially less guarded – perspective for her stories. The manager, clearly not worried about any alleged "dirt" that Kurt might know, excused himself, and Lena and Kurt followed him out of the office and out on the street. It was an incredibly warm August afternoon, and the short walk to the bar and the pleasant breeze gave Lena a chance to rid herself of the last vestige of irritation at the way Kurt had let her stand over the desk like an idiot an hour before.

Kurt was charming in low-key way. That afternoon and the several times they saw each other over the next month he didn't seem either to be trying to impress her or make excuses for his lack of a profession or his modest career aspirations. After years of dating doctors and lawyers who were attracted to her for her professional station and self-confidence but then quickly tried to establish their intellectual superiority, she found it refreshing that he neither had rank on her nor seemed concerned about it.

They slept together for the first time five weeks later, and Kurt surprised her by quickly expressing his love for her the week after – long before she felt any such thing. Sex was fine and really all she wanted from him at the time; she'd never even considered that she might fall in love with a charming but strangely juvenile man. But, it was clear – not only because he said it – that Kurt wanted something more. He was vulnerable to any slight criticism from her, and shrunk into a pouting funk whenever she had to leave town for a day or two of reporting.

He wasn't without merit as a boyfriend. On their first "date" in the bar in Washington Park, he professed a sincere interest in philosophy when she told him it was her minor in college. He'd started out at the University of Colorado in Boulder as a philosophy major before dropping for lack of funds, he told her. Occasionally, to impress her, he threw out a phrase that came straight out of philosophy textbooks – "categorical imperative" and "slave morality" and he was clearly intelligent and articulate enough to use them convincingly. His confidence meant that she never questioned his history, even though she'd never seen a book larger or more scholarly than a mass-market paperback in the shabby, one-bedroom apartment where he lived south of the University of Denver.

When she was in town and available for a date, he was always agreeable to whatever she wanted to do for the evening – a play, an outdoor concert, a new restaurant. She was impressed with his willingness to try new things and the energy he put into pursuing them with her. The doctors, lawyers and finance chiefs she had dated in the past always seemed to run out of steam after a couple of months, and the relationships had not so much ended as petered out for lack of interest.

But it was also clear that sports and drinking were his true avocations, whatever he had majored in those years he had attended college. When she was out of town, he reported in their phone conversations that he was doing "nothing," and she could always hear sports on the TV behind him.

Their wedding date was set before his façade started to crack. But in the months between the time she agreed to get married and the wedding, he was increasingly vengeful, often taking pot-shots at her friends and plotting ways to get even with them for their apparent dislike of him. It was true – they didn't like him. They thought he was too willing to let her pay for everything, he seemed to have no ambition beyond his maintenance job, and over time they saw him begin to drink more and more, and get meaner and meaner when he did.

She tried not to complain about it, but Lena began to worry about Kurt's friends. Other than Kevin, his assistant maintenance man at the apartment complex, he didn't seem to have any. And for a one-time philosophy major, he was amazingly non-introspective about himself or his relationships.

"Why do you hang out with him?" Lena asked about Kevin one Saturday after Kurt had told her about an incident at work the week before. Kevin had been reprimanded – unfairly, Kurt thought – for insulting a resident of the apartment complex.

"He's my friend."

"He's your co-worker. You don't have to be friends with everyone you work with."

"He's the only one I work with. Other than the asshole boss."

"Ted did not seem like an asshole," she said, recalling her interview with him.

"You don't work with him."

"No. I guess people can be very different from what you think," she acknowledged. "But, still, why Kevin? He doesn't seem especially bright."

"He's a good guy. He's pretty simple, and I like that. He likes sports like I do – and you don't - and he works hard."

She was ready to drop the subject, but Kurt continued. "And, I think he's pretty religious, which is probably a good thing, don't you think?"

"Me? You think that I care about people's religions? You know I'm agnostic at best." They were sitting in her living room, watching a Saturday afternoon Rockies' game. With a sudden seriousness and ardor, Kurt put down his beer, turned toward her on the couch and reached for her hands.

"I want you to go to heaven with me," he said, looking pleadingly in her eyes. She stifled a laugh. For the prior two weeks, he'd barely spoken to her. She was surprised to see him trying to be intimate all of the sudden, in whatever clumsy way he thought to try. She had started to worry that neither of them would ever put much effort into their relationship; she knew she really wasn't working at it. But heaven?

"And what do you think heaven is? A place where you and I sit on the couch and drink beer? We wake up from the dead fully clothed and show up in heaven and God says, 'Hey, the Rockies are on?'"

Kurt looked hurt, but she was warming to the subject. "You really think we get our bodies back? We'll be physical humans and there will be beer? Will you still belch? Will we still get sweaty when we have sex? It'll be just like here except you won't have to go to work for Ted?"

Kurt was quickly getting angry, his face darkening. She stopped and tried to hide her smirk. He had dropped her hands, and a scowl was hardening his jaw. He picked up his beer and threw it back in a huge swallow.

"Yeah, actually that is what I think," he snarled. "Although, now that I think about it, I'm not sure I do want you to be there."

Kurt got up from the couch, pushing it back a couple of inches, scraping the wood floor. "Why do you always try to make me look stupid?"

"I wasn't trying," she stopped. Actually, she was. But to her, that hardly seemed to be the problem. The bigger problem was how wrong he was for her.

Kurt pulled the keys out of his coat pocket on the coat rack, knocking the coat on the floor. He didn't stop to pick it up before stomping heavily out the front door. The screen door slammed behind him, and she watched him retreat down the sidewalk to his truck.

She'd have the rest of the day to herself. She stood up slowly and turned off the TV, standing still for a moment, enjoying the silence. Too many of their conversations were turning into stark demonstrations of why they shouldn't get married, and too many times they ended with Kurt getting angry. But in many ways, she was okay with that. It left her with more time to herself to do what she wanted.

It wasn't long after they got married in a small, civil ceremony in the park that he retreated to the couch full-time and quit trying altogether. At first, he still went out to eat with her friends or to a concert in the arboretum, but he no longer tried to show any enthusiasm for it. And he couldn't make it through an evening without a six-pack of beer to lubricate his minimal contributions to conversation. Worse, while he needed four or five beers to be conversant, after six or seven, he became sullen and sour. The return to her – now their – bungalow after evenings out invariably involved a shouting argument that she was sure the neighbors could hear. She had lived in her house for five years and knew her neighbors casually. But now she began to avoid them, and quickly stepped into the car with a feeble wave anytime they were out in their yards.

Finally, she quit asking him to come along on her evenings with friends. Later, long after his trial was over, she considered – with the neutrality of time and distance – why she gave up so easily. By the time she got married, she was used to being alone, she concluded, and so their withdrawal to opposite corners felt normal to her. Alone on the farm in Nebraska, alone in college, alone on her assignments as a journalist. Being emotionally alone was comfortable and didn't require her to try to empathize, to try to share. And it meant she didn't have to face whether she even liked Kurt, let alone loved him.

As Kurt sank into lethargy, she started to avoid her own home. She went out with other reporters and editors. Meanwhile, he either went out drinking with Kevin, or came straight home from work, popped open a beer and sat down in front of the TV in his work uniform until he fell asleep. No wonder he stayed so skinny, she realized. He ate lunch at whatever fast-food restaurant piqued his interest in the middle of the day, but he rarely wanted dinner.

When she cooked at home, he rebuffed her with a look that said "I'm not interested," or with a scowl that turned the fault back on her: as, "Aren't you getting fat from eating all of the time?"

It was only a year from the time they met that he had gone from charming, infatuated, energetic and attractive to vengeful, bored, lazy and a slob. When it was all over, she looked back on the experience with a mixture of disbelief in how quickly it had deteriorated and relief: at least she hadn't spent any more of her life with this con artist. The fact that it ended in tragedy for others was horrible, but she knew the tragedy would probably have happened whether she had been in the picture or not, and when she left Denver shortly after, she felt no guilt or complicity. She just wanted to leave it behind her and find a place where no one had ever heard of Kurt Clayborn.

Of course, at Mount Si, Bob knew nothing about Kurt. Of her current friends, only Terry had heard the whole story. So when Bob winked at her over the pro-shop counter, he had no idea how little she wanted to get involved with Greg or anyone else.

But by the time she and Greg had finished their round, she had changed her mind.

AS FAR AS she could remember, her quick affair with Greg was the first time she'd experienced what other people called being swept off her feet. In some respects, that was a relief. She had begun to believe that infatuation would never happen to her – that she was immune or somehow lacked the appropriate emotional equipment. Further, she was both light-headed and slightly sick to her stomach for the three days following their round of golf, and had lost four pounds – something that usually took three weeks of serious dieting to accomplish. But, she wasn't thrilled by the way it distracted her. She was supposed to be looking for a job, not waiting for the phone to ring and checking her e-mail and cell phone every five minutes to see if he'd sent her a message.

Their first round of golf started with laughs and ended in drunken giggles. As she stepped up to the first tee, Bob in the pro shop turned to the microphone and announced to everyone within earshot: "Now, on the first tee: Lena Bettencourt from Seattle, Washington!" as if she were famous. Lena laughed so hard she could hardly catch her breath or hit the ball. Greg was still laughing when he lined up for his second shot on the fairway. He topped the ball badly and that set Lena to laughing again.

"Oh, and why is that so funny?" Greg turned to her, hands on hips, trying to look pissed off, but it just made him start laughing again. They didn't settle down until they reached the bench on the tee box of the par-three fourth hole. They sat and waited for the foursome in front of them to clear the green.

The ice having been broken, they shared abridged versions of their personal stories. Lena: unemployed former speech writer, looking for a job, living in Seattle, condo in Suncadia, loves dogs but doesn't have one right now. Greg: marketing vice president at a winery in Woodinville, divorced five years, two boys grown and through college, loves dogs too and doesn't have one right now either.

"Well, let's just move in together, you get a job, I'll quit mine, we'll get a dog and live happily ever after," Greg suggested.

"Or not," Lena said. "How about if instead we just leave all of this, fly off to Spain, tour the wineries and play golf for a year?"

"Better!" Greg agreed. "But first, I'll bet you a buck on a KP on this hole."

Lena took the challenge. She was very confident with her nine iron, which she needed to reach the hole 125 yards away, and she stood up to the tee with every intention of winning closest to the pin – the KP. They were both playing from the middle tees, and since she'd beat him on the last hole, she was first to tee up.

Her ball flew straight at the pin, but it was long. It smacked the top of the flag and bounced back off the manicured surface, landing six inches in front of the green in the fringe.

"Ah, too bad. No KP unless you're on the green," Greg said, stepping up to his ball and shanking it off the hosel only about 100 yards, both short and far right of the green.

"Ooooo, that was ugly!" Lena laughed, picked up her bag and reached down to collect his as well. "I'll get this. You go get your ball."

They played the rest of the round for a dollar a hole, straight up match play, and on the 18th hole, she held out her hand to collect two bucks from him. He grabbed her hand, laid two dollars in it, and then pulled her toward him and planted a congratulatory kiss on her lips.

The gesture didn't exactly take her by surprise, because by the end of the round, Greg was standing close when they talked, putting his hand on her back when they took off down the fairway together, and scrambling to pick up her sand wedge when she left it behind on the green. It was clear that, even if he wasn't ready to move in together or run off to Spain with her, he was interested in more than one, random round of golf in the company of Lena Bettencourt from Seattle, Washington.

Not making the same mistake she'd made with Kurt 10 years earlier, Lena calculated that her attraction to Greg was likely to be short-lived and mostly sexual. That was her pattern. In the six years since she divorced Kurt, she'd had many one-night stands. One was with a guy at work, who left the company shortly after their out-of-town indiscretion, saving them both long-term embarrassment and discomfort around the conference table. The truth was that she liked men as friends, and craved sex all her adult life, but she never felt that any man could be the soul-mate she was supposed find in a heterosexual relationship. On the other hand, sex with women held no fascination for her, and she continued to be sexually attracted to men for whom she had absolutely no emotional attraction.

Over a beer at the Mount Si Golf Course bar, she decided to keep this friendly encounter simple. Lena declined Greg's offer to follow her home in his car "just to make sure you make it alright." But when he texted her a slightly suggestive message the next morning and then called and asked her to dinner in her neighborhood, she could think of no reason to not let him pick her up at her condo in Seattle that night.

When she opened the door, she caught her breath. Maybe it was because she had seen him with a hat on his head the day before, but she was surprised how good looking he was. His thick shock of dark hair and dark eyes seemed to advertise a sexy dark side she hadn't noticed on the course, and when he stepped forward to kiss her hello, she didn't try to hide her attraction.

He let her go and moved inside and closed the door behind him. She turned to lead him into her tiny condo, but he grabbed her from behind, spun her around and kissed her again. Three hours later, they took a break from lovemaking to order pizza, which Lena retrieved at the door in her bathrobe. And, the next night they did the same, minus the pizza. On Thursday morning, as

Greg left at sunrise to go home to shower and change for work, Lena called Terry and left a message: "I won't be coming up this weekend. I'll explain later, but I think you're going to like this story." Always a writer, she loved creating suspense for her audience.

Saturday morning, Greg sat on the edge of her bed pulling on his socks and casually told her his sons were coming home for the weekend, and he was going to spend the next three days with them.

"I'll be thinking of you constantly," he said, absorbed by the work of aligning his socks and tying his shoes. "But I probably won't be able to text or call. I don't want lectures from them about getting involved again. They think I have horrid judgment in women – and they have good evidence."

"Oh, really?" Lena said. She was as puzzled by his sudden coolness as she was at his heretofore unspoken plans. She pulled the covers up over her shoulders and watched him without sitting up.

"I don't think they'd believe me if I told them about you. You're so terrific," he said, getting up from the bed and bending over to give her a quick kiss. The compliment fell flat, and he seemed to realize it. "We'll get the three of you together sometime later. They'll be impressed with how much my judgment has improved."

"So you won't even be able to sneak away for a quick text message?" Lena was going to miss the suggestive messages she'd been receiving from him the past four two days. Greg didn't answer, slipping into his jacket and walking down the stairs. Lena jumped up and scrambled to slip her nightgown over her head before he reached the door. There, Greg turned and bent down to give her another quick kiss, squeezing her butt cheeks with both hands. They had played with dozens of sexual exchanges the past two nights, but suddenly his hands on her ass felt demeaning in the context of his rapid escape.

But what did she know about having grown sons? she rationalized after closing the door and putting a teapot of water on the stove. Heady with four days of sex and one of the handful of relationships she'd had in her life in which she could truthfully admit a potential for emotional attraction, she wasn't about to let the quick exit ruin it.

Rather than sit and stew and worry for the weekend, Lena called Terry to announce that she was coming up to Roslyn after all, and she drove up to Suncadia that afternoon. She talked about little else with Terry all weekend, expanding on the wonder of the past week and then, alternately worrying aloud about what Greg's quick, unexpected exit might mean, finally inciting Terry to call a moratorium on the subject of Greg.

"I am very happy for you, but you haven't said a thing about your job search all weekend," Terry said. "This just isn't like you." They were sipping wine in Lena's condo, waiting out a rainstorm that had washed out Lena's Memorial Day golf plans. Summer rarely comes to either side of the Cascades until July 5, and this year looked like it was going to be no exception.

"Well, I'm sorry," Lena said. "I listen to your tales of romantic encounters all the time." Was her friend jealous? She wanted to be mad, but she knew that Terry was right. She was more than the object of Greg's lust – however long it ended up lasting, and she needed to get grounded in who she was again.

It didn't take long. When she returned to Seattle on Tuesday, she texted Greg a quick "Mist U" on his cell phone. He didn't answer. An hour later, she texted "How was the visit?" No response. She tried to call him later that afternoon, and he didn't answer. She texted again in the evening. At first she wasn't worried: Maybe his sons were staying a little longer, she thought. She wandered around in a daze on Wednesday, never getting out of her bathrobe all day. Still no Greg. By Thursday, she knew it was over.

Perhaps because the quick affair with Greg had more sexual energy than most of her liaisons of the past, she'd been fooled. Usually, she could read insincerity in a man, but in this case, they'd spent so much of their time together in bed that there hadn't been a lot of normal conversation.

A week later, she still had trouble sorting out her feelings about it. She imagined a TV reporter sticking a microphone in her face and asking the perennial TV-reporter question: "What was going through your mind when...?" She'd have no answer. And if they stuck a microphone in her face and asked her the second-most overused question, "How did it make you feel?" she'd have no answer for that either. The little "thing" as she referred to her four-day affair when she talked with Terry on the phone, wasn't that complicated, but she couldn't decide whether she was embarrassed, angry, hurt, furious, curious, humiliated or simply confused. She did know she wanted to get beyond it – way beyond it – so she wouldn't have to think about it anymore. She had serious work to do in the form of a job search.

By Friday, she decided the only way to get out of her funk and get on with her life was to pull up a blank spread sheet and make a plan that set tasks and deadlines for her job search that she would restart with fervor the next week. Then, she packed a bag for Suncadia, taking her computer with her. She could do her job search from the mountains.

SATURDAY, SHE PLAYED GOLF with Terry. She'd long before passed Terry in ability, but she still enjoyed rounds with her best friend. They played "bingo, bango, bongo" – one point for first on the green, one point for closest to the pin, and one point for holing the ball first. Terry won by a point, and they drove back to her wine store together to commiserate about the strange turn of events with Greg and Terry's most recent affair with a grocery store manager from Cle Elum.

"I have to admit that last weekend, I had the scary feeling that things were going to change a lot for you," said Terry, over a glass of a Syncline red blend. She pulled herself up to the barstool next to Lena. "I'm kind of glad they didn't."

"Yeah. I feel really, really ridiculous," Lena admitted, bending down to give into Rex's demands for a head scratch. "Now, go lay down," she ordered Rex, who obediently waddled back behind the bar and collapsed on his store doggie bed. "I barely knew the guy and I was already planning the next 30 years of golf vacations with him in my head."

Terry shook her head and tipped some more wine into each of their glasses. They sat at the tasting bar and listened to the music streamed over the Internet on a sound system that was well-oversized for a quiet wine tasting room. The building Terry had purchased with her divorce settlement had once been a bar, and with the town in the economic doldrums, she figured she probably paid less for the entire property than the former owners had paid for this stereo and all of its speakers.

A young couple walked into the store and browsed through the racks. Without leaving her perch at the bar, Terry called out an offer to help them find something, but they waved her off, and after a few minutes, left the store empty-handed.

"At least I have my appetite back," Lena said with a wry chuckle. "I lost some weight in the past week. Maybe if I could find a Greg every other week or so, I could finally shed these 20 extra pounds."

"Something to be said for that," Terry nodded. The mention of food must have made her hungry, and she got up, slipped behind the tasting bar and pulled some cheese and olives out of the small refrigerator where she kept appetizers for customers whom she deemed serious enough about buying wine to justify an investment of a little brie and crackers.

Terry sat the plate in front of them and scraped a little mold off of the brie with a knife, wiped the moldy cheese off of the knife with her finger and put it in her mouth. "Ick," Lena said. "That was moldy!"

"What do you think cheese is made of?" Terry laughed. "It's basically cream waiting to mold."

Lena spread some non-moldy cheese on a water cracker and topped it with a kalamata olive and tossed it in her mouth whole.

"I don't know what I'm going to do," she said, finishing chewing and washing the dry cracker down with a big swallow of wine. "I am getting nowhere with this job search. The Greg thing at least gave me a distraction for a week, which was good in a way. But now I've got to get back to it. The problem is, I really don't think there's anything out there I want to do right now. And, I'm thinking no one wants to hire someone my age anymore either."

"They can't ask your age," Terry said. "How do they know how old you are?"

"I have to put my graduation dates on my resume. If you don't, it just gives them an excuse to pass you over and go to the next resume," said Lena.

Lena realized it had been a very long time since her friend had tried to find a job. She envied Terry's self-employment, if not her financial struggles.

"Truth is, I've really lost any interest in finding a job at this point," Lena said, preparing another brie and cracker sandwich and biting it in half. "I'm getting kinda used to not having to get up and shower every morning and rush off to the office."

"Why don't you just play golf for a while?" Terry asked. "If you took a year off, would it really kill you? Would you be broke?" Lena knew that Terry knew the answer. It was a rhetorical question and Lena took it that way.

"I just don't know if playing golf would give me any kind of focus," she mused. "I've always seen my life as some kind of a progression – you know, getting better at something or making more money. Wow, that's pretty American of me, isn't it?" she laughed at herself.

"Yeah. It's also very you of you," Terry laughed. "But why can't you turn that drive into your golf game?"

"To what end?" Lena shook her head. "If I'm too old to get a job, I'm certainly too old for the LPGA."

"There's a lot of amateur tours, aren't there? Maybe you could hook up with one of those."

"I'm not good enough for amateur golf, either," Lena protested. "I only drive 220 at best. I don't think that's going to get me very far, even in amateur tournaments."

"Well, but you putt well. That's half the score isn't it? And I think it's probably easier to learn to drive farther than it is to learn how to putt."

"How do you know?" Lena laughed. While she was flattered by her friend's sudden interest in her golf game, and intrigued by her ideas about what it took to win in competition, she was also surprised that it seemed she'd actually put some thought into it.

"I've read that you have to make 10,000 putts before you start to get the groove," Terry said. "But, you've got that down. You could show them. You know they say: 'drive for show, putt for dough.' Turn it on its head."

"But you can't win by putting well if it takes you three shots to get to the green on every par-4," Lena argued.

"Well, you hit the ball straight, even if it's not far," Terry countered. "Get yourself a coach and a couple of lessons, and I'll bet it won't take much to add 20 yards to your long game."

"Huh," was all Lena could think of to say. She thought for a while without coming up with another excuse for rejecting Terry's suggestion, draining her wine glass and reaching for the bottle to pour another. She didn't want to argue with Terry, but she wasn't sure she wanted to ruin her love of golf by making it a full-time occupation, even if only for a few months.

Golf is a very hard game, she wanted to tell Terry, but her friend already knew that. It is hard even for people who are good at it – people who work full time at it. It's not just physically challenging and exacting, it's also mentally exhausting. Every single shot provides immediate feedback – you're good, you're bad, you can't hit the broad side of a barn. And for very, very few people is the feedback any more consistent than that. It's just plain exasperating. Lena had only played the sport for a few years, and had advanced fairly quickly for someone who started at her age. But she already knew it was maddening and cruel.

By the time they locked up the wine store and Terry drove Lena to her condo at the Lodge, she stopped thinking about it, and was back to musing about her short but intense obsession with Greg.

"Do you want to come in and have a drink?" Lena asked.

"Nah," Terry shook her head. "It's too early. There'll still be a bunch of kids around."

Lena laughed. She knew how much Terry disliked children, especially their noise. And the Lodge living room was usually filled with scrambling, running, screaming, laughing and undisciplined children.

"But, the kids can't come into the bar," Lena said.

"Still, you can hear them," Terry said, and Lena was tired enough to let her friend use the kid noise as an excuse to get back to Rex and her own warm house.

Lena stopped at the 56 Lounge next to the Lodge's big living room – named for the correct temperature for storing red wine – and ordered a glass of cabernet to take upstairs to her condo. She needed to stock her refrigerator and wine rack if she was going to stay for the week, regardless of what she decided to do with the next few months. Wending her way through the clamoring children in the Lodge great room, she barely managed to get to the elevator without spilling her wine. She was beginning to understand Terry's aversion to the place.

The next morning, she lay awake for a few minutes thinking about her conversation with Terry the night before. Golf. The sunlight flooded through her living room window. It looked like a perfect day for golf. With no other demands on her time, why not? And for that matter, why not play golf every day for the next few months? It could be her escape from the fruitless job search.

Maybe it was the change she needed. She didn't have to win anything. She could just relax and play.

She jumped out of bed. For the first time since she'd lost her job, she had a plan.

4 PRACTICE

Learning to play golf is like learning how to write well, Lena thought. Part of the key is working at it, practicing, watching – or in the case of writing, reading – the professionals and the artists. But, as she once heard Hank Haney tell one of his students in a Golf Channel episode, "you have to make it happen. It doesn't just happen." You have to *do* it.

Her old CEO liked to quote Malcolm Gladwell often – at least in the scripts she wrote for him – particularly on a couple of somewhat paradoxical values that he held dear – the power and virtue of hard work, and the acknowledgement that there's a lot of luck in success.

"Achievement is talent plus preparation," he frequently quoted his favorite author. Innate talent played a role in success, but probably a smaller role than preparation. In fact, practice and dedication were far more important to succeeding than original skills or talent. And, Gladwell suggested thousands of hours were needed to perfect any physical skill.

At nearly 50, there was good news and bad news for Lena in that prescription. First, she realized she probably wasn't a terribly talented golfer. If she had been, a lot of things would have come easier to her by now. And, she probably would have shown those innate talents in other sports as a child, even if she didn't take up golf at a later date. So if it was more preparation than talent, she at least had a chance at success, especially since she was willing to taking at least a year off from work to make it happen.

Of course, most of Gladwell's examples of talented, successful athletes had logged those hours of swinging – or at-bats or free-throws – before the age of 10. They weren't starting at 50. So, maybe she wouldn't ever make the LPGA. But, on the other hand, no amateur players probably logged more than eight hours a day, so Lena figured that she could still compete at the amateur level if she made it her fulltime job. Besides, she had met plenty of weekend golfers at Suncadia who said they had significantly improved their games during a year of unemployment – whether voluntarily unemployed or not.

But what really appealed to her about getting good at golf, when she thought about it, was the fact that maybe, just maybe, she could finally become someone special again. Being a journalist, she'd had the best job at her Denver newspaper, covering politics, always on everyone's A-list, invited to all the openings and first nights. That was nice, even though she'd come to hate her job and knew the only reason she was on the A-list was because of her position, not because people liked her. People wanted to be around someone of power, and she had it. But, she'd lost it – on purpose. She'd left her job, moved to a new city where no one knew her. And she became one of the millions of corporate minions hacking away at a mid-level job and one of a million weekend golfers who struggled to break 90.

But being a top amateur golfer would make her stand out in the crowd, if only among a small crowd of mainly over-50 female golfers. If only 25% of golfers ever break 100 following the rules, that still left her as one of millions. On the other hand, only one person a year could win any one of the USGA championships, and winning one would be the antithesis of normal.

The other benefit of a career in golf – however short and unpaid – was that she could be outside all of the time. Playing in the rain and wind didn't bother her nearly as much as it nagged her to be inside, working at her computer on a beautiful day. The day they held the funeral for her mom and dad had been a glorious one, a bright, sunny warm day in October, and she had struggled with the knowledge that they were missing it. Since that day, she was sickened with angst anytime she sat inside, looking out the window at a perfect day, worried that it would be the last one of her life, and that she'd spent it inside clocking another meaningless eight hours for the corporation instead of enjoying the sun and the fresh air outside.

It was early June when Lena moved her clothes out of the condo in Seattle, put it up for rent and settled into her tiny condo in Suncadia as a full-time resident. It wasn't a very big space, and it was boringly resort-conventional. Lena had turned the kid's bunk room into an office and TV room with a desk for her laptop and two small recliners. The small kitchen looked out over a breakfast bar into the combination dining and living room. Lena had no need for a dining table – her only meal-time company was Terry, and that was rare – so she had filled the room with a soft leather love seat and chaise, accompanied by a couple of leather, glass and cast iron end tables and matching coffee table, all set off by the new Tibetan rugs she'd bought the week after she was fired. The seating was arranged to face the stone-faced gas fireplace, and when Terry did visit, more often they sat staring at the fire with a plate of cheese and sausage and a bottle of wine on the coffee table than they sat at the breakfast bar.

Together with the small master bedroom and bath, the entire unit was only 600 square feet. Lena had been glad for its small size when she paid the bill for removing the carpet and put down a hardwood floor so that she could use the Persian rugs she had collected over time. They weren't for show – no one but Terry ever came to visit – but to her, they made her simple condo feel luxurious.

What the unit lacked in space, it made up for in convenience. She had access to a bar, restaurant and coffee shop on the first floor of the Lodge, regular housecleaning by the Lodge staff, and the Suncadia driving range right across the street.

In one month, Lena had gone from thinking she'd take a year and a half off to play leisurely rounds of golf to having a goal: she figured she had a year and three months to get ready for next year's USGA Senior Women's Amateur, which fell in mid-September. The qualifying tournaments were open to women with an index of 18.4 and below who were at least 50 years old. She would turn 50 in 10 months, and already her handicap was 14. Unless she really screwed things up over the next year, she shouldn't have any problem getting into one of the regional qualifiers.

Now she had to organize her practice and develop a routine that was not only effective but interesting – interesting enough that she could stick with it for a year. Her putting was probably her best golf asset, as Terry had pointed out. Her short game was good, but not excellent, and her short to mid-irons were decent but not good. Her biggest weakness was her drives.

"WHAT DO YOU THINK you need?" asked Erin Kutchar, the female assistant golf pro at Suncadia. Lena had walked over to the pro shop to see about getting some regular lessons and coaching. If she was going to be serious enough about golf to dedicate a year off of work, she was going to have to be serious enough to spend some money on lessons as well. Plenty of golfers think they don't need lessons, and then spend a lifetime honing bad habits instead of improving. Lena was humble enough about her game to ask for help. Besides, if Tiger still needs a coach, why wouldn't she?

"I was hoping that you would be able to help me organize a practice schedule and get into a routine," Lena told her, sitting in the tiny pros' office that opened to the pro shop. She liked Erin and had admired her golf swing. Erin's arms always extended through her shots, making her swing look like a long, languid affair, but she generated enough club speed with the late release of the club head through the ball and her large wingspan – she was nearly six feet tall – that her drives averaged well over 280 yards, which was long for a woman, even for a club pro.

"I'm worried that I won't stick it out the whole year, that I'll get bored or discouraged or both," Lena explained, sipping the late afternoon beer that she'd fetched at the Lodge bar on the way over. "This is going to be a one-shot deal, and I'm never going to have another chance. I really need to do it right."

Up to that point, Lena had been self-taught. When she started playing golf in Seattle with a co-worker a few years earlier, she rented a practice booth at a high-tech, indoors teaching facility east of downtown. She could have taken lessons, too, but she saved a lot of money by using the video capability in the booth – taping each swing and comparing it with the swing of a pro. She refused to use Lorena Ochoa as her model; that head jerk at the start of her downswing drove Lena nuts. But she loved Michelle Wie's swing. Of course, she was 10 inches shorter than the once-child-prodigy, but Wie's extension and the way she started her hips rotating back toward the target before her club even reached the apex of the backswing was awesome.

But now, it was time to get some help.

"I'm quite sure there isn't just one right way," Erin mused, pushing the paperwork on her desk to the side to make room for her elbows. "There's an awful lot of ways to waste time, but I've never seen the one good routine that works for everyone."

"How'd you get where you are?"

"Oh, I started when I was seven. I had a pretty good swing before I knew that there was such a thing as a bad one. And my mom had played a year on the tour. She taught me."

"Nice. I guess I'm a little late for that train, though."

"Yup. It's left the station for you, girl," Erin laughed. "But it's not hopeless."

"How do I keep from getting bored or discouraged?" Lena wasn't going to leave Erin's office until she got a plan, or until her beer was empty, anyway.

"They say lesson, practice, practice, play, practice, practice, play. One lesson a week with four practice sessions and two rounds. That way you don't try to work on too much new stuff each week, and the playing helps keep down the boredom and helps you see your progress."

Lena cringed. "I don't know that I can do this seven days a week."

"Then practice and play on the same day," said Erin. "Practice doesn't have to be eight hours. Maybe you just putt for two hours."

"Yikes. Thank god I'm a good putter. My back would kill me if I putted for two hours."

"Ha! That's why you should have started when you were seven like I did," Erin laughed. "I didn't even know I had a back. Now, I'm good for about five minutes. I don't compete anymore so my mantra is now 'Fuck putting.'"

Lena laughed. Unlike the men pros at the club, Erin didn't try to project a buttoned-up image. Sure, Prospector and the neighboring private course of Tumble Creek were pricey and well-regarded as tough, well-designed courses. But, up here in the foothills of the Cascades, nestled right up against the gritty old coal town of Roslyn and down the road from the plain-Jane railroad town of Cle Elum, Suncadia couldn't turn its back on its humble environs.

"I'd like to work with you," Erin said. "I'm not sure that your goal is realistic, but I really like working with someone who has one. It's great discipline. But I understand if you'd rather work with one of the guys. It's no problem."

"I'd much rather work with you," Lena assured her. "We'll start tomorrow, okay?" They toasted their agreement – empty beer bottle to plastic water bottle – and negotiated a package deal for three months of instruction.

Walking back to her condo, Lena tried to remember what she was doing at the age of seven. She was pretty sure she'd never seen a golf course at that point in her life. She didn't even realize golf was a sport until she was in college. And even then, the cost of the greens fees and the equipment put it out of reach for her.

WHEN LENA WAS SEVEN, she lived with her parents in a modest farmhouse outside of a small Nebraska town, 30 miles from Lincoln. Instead of golf practice after school, she rode the bus home, helped her mom with the housecleaning, weeded the garden and did her homework. It was well before the age of soccer moms, and her parents would never have imagined driving her around to school events or sports practices.

Her mother worked from seven in the morning to three in the afternoon at the police department, answering the emergency phones for the small town's police force and ambulance and fire departments. It was usually quiet, so she also did the bookkeeping for all of the departments while she monitored the police scanner and waited for emergency calls.

Lena's weekends were just as quiet and as isolated as the family's home. She saw her friends only at school and some of them at church on Sunday mornings. They attended the Methodist church in town for a while, until her father had a disagreement with the pastor over a sermon that her father thought insulted Jews – although up to that point, Lena had never heard her father mention Jews or any other ethnic group. They then joined the Lutheran church.

Religion as discussed in Sunday school was basic and dominated by rules. The 10 Commandments. Good people go to heaven and bad people go to hell. But at home, it was a bit more complicated.

"Why are we Lutherans?" she asked at the dinner table one night after her history class had exposed her to the Reformation and the religious wars of Europe, which had immediately expanded her religious vocabulary and curiosity beyond Martin Luther to Calvinists, heretics and St. Augustine.

"Because Lutherans are good people," her mother quickly answered. Undoubtedly, she wanted her daughter to be saved, and questioning the church wasn't going to help it happen. "Lutherans go to heaven. They are following the word of God more closely than others do."

Her mother's answers to any kind of philosophical question were usually phrased in such a way as to cut off debate, not encourage it, but this answer was too silly even for Lena's youthful world view. The notion that one could label all Lutherans "good people" made her snicker reflexively. Immediately, she felt bad for it; her mother seemed fairly fragile whenever a debate in the house turned away from strictly financial or household matters.

"Huh!" her father exploded over his plate, coming close to spitting a mouthful of meatloaf and mashed potatoes across the table. "We're Lutherans because we live in a town where one of the churches is Lutheran and the other has an idiot pastor. Don't kid yourself, Lena. They're all the same."

Lena suspected that they weren't all the same, if so many bloody wars had been fought over the differences, but she decided that this was probably not a good conversation to have over dinner. Her mother seemed to shrink in her chair at her husband's outburst, and Lena felt guilty for causing it.

Lena hated dinner table arguments – not so much those between her and her father, or between her and her mother. What scared her were the arguments that started between her parents at the table and then migrated into the night, ending in a slammed door and screeching tires when her father sped to the male camaraderie and equanimity of the bar at the corner of the highway and county road they lived on. Until he left, she held her breath and waited to hear a slap, or the tumble of furniture or dishes when her father's verbal abuse turned physical. It rarely did, but it was always a frightening possibility.

The Lutheran church pastor managed to steer clear of subjects that set her father off for a couple of years, and Lena saw a few different friends from school there on Sundays. But eventually, her father got mad at the Lutheran minister as well, and one Sunday, he told Lena she didn't have to go to church anymore. Lena was 12, and she didn't see any reason to go to church either. She'd prefer to stay home and spend the quiet Sunday reading a book or wandering with her dog, Stripe, down along the creek that bordered their farm. It was the only day of the week she wasn't required to do something – housework, homework – for someone else.

Their abstinence from church services might have hurt the family's reputation in that properly Protestant Midwestern small town if they'd had any reputation to hurt. But with her father's professional inertia – he worked a line job in a small factory in Lincoln, his temper and problems with authority ensuring that he would never ascend to the management ranks – and her mother's minimum-wage municipal job, they struggled at the edge of poverty, with only the expansive backyard garden and pride keeping them from applying for food stamps.

Introverted and oblivious to her socio-economic status, Lena wasn't aware of the family's relative poverty for most of her elementary school years. That is, until Laurie Peterson confronted her in the locker room after PE class in the fifth grade and demanded to know when Lena was going to start wearing her "winter clothes."

Lena was not intimidated by Laurie's higher status in town – she didn't care that Laurie's father owned the town bank – but the question confused her. Quickly she glanced around the room; the rest of the girls had stopped dressing to enjoy the exchange. Surveying her half-dressed classmates, Lena realized for the first time that there were winter clothes and non-winter clothes. There were school shoes and play shoes, she knew that. She didn't wear her good shoes outside to help her father with the chores around the farm or to walk with her mutt Stripe down to the creek. And there were Sunday clothes – or a Sunday dress, anyway – and school clothes. But the fact that the other girls were wearing different clothes for the seasons had up to then escaped her.

It was an epiphany, and from that day on, Lena realized she and her parents were poor. Not that it made a lot of difference in that town. No one was rich the way she'd come to know of wealth in college and later as a reporter, and home gardens and the cultural persistence of extended families limited suffering at their end of the economic scale for lots of rural families. But while the scale was more limited on the upside and the downside, everyone in that small town seemed to know their place on it, and once she recognized how low her rung on that ladder hung, Lena began plotting her escape.

Talk of going to college only made her mother roll her eyes and her father scoff with scorn, so she broached the subject with them only a couple of times before abandoning hope of getting any help from her parents. Her relationship with her mother, always strangely distant given the small size of the family, became colder, as if her mother resented her plans to rise above her parents. But Lena continued to look up information on different colleges in the library at school without any idea of how she was going to pay for one.

Then, long before the time came that she needed to start planning for scholarships or financial aid, her parents had died in a Friday afternoon car accident on the way home from work.

IMPATIENCE WAS ONE OF LENA'S strongest suits. Whenever she was asked in a job interview to discuss her biggest faults, she always admitted to impatience first. It not only was the truth, but it helped her build an image of a high-energy, hard-working, non-procrastinating employee – the kind that would make the co-workers around her step up to her challenge. Employers loved it.

But, it also meant that she usually ran out of patience with any task, location, job or activity that lasted too long. Planning ahead for a year of serious golf lessons and practice scared the hell out of her. The only way to deal with it was to break it down into pieces that could be tackled one at a time, and each for a shorter period of time.

The first piece she decided to tackle was building up her stamina and getting in better shape. She started playing 18 holes at least two days during the work week, and walking with her clubs. She'd usually ridden a cart before, largely because it was tiring to walk with a push cart around long and hilly Prospector. If she walked, she returned to Seattle on Monday mornings tired and sore. But now, without a job to sap her energy, she decided that everything would be easier if she lost a few pounds and built up some leg muscles. Ever since Tiger Woods had entered the golf scene, golfers everywhere had discovered the difference that getting in shape could mean. They lifted weights and ran on treadmills, further separating themselves from the rest of Americans, who seemed to be getting fatter by the week.

But, Lena hated gyms. She'd hated them in high school PE classes, and she hated them now. Getting in shape would have to come naturally, from walking the course and from lifting her bag onto her shoulders some 60 times per round.

It worked. After only three weeks, the fatigue of walking 18 holes began to fade and she started to notice a bit of extra room in the waistband of her golf pants. Lena knew she should have been happy with the fact that she could eat virtually nothing and never be at risk of starvation. Short and small boned, she didn't need more than 800 calories a day, but in a world that provided – even pushed – thousands of calories or more at each meal, staying thin was a struggle. She tried to eat reasonably – pushing herself back from the plate long before she was full, ordering fish and chicken and vegetables at restaurants and fixing salads for dinner at home. She stocked her refrigerator with fresh vegetables and salad fixings, but much of them turned brown and gooey before she got around to eating them. And the more she learned about wine, the more she wanted to drink it, and the better cook she became, the more she wanted to cook and eat the results.

Traveling for work was probably the biggest weight-inducing problem she'd faced in recent years – not only did the healthy, expensive stuff in her refrigerator go bad while she was on the road, but finding healthy food on hotel menus was difficult, and when it was available, it was unsatisfying, especially after a stressful day of dealing with TSA agents at the airport and schlepping luggage in and out of cabs and hotels. She'd read articles with tips for eating well on the road, but they were totally irrelevant once she'd checked into a dreary hotel room and perused the in-room food service menu. A bowl of lobster bisque was far more appealing than a bland, iceberg lettuce wedge, unless that wedge was smothered in blue cheese.

But, now, with work travel in the past, and walking an average of six miles a round, pushing a bag cart or carrying her bag, the pounds were falling off. The other benefit of walking instead of taking a cart was the feeling that she was closer to the game. She walked the same route that her ball had taken. When she lined up for her shot, the ground under her feet felt more solid. The distance between her hands and the ground didn't change as it did when she got in and out of a golf cart. Somehow, it made the swing path more predictable and her shots more solid.

When it came to her lessons, she and Erin started with the short game. It was all about touch. Anyone who played more than a couple of rounds of golf in their life knew that the short game could gobble up strokes. A short drive could add a stroke, but a bad chip or a poor bunker shot could easily cost two or three.

It took discipline to practice the small, delicate pitches and chips that could save par. A 12-foot chip wasn't impressive as a big drive or a long, arcing fairway shot, and it was hard to get excited about a couple of hours of making 10- to 20-footers from the edge of the practice green. But Erin convinced her it would be worth it.

Lena had a decent swing – the kind that had occasionally elicited praise from strangers who were paired with her on weekend rounds – but she didn't hit the ball far enough to get where she wanted to go – to the top of the amateur ranks in her age bracket. And when she tried to get more distance, her swing flew off course and she sliced the ball out of bounds more often than not. But Erin convinced her that there, too, short game practice would help. If she started hitting her short irons better, her drives would naturally improve as well.

They started with chipping and pitching and worked backwards toward the tee. Even though she putted well, Erin insisted she continue to practice putting a few hours each week so that she wouldn't lose a skill that might eventually end up being the difference between being competitive and not having a chance.

Terry joined her on the range or on the course about once a week – usually on Mondays when her shop was closed. But generally, Lena went out alone. The weather was still cool and rainy most days, and it wasn't hard to find herself alone on the first tee box.

"You're quite the loner, aren't you?" one of the assistant pros in the pro shop, asked her after she'd been working on her game for about three weeks.

"I guess," Lena said, feeling a bit defensive. "It's just that most people are working when I'm playing these days," she excused herself. Certainly the cool, rainy weather in Suncadia in June kept potential playing partners inside. But, it was more than that. It wasn't just the golf course where she spent time alone. She still preferred a good glass of wine and a good book at home to a partying with the Suncadia staff and regulars at the bar at night.

And there were definite benefits to playing alone. Lena had discovered that she could concentrate on each shot when she was alone in a way that she couldn't when some – however minimal – interaction with playing partners was required. It was easier to keep focused on the intent of each shot, the aim, her balance, the shoulder turn, staying over the ball, turning her hips – all the things that made a shot better – when she didn't have to make any conversation at all.

It was a bit like her work as a reporter back in her newspaper days. After all of the interviews and the research was done on a story, it was a solitary effort to put a story together. She liked that – crafting a story alone, absorbed in her computer screen and her notes, oblivious, often, to the waning daylight and approach of night. While it meant she couldn't lean on anyone else to make an article successful, she didn't have to worry about someone holding up their end of the deal, either. She avoided joint projects in the newsroom, and abhorred the "group grope" – the morning news meetings when reporters and editors were supposed to gather and share their projects, supposedly to get help, sources and ideas from each other. In her experience it had been less of a help session than a one-upsmanship with the key audience for reportorial brilliance and insight being the senior editors in the room.

Another thing that happened once she started her solo practice routine – one that took her a while to realize – was the end of the dreams about Kurt. At least once a week in the dead of night for the past five years, she had relived the inertia, the dread, the hard knot in her stomach that characterized her 18 months with Kurt. She dreamed he was still there, she still hadn't found the nerve or the energy to get out or kick him out. There he was on her couch, and they were arguing about dinner, about house cleaning, about everything.

Perhaps it was the incredible amount of concentration required to create a replicable, effective golf swing and a predictable, solid chipping stroke that purged him from her dreams. But, whatever golf was doing for her body, she felt it was doing even more for her emotional health. She was focused and calm, and there was no place in her head for Kurt.

One quiet solo day, she played through three foursomes of men on her way through a quick and pleasant two-and-a-half-hour round. When she walked up behind a third group on the par-three

12th hole, they moved off of the green ahead of her and waved her onto her tee while they waited. For some, teeing up with four strangers watching can be intimidating, but Lena found the audience helped her concentrate on the shot – instead of letting her mind wander off-course. She hit a crisp nine iron and lofted the ball smartly onto the green, and it spun to a stop about 8 feet below the pin.

"So that's what the ball looks like on the green," one of the men quipped when she walked up to putt, and Lena realized that none of their balls had made the putting surface. By the time she had putted out, they still had not located all of their balls in the weeds and woods around the green. She waved a cheerful good-bye, picked up her bag and moved along, feeling immensely happy about how the day was turning out.

Her progress, however, was anything but linear. In fact it resembled the random ups and downs of any beginning golfer's trajectory. Two good days followed by five horrid ones, followed by a great day, and then two more mediocre performances. Sometimes it was her drive that wouldn't work, and sometimes she couldn't hit a wood off the fairway for love or money. Some days, she couldn't miss a chip or a bunker shot, and then others she was left with nothing less than a 20-foot putt thanks to poor approach shots.

So much of the golf round is played between the ears, and Lena knew that in order to get consistent enough to be able to win in serious competition, like the USGA Senior Women's Amateur Tournament, she needed to learn how to control her emotions during a round. She had to learn how to keep from turning a blow-up hole into two consecutive blow-up holes because she couldn't control her reaction to a lost ball or a bad-luck, back-of-the-bunker sand lie.

Even worse than managing the mental trick of getting past a bad hole was getting out of a serious bad-golf streak. And, the only advice she could find in books, Erin or her friends was "you have to get over it." It wasn't helpful. If anything, it made her feel inadequate, like everyone else knew how to do that, but in her arrested development, she'd never learned it.

More than once in the first month, Lena considered giving up. It was a pleasant daydream to imagine waking up 14 months later, after the amateur tournament was over, all of the concentration behind her and her future ahead. But then, she'd have to figure out what that future was going to be. Without any idea of what she wanted to do with the rest of her career – or life – she returned to golf and eventually, the practice and repetitions started to pay off. She was still erratic and inconsistent, but, her drives were longer, her fairway woods less unpredictable and her chips a little more accurate, on average. The bad shots, she rationalized, were just golf.

5 RYNE

Summer arrived in earnest at the end of June, a couple of weeks earlier than usual for Seattle and Suncadia. Along with it, came a regular schedule of tournament and member events at Prospector. For the first two years she belonged to the golf club, Lena didn't participate much, thanks to work and her lack of enthusiasm for joining things. And, this year, she had enjoyed the quiet and concentration of more than a month of mostly solo rounds. But now she had a reason to get in on the action – she needed practice playing in competitions, however laid-back and friendly the club events were at Suncadia.

During the year's first sunny, warm weekend, on the last day of June, she was teamed up with three other club golfers she'd seen around, but never officially met. Brandt and Carly lived along one of Prospector's fairways and they seemed to know everyone in Suncadia – residents and staff alike. Lena was a little reluctant to become another in their stable of great friends. How can anyone know that many people and bring any sincerity to the relationships? she wondered.

But Brandt won her over quickly. Gregarious with a contagious enthusiasm, Brandt had a way of making her feel like she was the most interesting person he'd ever met. He quickly figured out the strengths and weaknesses of her game and what helped and what hurt when it came to pre- and post-shot commentary. Meanwhile, compared with Brandt's high-energy level and quick temper,

Carly's manner was cool and calm. She played well and steady, but what appealed to Lena was her quick wit and the practiced and sure, yet warm, way she managed her relationship with Brandt. If Lena ever ended up getting into a long-term relationship, she hoped she could manage it with Carly's grace.

The third partner of the day was a tall, athletic man in his mid-40s who puffed up his chest, stuck out his large hand for a shake and, with a perfectly straight face, introduced himself on the first tee as "Ripped Buffington." Watching the introduction, Brandt dropped his club and bent to the ground laughing. "Come on Ryne," he laughed. "Give the woman a break. She'll probably outdrive you anyway!"

Ryne, as her cart partner for the day turned out to be, was a newspaper editor in Seattle, and he had a newsroom-like cynicism and irreverence that made her feel comfortable with him. He had a huge wingspan, thanks to his 6-foot, five-inch height, and hit the ball 250 yards. But many of those yards were along an arc that ended well into the trees on the right or left. His chipping and pitching were erratic and he had obviously never taken a lesson on how to hit out of a bunker. If he failed to get out of the bunker on the first try or couldn't find his drive off in the trees, he swore at the top of his lungs and threw a club. And, more than once he stormed across the entire length of a large green, trailing a string of swear words as he retrieved a chip that skipped out of the rough on one side and merrily bounced all of the way across to a bunker on the other side.

But his putting was nearly magical. She'd never seen anyone make so many putts outside of 30 feet in her whole, albeit short, golf life. And whatever happened on a hole, stayed on that hole. By the time they arrived at the next tee box, Ryne had totally wiped his memory clear of the disaster that had just occurred on the last hole and was back to his jolly self.

Before long, Lena saw that Ryne's blustery behavior was a cover for shyness. He and Lena chatted amiably in the cart while waiting for Carly and Brandt to hit their balls, but he never looked her in the eye. His gaze was always focused on the distant horizon. Their conversation stayed safely on the subjects of golf and working in a newsroom, two things they had in common. For once, Lena was willing to let her curiosity about his love life remain unsatisfied.

She'd have many more chances that summer to delve into those subjects, if she decided to, she guessed.

Generally, Lena didn't like playing in foursomes because they usually were too slow. Equally, she hated waiting on the tee box for the group ahead to move along, but Brandt, Carly and Ryne kept her entertained all day. They teased and lobbed ersatz insults at each other on the tee boxes, and pretended to have sudden attacks of Tourette's syndrome in the midst of each other's putting strokes. Lena wasn't left out. She played from the forward tees with Carly and outdrove all of them on the first tee, so they figured that even though she was new to them, she was fair game. They delivered a continuous funny mix of encouragement and harassment for 18 holes.

By the 17th hole, Ryne was on his sixth or seventh beer of the round, and the alcohol seemed to be straightening out his drives. But, it wasn't helping either his composure or his short game. He hit a great drive into the middle of the long par four, leaving only about 125 yards to the green. Then, he hit a dreadful nine-iron into the deep bunkers to the left of the green, and Lena knew he was going to create a scene getting out. On his first attempt, he swung the club straight down, sticking it deep in the sand, making no impact on the ball at all.

Brandt and Carly pulled their cart up to the green and wandered back to stand by Lena and watch as Ryne seethed and took his stance to try again. His second shot took no sand at all, and he bladed the ball straight into the bunker's steep green-side lip. Now, his ball was not only in the worst bunker on the course, but it stuck in the sand with only a small bit of the white of the ball showing.

Ryne lost it. "This is a game for fucking retarded monkeys!" he yelled, leaning back and holding his club over his head as if addressing God with his complaint. "Only retarded monkeys should play this game!" Spit flew out of his mouth as violently as his words, and Lena tried not to laugh. She didn't want make him angrier, but it was hard to hold it in. Beside her, Brandt snorted loudly and turned around so he wouldn't have to watch anymore. Carly turned and walked up onto the green shaking her head, unconcerned that Ryne would ever be able to hit the ball out of the sand and onto the green. After two more uncontrolled, violent swats at the ball and the sand – each of which renewed his hysteria – Ryne picked up the ball. "Why does anybody but a retarded monkey ever play this game!" he yelled and heaved the ball out of the sand trap and a hundred yards beyond the green into the woods.

"How the hell am I supposed to putt when I'm laughing so hard?" Carly called out, calmly taking her stance over her ball on the green. Brandt, picked himself up from the fringe, where he'd sat down to wait out the tirade, and wiped the tears from his face. He turned to Lena. "That was precious. That was vintage Ryne."

WITH THAT AUSPICIOUS START, the four new friends began a regular routine of playing together on Saturdays about 8 a.m., whenever there wasn't a tournament or other member event going on. Ryne usually only played on Saturdays, due to his duties on the city desk at the Seattle Times on Sundays. When Carly and Brandt had other commitments, Ryne and Lena were still usually paired up on the first tee.

Ryne and Lena became easy pals. But, having avoided the lifestyle questions the first day out, she found it hard to broach the subject later on. She liked him though, and found herself thinking about him during the week, as she was practicing or playing her solo rounds. She wasn't really interested in a complicating relationship, but he looked good enough to be a cast member for a sexual fantasy or two. Ever since the quick affair with Greg, she'd been celibate, and not necessarily voluntarily. Between spending so much time on the golf course and living in Suncadia, there wasn't much occasion for romance. She was beginning to feel Terry's isolated-in-Roslyn pain.

One Saturday afternoon after the foursome finished their round, Ryne had a quick beer at the clubhouse bar and then took off in a hurry, as usual. Lena asked Brandt and Carly what they knew about him.

"I think he has a girlfriend, but he never wants to talk about her," said Brandt.

"Why not?"

"Who knows. But one time, I asked him if he was married or had someone, and he just made a joke. Why?" he asked Lena. "Are you interested?"

"Do you think I should be?"

"Hell, yes!" Carly answered for him, a little too enthusiastically for Brandt. He looked at her sideways and raised his eyebrows.

"Oh, get over it," Carly laughed at him. "You aren't in any danger. I just think he's kind of a hunk, of sorts. And smart," she paused. "But he is a bad golfer. If you can handle that."

"What time is the golf tournament on today?" Brandt interrupted to change the subject, either uncomfortable at watching two women size up another man, or simply bored with the topic. Carly and Lena dropped it too, having little more to say about the mystery man.

The next Saturday, while they were waiting on the third tee - a par three that frequently backed up as duffers wasted a few shots getting out of the deep bunkers that guarded the front of the green - Lena decided it was time to see if she could nudge her relationship with Ryne past golf.

"There's a concert tonight at the winery," she chummily bumped Ryne with her elbow as they waited in the cart for the group ahead to clear the green. "You want to go and hear them, and have a drink with Brandt and Carly and me?" A double date, she figured would seem less forward or scary to him. It would be a lot like Saturday morning golf. "Or do you have to get back to Seattle?" she said, giving Ryne an escape route, if he wanted it.

"Who's playing?"

"I'm not sure. But Brandt and Carly said they're good."

"Oh," Ryne said, and paused as if he were trying to figure out whether he wanted to come or not. "But I can't. I have plans."

Frustrated, Lena decided this was finally the time to try to punch through his opaque facade.

"What plans? You always have plans. Do you have a girlfriend? A boyfriend? Why don't you ever stick around with us?"

"Twenty questions? Or the Spanish Inquisition?" Ryne laughed, standing up to pull a club out of the bag and stride up to the tee box.

"Oh, you're not getting by with walking away from this," Lena insisted, jumping out of the cart and trotting after him. "What's the deal?"

Ryne pushed his tee in the ground, balanced his ball on it and backed up to line up his shot. "Let's just say it's complicated," he said, not looking at her.

"That's a Facebook answer," Lena laughed, standing back to give him room to take a practice swing. "Complicated how?"

Ryne took his stance and waggled his eight iron, at least giving the impression that her questioning wasn't interfering with his concentration. He swung smoothly, aiming the ball toward the left side of the green, fading it perfectly to land just a couple of feet from the pin. It was one of his best shots of the past two weeks.

Apparently, her questions weren't hurting his game.

"Complicated how?" Lena repeated, watching his ball slowly roll closer to the hole.

Ryne sighed, and avoided her eyes. "Why don't you think about your shot instead of worrying about me?" he suggested, walking away from her and from the topic.

Lena gave up, later confessing to Carly that she didn't want to jeopardize their friendship by quizzing him further. They were friends now, but he still seemed shy at times. He obviously didn't want to share whatever it was that was occupying all of the time he wasn't on the course.

But a week later, Carly brought news that she'd Googled Ryne at work, and while she couldn't find much about his personal life, she had discovered that his birthday was coming up at the end of July. Maybe that was an opening, she suggested.

Lena went online that night and ordered a dozen ProV1s with Retarded Monkey stamped on them, and the next Saturday, following their round, she parked her car behind his in the driveway of his house in Prospector's Reach, a housing development along Prospector's 18th fairway, and strode up to his door.

She rang the doorbell and stuck her sunglasses on top of her head. She was ready to give Ryne a big birthday hug when he appeared, but instead, a tiny sprite of a woman with long, straight blond hair opened the door. The two women stared at each other for an uncomfortable minute before Lena stammered something about wishing Ryne a happy birthday. She shoved the box of Pro-V1s at the tiny blond and ran back to her car. She didn't look back to the front door as she started her car, threw it in reverse and sped away.

The next Saturday, Lena showed up for their tee-time with dread. She considered calling the pro-shop and pleading a sudden bout of the flu, but she decided that would be too obvious to Ryne why she was avoiding him. And besides, she didn't have anything to be embarrassed about – she'd just delivered an appropriate gift to a friend, even though she had fled the scene as if she had crossed some kind of illicit boundary. Still, it took some guts to look up from her putting practice with a poker face when Ryne walked up to her on the putting green.

"Hey," he began, not terribly enthusiastically.

"Hey," Lena responded, quickly returning her focus to her two-foot putts.

"Thanks for the Pro-V1s."

"Sure." Lena said, and then paused. She was inclined to let the subject drop, but she couldn't. She was tired of his secrecy and impatient with his shyness. She stood up straight, and looked Ryne directly in the eye, even as he avoided her gaze. He didn't move and didn't speak, so she plunged ahead.

"Who's the young chick? Don't tell me you have a daughter that you failed to mention."

Ryne winced. Lena's observation of the differences in their ages hit its mark.

"She's older than she looks. She's a reporter at the paper."

"She works for you? Oh, that's *much* better than I thought," Lena retorted, not trying to mask her sarcasm. "No wonder she's a big secret,"

"She doesn't work for me, but it probably looks just as bad," Ryne admitted with a sideways nod. "I don't mention her because I know how it looks, and no one at work knows about this."

"And what do you mean by 'this?'" Lena retorted. She had a pretty good idea what he was talking about, but she didn't want to let him get away without clearly delineating the relationship. Then, she could commit to forgetting about any possibility of a relationship beyond their golf one.

"We spend weekends together. We sleep together. I like her. She loves me. That's what I mean."

Lena paused, amazed that he was so quick to drill down to the discrepancy in the relationship. He liked her. She loved him. Lena stood with her putter in her hands and took in the man in front of her. He certainly was lovable, at least as far as she could tell from their casual Saturday golf dates. It was also easy to imagine that a man in his late 40s, at least one with a modicum of self-awareness and maturity, would find it hard to be serious about someone just slightly more than half his age – the prevalence of trophy wives notwithstanding.

But did she care anymore? Or was the humility of the weekend before enough to neutralize any attraction?

Ryne stood still in front of her, as if inviting her scrutiny. When she didn't continue her interrogation, he volunteered a bit more.

"I don't talk about her because she's a reporter who works at the paper, and no one there knows about our relationship. I'm sorry I didn't tell you. She doesn't play golf. I didn't think you'd ever meet her, so I haven't talked about her. I'm sorry."

"Yeah, well, okay," Lena turned back to her putting so he couldn't read the disappointment in her face. She wasn't angry. She was disappointed. She had spent a couple of hours the night before with Terry, speculating that it was a younger sister – maybe even a daughter. Now she knew. "You have as much of a right to privacy as the rest of us," she said, dismissing him and blasting her two-foot putt three feet past the hole.

Ryne walked away, and by the time they met at the cart for the trip to the first tee with Carly and Brandt, they'd reached a tacit agreement to drop the matter and play golf as usual.

LENA MET KIM the next month. She was already in the routine of playing with Carly, Brandt and Ryne on Saturdays, but Sunday's pairing was always a crap shoot. She usually ended up playing with three guys, which didn't bother her, but that typically meant that she drove her own cart, played from the forward tees by herself, and wasn't included in much of the threesome's conversation.

But one August Sunday, her tee-time included herself, another single, and a couple from Issaquah who was staying at the Lodge for a romantic weekend. The couple was so focused on each other that Lena was guessing that they were either not married yet or just newlywed.

Her single partner, Kim, was tall, broad-shouldered and good-looking in a kind of Sam Waterston way with grey eyes, a close-trimmed beard and bushy eyebrows. It was busier than usual that weekend at Suncadia, the weather having turned nice and attracting more golfers from Seattle, so Kim and Lena ended up sharing a cart.

"Does your wife play?" Lena asked Kim on the first hole as they waited until the group ahead moved on to the green so they could tee off. Lena had never subscribed to the Marquis de Sade's contention that all relationships are sexual. But, whatever her relationship with Kim was going to be – one day or a life time, platonic or not – she wanted to get the basic information up front. She'd made the mistake of not clearing the air with Greg or Ryne right away, and having embarrassed herself with both men, she wanted to set her expectations – and Kim's – quickly, so they could get on with focusing on golf.

With her question, she was really asking three things: why was he playing alone, was he married and, if so, how was the marriage. Usually, the answers she got when she asked the simple question covered all three grounds – the first two intentionally and the third was usually discernible from the tone of the answer.

"No," Kim answered. "She used to but she can't play anymore. She has advanced Parkinson's." Kim tapped the head of his driver on the ground and watched it leave a line of small dents in the dry turf as he waited for his turn to tee up his first drive.

"Oh, I'm sorry," Lena never expected this kind of answer, although she'd heard something like it more than once on the course. She wanted to be sympathetic, but not pry into a family or health issue that was none of her business. "But she doesn't mind that you come out here?"

"No, she insists that I do. And, I think she's right. It is good for both of us," he said, walking up to the tee markers and sticking his tee in the ground. He stood behind his ball on the tee and aimed his driver down the fairway. The young couple was oblivious, giggling over some private joke behind them. "We spend hours together whenever I'm not at work during the week, and she thinks I should get out and get away from our troubles at least once a weekend. I didn't want to do it at first, but I started following her orders to get out of the house after her mother convinced me that it was what she really wanted. Now, it's just part of our routine."

"That must be hard," Lena said quietly, wishing that the golfers at the 150 yard marker would pick up the pace and move along. She was worried that as long as Kim waited to hit his tee shot, he would feel that he had to keep talking about the situation even if he didn't want to. But he continued in a steady voice that told her he was accustomed to talking with strangers about his wife's illness.

"In the winter, I play courses around Seattle or spend a few hours at Home Depot or a golf shop. I buy her – her name is Stacy, by the way – I buy her flowers and books and come home earlier. It's not as good as a day of golf up here, but I still enjoy the time away."

He stopped, and looked embarrassed, like had said something he realized was insensitive. "I don't mean I enjoy it. I mean it's helpful. We seem to have more to say to each other after I've been out doing something without her for a while."

"I think you can hit," Lena nodded down the fairway where the group in front had moved toward the green, and Kim stepped up to his tee. They didn't talk about his wife any more that day, but fell into an easy rhythm of taking their turns hitting their balls and waiting on the other couple. Playing with better players like Kim always helped her pick up an idea or two about how to play her own game better.

When the round was over, they drove the cart into the parking lot, and Kim loaded his clubs in the car. Lena grabbed hers out of the cart, said a cheery goodbye and started the trek back to the Lodge. "If you don't mind, I'd love to hook up with you for a round again next Sunday," Kim called after her. "I would much rather have someone I like to play with than get paired with a stranger."

And with that nice compliment, Kim and Lena began playing a regular tee-time on Sundays at 8:00. Twice before the end of summer, Terry joined them, and the three of them played the same quick, no-nonsense pace.

The first time they played, Kim was a significantly better player than Lena. He drove the ball 225 to 250 yards, and straight. His short game was decent, but he had no patience for putting. He broke 90 consistently, and occasionally shot in the low 80s. But, as the weeks passed, Lena's daily practice began to trump his once-a-week play, and she started to outscore him. She considered moving back to the white tees to make it a more fair fight, but her plan was to make that move in Palm Springs in the coming winter, and she didn't want to rush it and get discouraged.

Starting with the second Sunday, Kim and Lena began stopping for a beer at the bar next to the pro shop after their rounds, but other than that, their friendship was limited to the course, and it seemed to work for both of them. Lena didn't want Kim to think of her as anything but a golfing buddy, and Kim was usually eager to get on the road, over the pass and back home to his wife. Lena always asked how Stacy was doing, and Kim shared increasingly intimate details of the trials of Parkinson's disease and how it was affecting his wife's mobility and their relationship. Lena began to feel that their conversations about Stacy had become an important part of Kim's Sunday get-away. He said he had told Stacy about their rounds together, and Lena found it incredibly generous of Stacy to embrace their friendship, even as she was slowly losing everything.

With her weekends filled playing golf with her friends, her weekdays dedicated to practice, practice, practice, and a couple of evenings a week saved for getting together with Terry, the summer sped by, and autumn caught Lena by surprise. She woke up one morning early in September to find frost on her walk to the course. The end of the season was approaching, and Lena had to make a decision – was she making enough progress with her golf game to invest in a trip to the California desert for the winter, or was it time to cut her losses and try to get back into the job market?

The next weekend, as her Saturday companions packed their clubs into their cars after their round, Ryne surprised them all and suggested they toast the imminent end of summer and their golf season with a trip to the winery.

"Are you sure you want to be seen with us?" Brandt chided him. "We think you've been avoiding us because you're embarrassed to be known as our friend."

"Yeah, right. A journalist worried that his friends will ruin his reputation. Give me a break," Ryne laughed. "Come on, Lena, ride over to the winery with me."

It was only a mile to the winery, and Lena had to scramble to call Terry on her cell phone and cancel their dinner date at the Brick, inviting her instead to come over to the winery and join the four of them. Terry quickly agreed – she'd yet to meet Ryne, although she'd heard everything Lena knew about him – about his golf, his drinking and smoking (it made Lena feel a little less guilty about her occasional cigarette), his good looks, his sense of humor and – of course – about his girlfriend and the embarrassing way Lena had met her.

They pulled an extra chair up to a bar table in the winery tasting room, and Lena sat between Ryne and Terry with Brandt and Carly across the table from them. They ordered a dozen appetizers for the five of them with a couple of bottles of wine. As soon as the wine was opened and the glasses filled, Ryne stood up and lifted his glass.

"I propose a toast to Lena's winter of discontent in Palm Springs!"

"Hear, hear," cheered Brandt, clinking his glass to Ryne's and taking a quick swallow, not waiting for all of the other glasses to meet his first.

"Wait a minute," Lena laughed. "I haven't decided whether I'm going yet. And what do you mean by 'discontent?'"

"Lena, dear," Ryne said with mock sincerity, "you've already wasted four months of your life on this quest. If you quit now, what will you tell your grandchildren?"

"I have no children. What grandchildren?" Lena protested, confused about what part of his pronouncement she should argue about first. "And why do you say wasted? And – again – why discontent?"

"You are going to go to Palm Springs, aren't you?" Carly interjected. "I need to have a place to visit this winter. I can't take another Seattle winter without a sun break."

"I'll go with you," Terry announced, and before the appetizers arrived, it had been decided by the Saturday gang that Lena was going to Palm Springs for the winter and everyone except Ryne was coming to visit.

Once the food was in front of them, Ryne lowered his voice and turned to Lena. "I'm sorry I can't make it. I could use the sunshine, too."

"Oh, I think that would be a little awkward anyway," Lena said low enough to keep their conversation private. "What would your girlfriend think?"

"Yeah. Well. She's not my girlfriend anymore." Ryne reached for his wine glass and took a bit swallow, allowing Lena time to process the news. "I needed a little more space than she could give me, and I think she was really too young for me anyway."

"No shit she's too young. When did this happen?" Lena asked, noticing how Terry was leaning across her to hear what Ryne was saying. Lena poked Terry with her elbow and threw her a quick frown.

Terry backed off and shrugged. "I'm just trying to be part of the party," she pouted.

"So, when did this happen?" Lena repeated, turning back to Ryne. But he'd taken the interruption as an excuse to get deeply interested in Carly's and Brandt's conversation. He pretended not to hear her.

"He's a bit passive-aggressive, if you ask me," Terry noted in a conspiratorial whisper, motioning to Ryne with a chicken wing. "I don't think he really knows what he wants."

Lena just took a deep sigh and shook her head. There really didn't seem to be any reason to worry about Ryne. He was simply too difficult to consider as eligible for a relationship, and now she had to start planning her trip to California.

ONCE SHE CAME to accept her friends' decision that she would continue her pursuit of the USGA tournament by going to Palm Springs, Lena backed off her practice schedule a bit, and spent a little more time in the gym at the Suncadia fitness center. Even in the winter, Palm Springs called for less clothing and more skin, and she wanted to work off as many pounds as she could before she left. The short Suncadia summer had ended fairly suddenly, as usual, and the return of the wind and rains made golf a chore at the same time they increased her appetite for comfort food.

She still played chilly, windy golf on Sundays with Kim, although the regular Saturday group didn't get back together after their evening at the winery. Leaving Kim for the winter was one of only a few things that worried her about leaving for Palm Springs later that fall. She wasn't so worried about him – he wasn't alone. He and Stacy were still best friends. and they had many other friends and neighbors who were probably a far more important part of their lives than she was. But, Kim had become a routine of sorts for her – a steady friend she saw on Sunday mornings, who, along with Terry, was one of the few anchors mooring what had become a rootless life over the past few months. With no job, no idea what she'd do once her golf year was over, and no interest in a long-term relationship, Kim and the Saturday foursome had become a larger part of her life than friends had ever been.

6 TRIAL

Having a steady stable of friends was a benefit of playing serious golf that Lena had not really expected. She hadn't had many close friends over the past five years she had been in Seattle, except for Terry. But, back when she was married in Denver, Lena had become almost maniacally gregarious, gathering friends and social commitments to fill up the emptiness of her cold marriage, and to avoid having to go home to watch Kurt slouch in front of the TV and drink. By staying out until 9 or 10 every night after work, she often managed to return after he fell asleep on the couch, where he frequently slept the entire night. Weekends, she went shopping or on short trips to San Francisco or Palm Springs with friends who had been mere acquaintances before she got married.

The night Kurt was arrested for murder, she had returned home from a casual dinner party at a fellow reporter's house with a half-dozen other reporters and editors from the paper. She was pleasantly surprised to find her front door locked. Expecting that Kurt had gone out bar-hopping with Kevin, she unlocked the door, pushed it open with her briefcase and once inside, closed it behind her with a foot. To her surprise, Kurt was hunched over on the couch with his elbows on his knees, and she let out a startled "oh!"

Kurt didn't look up. The TV was silent and dark, and he sat under the dim light of a lamp next to the couch.

"What's wrong?" Lena asked, putting down her briefcase and putting a hand on his hunched shoulders. It was the first time that she'd touched him or felt anything like sympathy for him in months.

Kurt didn't answer. He shook off her hand and kept his face buried in his hands. He hadn't changed out of his maintenance uniform. She looked around the living room and saw the phone smashed into pieces on the end table. Six empty Bud Light cans lay on their side on the table and the floor next to him.

"What happened?" she tried again. "Is everything alright?"

"NO!" Kurt still didn't lift his head to look at her. "Everything is NOT alright. Now leave me alone!"

"Uh … this is my house," Lena said, hearing the anger quickly rise in her throat. She'd put up with enough from this man over the past few months – their miserable marriage, his belligerence, drunkenness and sloth. Whatever problem he had now she couldn't imagine how it could be worse than what she was going through, being married to him.

"You mean OUR house," he said, looking up at her so she could see his bloodshot eyes. "This is also MY house. Remember?!" He got up and staggered heavily toward the bedroom, brusquely brushing past her, knocking his elbow into her shoulder. She stepped back to keep her balance and let him pass.

"Well, you wouldn't know it from the amount of help I get around her taking care of it. Or paying for it," she started down the path of one of their usual arguments. She picked up the largest piece of the broken phone and waved it at him. But Kurt turned at the bedroom door and shot her a look that made her stop and hold her breath. She had seen belligerent drunkenness many times, but this was wilder and much more frightening.

"I'm not in the mood for your superiority. Get the fuck out of here!" he yelled, and he slammed the bedroom door so hard that two more beer cans rolled off of the end table onto the living room floor.

Lena stood still, holding her breath. She wondered if, in a strange way, Kurt wasn't right; she should probably leave while she was unharmed. For the first time in their marriage she was afraid of him. She still hadn't moved five seconds later when the front door flew open with a crash, and she fell to her knees and covered her head with her arms.

"Freeze!"

Lena didn't look up. She tried to fold herself closer to the floor as she heard the heavy boots of large men burst into the living room. A pair of heavy black boots stopped on the rug in front of her, nearly touching her nose, and she cringed as someone roughly pulled her upright by her arm. She wasn't quite standing on her own as she looked around at the policeman who held her and three more policemen holding their guns out in front of them, all pointing at her. One stray, stupid move, she thought, and they'll all shoot me.

"Whatever happened to 'hello, is anyone home?'" she heard herself quip, even as she crouched. She felt dizzy, her heart pounding loudly.

The policeman in front of her dropped her arm and squinted at her as if he was thinking of slapping her. Instead, he pointed his gun at her face. "Where's Kurt?" he shouted at her far louder than necessary, given he stood only a foot away.

"He's in there," she said, pointing toward the bedroom with a shaking hand, trying not to make any quick movements that might trigger a reaction from one of the swat squad. She didn't think about protecting her husband; she just wanted to get the guns out of her face.

Kurt should have come out of the bedroom, given all the racket. That he didn't made Lena realize how bad things were going to turn out. Her personal policeman stayed in front of her, pointing the gun in her face, while the three others pushed open the bedroom door, letting in a cold draft from an open window. Kurt had run, apparently out the bedroom window.

For the next two hours, Lena sat in a hard wooden chair next to a detective's desk at the police station, answering questions. After determining that Lena was unlikely to be an accomplice, Detective Jan Hauer gave her the basics: a young woman had been stabbed, strangled and possibly raped in the building where Kurt worked as a maintenance man. Both Kurt and his friend Kevin were considered the prime suspects, as they were the last people known to be in her apartment before the young woman's boyfriend had come home from work and found her twisted, naked body, face down on her bed.

Jan asked Lena about Kurt's behavior that night, how he typically treated or talked about women, whether he was ever violent or assaulted her. By the time the interview was over, Lena caught Jan shaking her head ever so slightly at times, as if she couldn't understand why Lena was married to him. And when Lena finally got up to leave, the detective suggested that she not return home until her husband was apprehended. Jan called an officer over to the desk and asked him to drive Lena to wherever she decided to stay for the night.

Lena wished she had a friend she could call, not relishing the idea of a sterile hotel room, but it was 2 a.m., and she knew that if she called one of her reporter friends, they would be up all of the rest of the night, talking and speculating about Kurt and the crime. That wouldn't be fair to any friend, and she was sure she wasn't ready to talk to anyone about it yet. Instead, she spent the night in a suite in the Westin downtown, an extravagance that made no sense except for the fact that nothing else made sense to her right then either.

With Kurt's arrest at a car rental counter south of downtown the next day, Lena's days began to swirl around her, a confusing passage of time that never seemed to square with what 24 hours had always felt like before. Before this crazy thing had happened, she had spent the minutes it took her to fall asleep at night reading. Now those sleepless minutes had stretched to hours, as she struggled to imagine how her life could ever return to normal. She couldn't read; her eyes wouldn't focus on the page of any book, and with the unfenced freedom of seemingly endless, solitary, undedicated hours, her mind refused to settle down and let her sleep.

THE INVESTIGATION into the murder of the woman in the apartment complex where she'd first met Kurt took two months, and the preparations for the trial lasted another month. By the time Kurt's trial began, Lena had missed three months of work, not because she was asked to take a leave of absence, but because she found it impossible to concentrate on reporting and writing. After a month, her friends had stopped trying to get her to go out at night, and she sat like a prisoner in her house, the doors locked and the windows secured with steel rods.

Thankfully, she wasn't really afraid of Kurt returning – he was tightly locked away after the judge had refused to release him on the bail that his defense attorneys had requested. But, she wanted to shut out the outside world, especially at night, when her own self-loathing reached its peak. She didn't so much think about his trial or their future. She simply played the past two years over and over in her mind, trying to make sense of what choices she had made, making no progress.

None of her friends had any experience like hers. By the time the trial was over, though, Lena had developed a new friendship in the one person she never would have imagined getting to know: one of Kurt's ex-girlfriends.

They first met outside the interrogation room at the police station. Lena often met with detective Jan or the attorneys on either side of Kurt's case there. She knew that someone could listen to their conversation on the other side of the one-way mirror, but she no longer cared. She had nothing to hide except her own shame in being Kurt's wife, and everyone already knew about that.

Lena had wiped her eyes and composed herself in solitude in the room for a few minutes after the attorneys left, and as she walked out, she bumped into Jan and Jo, nearly knocking them both over in the doorway.

"Have you two met?" Jan asked them, as she recovered her balance and stepped aside to introduce the two women. They shook their heads and Jan placed a hand on each of their backs. "You might find some comfort in getting to know each other," Jan suggested.

The detective had become the only person in whom Lena felt comfortable confiding about her marriage with Kurt over the past couple of months. As on the night of Kurt's arrest, Jan had adopted what you might call bed-side manner, if she'd been a priest or a nurse or a hospice worker. She was never in a hurry to get an answer or reach a quick conclusion when she talked with Lena about Kurt's behavior and activities before the murder. She seemed to genuinely feel sorry for Lena's situation, and gave Lena her phone number for what she called "nighttime crises of confidence" that Lena experienced while the investigation was on-going. Lena had never used the privilege, but was comforted by the option.

"Lena Bettencourt, this is Jo Blandin. Jo, this is Kurt's wife, Lena," the detective gave the formal introduction. "Jo was Kurt's girlfriend before he met you," she explained to Lena.

The two women locked eyes. With a bit of panic, Lena wondered what Jo must have thought of her for having married Kurt, but Jo's gaze softened in apparent empathy, and Lena finally held out her hand to shake. Jo took her hand in both of hers, and held it warmly.

"I'm so sorry for what you're going through," she said. "Maybe we can get together and help each other get through this."

"Sure," Lena said apprehensively, not wanting to commit to anything yet. Anyway, what did Jo have to get through? She was just an ex-girlfriend. It seemed that Jo's reaction was leaning toward pity, something she didn't want. "I'll ask Jan to help us set something up," Jo offered as Lena started to walk away, sliding her coat over her shoulders as she turned.

"No, seriously," the detective said, reaching out to stop Lena before she reached the door to the police station. "Let's set something up right now."

IT TURNED OUT THAT, oddly, Jo had a lot more experience with Kurt's anger and anti-social behavior than Lena had. The two women met a week later at the Ship Tavern in the Brown Palace Hotel. The 100-year-old hotel was a Denver landmark, and its charms stood the test of time. The atrium's stained glass ceiling and grilled balconies alone were worth at least 15 minutes of gawking, and the Ship Tavern, afternoon teas in the lobby, Churchill's cigar bar and Palace Arms Restaurant were all worthy of a tourist's visit, and yet still attracted Denver residents who never tired of the setting.

When Lena walked into the atrium for their meeting, Jo was standing in the middle, looking up. It was a favorite pastime of locals to try to identify the two wrought-iron grills that had been installed upside down along the hallway balconies that surrounded the atrium's nine-story open space. Lena loved to do it too, and she knew she wasn't alone in that she could never remember where they were, and had to discover them over again each time she looked.

"Hey," they greeted each other in unison. They didn't shake hands and didn't hug, but Jo seemed much more comfortable than

Lena, as she motioned for Lena to lead the way into the tavern. With a wave of her hand, Lena suggested they sit at the bar. If things didn't go well, it would be easier to leave Jo sitting alone on a bar stool than at a table, she thought.

Lena asked for a wine list, ordered a glass of Pinot Grigio and waited for Jo to decide what to drink, relieved when she, too, ordered alcohol. Watching Jo peruse the menu and order, Lena noticed for the first time their similarities. They were both short, brunette, slightly overweight in the way you are if you don't stop eating at the age of 40, and olive skinned. They even dressed alike, in jeans and a cotton sweater with low-heeled boots. Jo, if anything, looked younger than Lena's 44, but age was difficult to assess, she thought, ever since people had stopped smoking, exercised more and started using moisturizer around the time of their 30th birthday.

"I can't imagine how hard this is for you," Jo said, magnanimously, turning toward Lena as soon as the bartender left to fix their drinks. "It's hard for me, and I'm five years away from him."

Already Lena wished she hadn't come. She didn't want to "share" her feelings about Kurt or the crime – Jan was her only confidant and she was enough. Lena didn't want to talk about it with anyone else, not even someone who had obviously made the same mistake she had in choosing to spend time with a probable murderer.

She waited for her wine to arrive and took a sip before answering.

"I'm not sure I want to talk about this," she said, staring at the wine glass in her hands, avoiding Jo's intimidating steady eyes. "I don't know what good it will do. I don't know what talking about Kurt can do for either of us. It might be better if we both forget about him altogether."

"I understand," Jo said, taking a sip of her dirty martini. They sat in silence for a couple more awkward minutes.

"I don't know what I'm supposed to get out of this," Lena finally broke the silence by repeating herself, hoping to speed their meeting to a quick conclusion. "Do you know something I don't? Are you some kind of psychiatrist or therapist?" She turned to look at Jo.

Jo didn't meet her eyes, but continued to look beyond her drink along an infinite line through the bar in front of them. "I think maybe we have more in common than you think," she said. "At least, I think maybe we can help each other understand what's happening to us."

"I know what's happening. I made a big mistake. Probably the biggest in my life. No, definitely the biggest in my life. I don't understand why I married the man. But, I also don't understand what that has to do with you."

"I think I have some ideas."

"What? Do you see into souls? Or maybe God told you why we're here together," Lena said, pitch, anger and impatience building with every loony sentence. She wanted to get up and leave. There was no way this meeting was going to do anything to change her situation, and Jo's calm behavior didn't help. It just made Lena feel crazy in comparison.

"Look," Jo raised her hand to stop Lena. Her voice rose, too, agitated finally with Lena's belligerence. "I'm no more sure of this than you are, but I do have a little information that Detective Hauer thought might help you. That's why I agreed to meet you here, but if you don't want to hear it, that's fine with me."

Jo's reciprocal anger helped. Lena didn't want to be the emotional basket case in the midst of an intellectual interchange. If Jo was mad, too, that was better. They might have more in common than she thought – and maybe Jo did know something that would help her stop turning the same questions over and over in her head every night.

"Okay, okay. So talk, " Lena said in the calmest voice she could muster. "I've got at least five minutes before I'm finished with my wine anyway. Might as well hear what you know."

"What I want to share with you is my perspective of being in the middle of a string of Kurt's relationships," Jo said, starting slowly. "Before me, it was Susan. After me, it was you. I have to admit that my relationship with Kurt was fairly brief, but it was pretty eventful, and I thought maybe letting you know about it might help you get through this. It isn't your fault."

"I never thought it was my fault!"

"I know..."

"I didn't rape that woman. I wasn't there. I didn't tell him that was okay, and I certainly never approved of Kevin as a friend and role model." Lena fumed. "How could it have been my fault?"

"No. No. I know. I'm not saying that. I mean, I don't think it was your fault that you two ended up together," Jo said, gesturing with her hand in a way that signaled "calm down."

Lena glanced around the bar and was grateful to see that it was empty except for a couple that was smooching in a booth at the far end of the room.

"I'm sorry. I don't know what you know, and I guess I should be willing to hear it," Lena said, trying to modulate her voice in spite of the tightness in her throat. It didn't help that Jo, in spite of looking younger, seemed so mature. So in control. The younger woman's relatively better composure seemed to sap her confidence instead of calm her down.

"Hey, we're all his victims and enablers in a way," Jo said, "victims of an intention that we had no idea we were enabling."

Lena studied Jo's face. The younger woman returned her gaze, and Lena started to feel a bit of respect. Jo was likely as hurt by Kurt as Lena, but she had apparently risen above it, even to the point of reaching out to help someone to whom she owed nothing.

"How'd you get so smart about this?"

"I have just spent six years volunteering on a police crisis line. I've had to take a lot of training. But, to be honest, I've also spent most of the past five years in therapy," Jo said, looking down at her drink as if afraid to see Lena's reaction to that admission. It was the first crack in her steady demeanor, and Lena started to warm to her.

They sat in silence for a long minute, as neither of them seemed to know how to get re-started.

"I heard that you're going to testify at the trial," Lena finally said.

"I might. But, it depends on whether I can tell the jury anything that will be allowed in court."

"Would it hurt Kurt or Kevin if you did?"

"Kurt. I don't know anything about Kevin. He was not Kurt's friend when I knew him. But, I also don't want to help make a case that Kurt is insane or sick. I don't want to see him out on the street spreading his trouble or hurting any more women," Jo said. She shook her head as if she'd seen far too much of that already.

"I don't really know what you're talking about," Lena said, feeling silly for being so ignorant of Kurt's past. She'd married a man she knew little about. If she'd been smart she wouldn't even have dated a man she knew as little about as she did about Kurt. It was embarrassing, but the information was likely to get worse, not better, she realized.

"I guess you've probably noticed the similarity between us," Jo started slowly. Lena nodded.

"Well, Susan would pass for our sister. She was a journalist like you, back in Kansas where Kurt grew up. She disappeared seven years ago, and the only way I know any of this is because I did some research after what happened to me."

Jo's theory, as she continued to explain it was that Kurt's behavior clearly demonstrated some patterns, and those patterns had made Lena an obvious choice for him. She wasn't the only one who had been fooled by Kurt's earlier enthusiasm for a relationship, and she wasn't the only one who had failed to take his quick slide into sloth seriously when it happened.

Jo was a philosophy major in college. She had gone on to get her PhD and was now working on tenure as a professor at the University of Denver. At first, Kurt impressed her with his desire to make a life together, in spite of their obvious mismatch. She was well-educated and ambitious. But he never seemed ashamed of his blue-collar position or lack of schooling. He was at ease talking about philosophy or current politics or modern art; in fact, his mastery of so many subjects played right into Jo's progressive politics. Just because you weren't born into an educated, wealthy family didn't mean you weren't intelligent or worthy, after all. It just meant that you started from a different place. Given enough generations to allow your offspring to overcome those early disadvantages, even your family would eventually spawn brilliant leaders of politics or academics or business.

But as soon as they had moved in together, Kurt's behavior changed. Like with Lena, he'd become a sedentary, disinterested and uncommunicative drunk. As Jo explained it, it was as if he were trying to goad Jo into acknowledging he wasn't worthy and leaving him. Also like Lena, she was too busy and absorbed in her own career to focus on the deterioration of the relationship.

One night, while she was at school, grading papers, he brought one of his rough friends home with him. When Jo returned to their condo, Kurt was passed out drunk on the couch and the other man was watching reruns of "Friends" by himself.

Jo thought she had managed to slip unnoticed from the back entrance, through the kitchen and into the bedroom. But she was hanging up her blouse in the closet when she heard the bedroom door scrape open slowly. Kurt's friend stood in the open door, smirking as if her half-dressed state was an admission of her weakness.

Jo told the rest of the story quickly, obviously leaving out many awful details. Without Kurt waking up – let alone coming to her rescue – the man gagged her, beat her, raped her and left her in a heap on the bedroom floor with her nylons tied around her hands behind her back and another pair tied across her mouth. The next morning, Kurt woke her from an exhausted clump of sleep, pulled her to her feet, yanked the nylons off of her face and demanded an explanation. Exhausted and in horrible pain from the rape and from spending the night on her knees, she simply cowered in fear and humiliation, two things she'd never experienced before in her life.

After he left for work, Jo called the police, and before Kurt returned home that afternoon, she had packed everything she cared to keep and moved to a hotel room. From there, she filed for a restraining order, and went about erasing what she could of her year with Kurt. At first she was a bit surprised but relieved that he didn't seem to make any effort to get her back. But eventually curiosity got the best of her and she began looking into his past with the help of a law school professor at the university who specialized in criminal law.

The short story of Kurt's "issues," according to Jo's theory, was that he and his father had been abandoned by Kurt's mother in a small town in Kansas when Kurt was seven. His mother had been a college graduate, a bright sociologist working as a high school counselor. Apparently, Kurt's father was a charming, good-looking local carpenter who had been hired to remodel her small home when she'd moved to town. But, Kurt's father was also an alcoholic and a mean drunk, and one day Kurt came home from school and found her farewell note for his father.

After dropping out of high school, Kurt had moved to Kansas City for work, had been married for only a short time before the woman sued for divorce. There wasn't any evidence of what happened to the marriage or where the woman had gone afterwards, but, shortly after that Kurt had moved in with Susan, a bright, young reporter at the Star. They were engaged to be married, but according to stories in the paper at the time, she disappeared about a month after agreeing to be his wife. The stories also quoted friends who said she was afraid of him and was secretly planning to leave and move as far away as she needed to so that he couldn't find her. He wasn't the man she thought he was, they reported, and she was afraid he might become violent if she admitted that she wanted to leave him.

In spite of her relative notoriety as a newspaper reporter, the police treated Susan's disappearance as a case of a run-away bride and investigated no further. It was three years later when the local newspaper reported that a friend of Kurt's had bragged to cellmates in the Kansas State Penitentiary that he'd been let into the house by Kurt late one night and allowed to rape Susan while Kurt watched from outside, looking through the bedroom window.

"I think the bottom line is this," Jo said. "Susan probably did run away. And that once again completed the pattern that Kurt expected to see – women would leave him like his mother had left him and his father, and if he had to hurry that along with violence, he would. Even if meant betraying and hurting us. Even if it meant encouraging rape. It was as if he couldn't stand the suspense of waiting for all of us to reject him. What's sort of weird is that he keeps choosing the same woman over and over – petite, brunette, educated, professional. Us."

Jo had finished her story and waited for Lena to take it in. Lena couldn't seem to make a sentence form in her mouth. She was confused more than frightened by Jo's version of things. She hadn't been raped, but if Jo was right, was it only a matter of time before that would have happened? She hadn't left Kurt, but only because she wasn't committed enough to her marriage to care about how rotten it had become. She simply wasn't paying any attention. How could she have been so naïve about her own danger?

That night, lying in bed, waiting for sleep to come, she played her old mind game of "what's the worst?" Whenever she hated her job, felt overwhelmed by the size of her bills and the limits of her paycheck, or wondered if she should leave Kurt or if he would leave her, she always calmed herself down by asking, "what's the worst that could happen?" If she lost her job, she had options. If Kurt divorced her and she lost half of the house she'd paid for all by herself, she'd still have time to recover without retiring in poverty. If she left Kurt, she'd just move far away and change her name and start over.

But now, she realized, staring blindly into the dark of her bedroom, she'd never come close to knowing the worst that could have happened to her. If Kurt hadn't hooked up with Kevin, if he hadn't exited her life so suddenly, what could have happened would likely have been worse than anything she'd ever imagined. Much worse.

THE TRIAL lasted a brutally long three weeks. Kurt and Kevin were tried separately, and while the police never tried to prove that Kurt had actually raped the victim or handled the knife that killed her, it had been clear that he was present throughout the crime. That was enough. The district attorney was seeking a first-degree murder conviction, but was offering the jury second-degree as an option.

He and Kevin had been working on a week-long project to clean out the dryer vents in the apartment complex where Lena had first met him. On the Friday that the police barged into her house, the two men had finished up in the apartment of a young woman who had earlier snubbed Kevin's invitations to go out. The woman was home during the day, unlike most of the apartment residents, because she worked the 3-to-11 shift as a nurse at Denver General. When she didn't report for work that afternoon, her co-workers tried to phone her and then contacted her boyfriend, who found her raped and stabbed body. It didn't take long to trace the evidence to the two maintenance workers. It had been less than eight hours after the murder when the police had barged into her house.

Through most of the trial, Lena sat in the back of the courtroom seething in anger. Not anger at Kurt, but at herself for being part of the disgusting scene. In between the hours of the trial, sitting over frozen diet meals she subsisted on through those three weeks, she tried to recall what Kurt looked like to her when they met, when they got married, those first few weeks of their marriage.

As hard as she dug into her memory, she couldn't uncover many solid impressions. The way she laughed when he first suggested marriage remained fairly vivid. So did the time she drove to his apartment complex to pick him up for a movie date and didn't recognize him when he came out the front door and walked toward her car. He looked like a much younger person than she had started to construct in her head. Less solid, less mature.

That she couldn't unearth much else scared her. She wasn't afraid of Kurt – he was safely behind bars. But she was afraid that if she could date, marry and live with a person for whom she had so little regard, how well connected was she with anyone in her life? Were her friends really the good, funny people she assumed they were? Was her managing editor really the insecure, petty man she thought he was, or was she missing out on getting to know a complex, sympathetic, deeply spiritual human being? How was it she continued to go through life as if she were an only child living on the farm, miles away from her closest schoolmates? How selfish was she that she never really abandoned the safe, private life of her own thoughts and emotions and that she declined to get to know the internal life of another person?

Finally, the trial was over and the jury quickly convicted Kurt of second-degree murder. While Kevin's actions were pre-meditated, according to the prosecutor's case – now proven, Kurt's were those of opportunity, anger and at least cowardice if not complicity. Lena didn't come close enough to him in the courtroom to make eye contact, let alone exchange words, after the verdict. From a hard bench at the back of the room, she sat and watched the courtroom empty of spectators, reporters, the attorneys and finally the court security, and cried. She wasn't crying for Kurt, as some of those who filed past her out the big double doors behind her probably thought. She was crying out of loneliness – a loneliness that wasn't new, but that was raw and present in a new way.

Later, Kurt's defense attorney asked her if she would speak for him in the pre-sentencing hearing, but she declined.

"I don't know him well enough," she said.

"What do you mean? You were married to him."

"Only nominally, I realize now."

"Look, I know that you're probably angry to have been brought into this," he said. "But don't take that out on Kurt now." The defense attorney begged. He had apparently also been blinded by Kurt's charisma and seemed to really care about his client. "He really needs your help to avoid a longer sentence than he deserves.

He really doesn't know anyone else who he thinks can support him."

"No," Lena was firm. "I really mean it. I don't think I ever knew him, and I'd feel like a fraud standing there talking about the goodness of a person when I'm not sure there was any. And, I really don't think he deserves any leniency."

The lawyer was surprised at her frostiness, but he shouldn't have been, Lena thought. They'd had plenty of conversations prior to the trial that should have painted a pretty clear picture of what had been a marriage of neglect, not of lovers.

AFTER HIS SENTENCING, and a couple of weeks after he had been shipped down to Canon City, she drove down to the penitentiary. She felt comforted rather than offended at the huge concrete façade, the high, solid metal fencing and the cold, all-business way she was treated by the officers who led her into the visitation room. If these hard surfaces and efficient guards did their jobs every day like they did that day, she could be certain that they would effectively stand between her and Kurt for at least 15 years, at which point he would be eligible for parole.

"You know, I didn't touch that woman," Kurt said as they sat across from each other with a thick pane of bullet-proof glass between them. Lena couldn't think of anything to say in response. Whether he had or had not laid a hand on the woman was totally irrelevant, she and the jury agreed. He had stood by and watched not once, but several times while women were abused, beaten, raped and now murdered. She shivered with the realization of how close she had been to a man with so little sense of right and wrong, and now with so little remorse.

She searched his face for some relic of familiarity. His square jaw that she had once seen as masculine and proud was a little fleshier than she remembered, although it was set, hard and defiant. His blue eyes seemed darker, smaller and colder than she had remembered them. But his hair, a big bush of resistance to age, still drew her eyes. She had run her fingers through it whenever she had had a chance, until they had stopped touching each other altogether. It was unfair that such a grand head of hair should be the property of a man with so little else to offer, she thought. As we age, women get thick in the waist and thighs, while men lose their hair. It's the natural order – a way of keeping things even

89

between the genders. Now it seemed like another sign that Kurt wasn't maturing like others, another way he refused to grow up and be an adult.

"Are you just going to sit there and stare?" he asked angrily. "What did you come here for?"

"I'm filing for divorce," she quickly answered. "I thought I should tell you to your face."

A smirk started to form at the corner of his mouth. "I expected this." He locked eyes with her for a long time. Finally, he slapped his hands heavily on the counter top in front of him, and slowly lifted himself to his feet, not moving his eyes from hers. He said nothing. The smirk fully formed, he turned and walked back toward the guard at the back of the room, and together, they disappeared through the heavy door.

Relieved that it was over without shouting or a messy scene, Lena sat and looked at her hands in her lap. Tears burned in her eyes, and she sat still until she felt calm and composed enough to get back through the locks and gates and leave Kurt's new home in her rear-view mirror.

7 CALIFORNIA

After leaving the traffic of Interstate 10 behind her, Lena found driving into Palm Springs on Highway 111 a bit disconcerting, as always. It was a relief to be out of the rat race of the freeway, but the dry, rough foothills that rose off the highway to her right, shading the narrow blacktop from the afternoon sun, were aggressively ugly. Dust blew across the road and formed sand drifts against the occasional curbs along the blacktop. This was the desert. That's why people flocked here from Los Angeles, San Francisco, Portland, Seattle and Vancouver all winter. Sun. Heat. And, for many, golf. But between I-10 and town, the dry desert seemed incapable of supporting anything, let alone a lush green fairway or tall and majestic palm trees.

Once she passed the welcome center and the slender sliver of asphalt that shot up the foothills toward the tramway, palm trees sprouted on both sides of the road, increasingly shading her entry into the center of town. Slowly, she drove out of the wind and dust of the highway into the oasis of Palm Springs.

Lena was not only looking forward to some desert sun and heat, she was looking forward to getting back to golf. Two weeks before she started the drive to Palm Springs, she pulled a muscle in her back while throwing her golf clubs into her car after an on-course short-game lesson with Erin. For those last two weeks in Suncadia, she had to rest it, ice it and feed it ibuprofen. She was just getting some flexibility back and had started waking up without pain when it was time to head to the desert. She made the trip in three days instead of two so that she could get out of the car more and keep her muscles from tightening up again.

Back spasms were nothing new to Lena. The first time she'd been temporarily paralyzed by one, she was covering the Western Governors Association conference at Tahoe. Getting ready to return to Denver, she sneezed while leaning over to zip her suitcase shut. She felt a big muscle in the lower left side of her back start to tighten like a middle-of-the-night Charley-horse and then suddenly it hardened into a painful, stabbing knot that dropped her to her knees. She spent two lonely days in traction in a hospital in Truckee, and unable to hold a book in front of her, she had nothing to do.

Since then, she was careful. She could retrigger the spasm either by tightening the muscle consciously or unconsciously, as often happened when she succumbed to an involuntary stretch when she woke up in the morning. She lifted things with her back vertical and her knees bent. She avoided any task that required her to stand while holding her arms out in front of her, like painting walls or cleaning windows. Even making the bed could be tricky. She stretched carefully.

Missing two weeks of golf at the end of the season at Suncadia due to her back pain wasn't the worst thing to happen to her golf game. It had started to rain again and the daytime temperatures hovered at 50 degrees at best. Carly, Brandt and Ryne stopped coming up to the mountains for weekends, and even Kim had stopped coming up for their Sunday rounds. When she had been going out for solo rounds, the fallen aspen and maple leaves cleverly camouflaged golf balls, and keeping her eye on her shot until it hit the ground was no guarantee that she would find it when she got to the landing spot. It was frustrating and uncomfortable golf, and if she had to be injured in the middle of her training, Lena figured the timing couldn't have been better.

As she drove into Palm Springs on her way to the condo she had rented for the winter, Lena took a detour past a couple of her favorite golf courses, pulling up into the parking lots and walking to the edge of the nearest fairways for a long look. The manicured grass and sparkling water hazards triggered hot flashes of sorts - the kind of sudden warmth in her gut that reminded her of sexual attraction.

What attracted Lena to golf in the first place had been the setting, and nowhere she'd ever played – even Hawaii – were the golf courses more beautiful and peaceful than the desert courses of Palm Springs. Nowhere else had she found as sharp a contrast between bright-green neatly manicured fairways and expansive sandy waste areas. The sandy hazards were haphazardly sprinkled with wispy desert willows, lime-green palo verde, spiny cacti and massive agave. Nowhere had she seen the mountains loom in such a dramatic, layered rise to the west, changing colors from bright pink in the morning to dark purple at dusk. And, as a child of the Midwest, she still found it hard to believe that the tall, swaying palm trees that lined the fairways were real.

Lena took a week to get settled into the condo she had rented for the next five months. It was vintage 1970s – with plywood kitchen and bath cabinets, a mirrored breakfast nook and a conversation pit in the living room that cozied up to a small gas fireplace surrounded by ersatz sandstone. There must have been some fascination with below-grade accoutrements in the 70s, Lena guessed, as the bathroom also featured a sunken tub that functioned but looked too dangerous to get into. Someone had replaced what was probably an avocado refrigerator sometime in the past few decades, but the avocado stove remained, and behind it, a pale orange wall. The rest of the condo had been painted white, including the cabinets and the plastic tile in the bathroom. The total effect of the fake surfaces, the paint-over and the vintage architectural elements was somehow comforting in an I-can't-do-anything-to-this-place-that-could-jeopardize-my-security-deposit way.

Lena had stayed in the same place three years before for a two-week winter vacation, so she knew what to bring with her from Suncadia: a bathroom scale, a juicer for fresh grapefruit, and a decent floor lamp for reading. She stocked the kitchen with canned tuna, salad greens and vegetables; she intended to make the change of scenery an opportunity to clean up her act and eat better.

She unpacked her suitcases and nearly filled the second-hand dresser and the small mirror-door closet, even though she'd brought little more than a bathing suit, hiking boots and golf clothes, not planning to spend much effort socializing off the golf course. She figured that a few laps across the condo complex swimming pool and a movie at a theater every now and then might be a nice idea, but otherwise, she had no desire to join the desert's snowbird society. She signed up for a Netflix subscription and called for basic cable so she could get the Golf Channel. If Terry and Carly came down as they'd promised, she expected that they'd go for a hike up Indian Canyon and maybe spend an afternoon window shopping on El Paseo. But she didn't have any plans to entertain the neighbors or look for new friends. This was her chance to focus on her golf game with few interruptions or distractions.

Once she was settled and all traces of soreness in her back had retreated, Lena's next order of business in the desert was to find an instructor to work with over the winter. She had three names of people that Erin knew in the valley, and she called to make appointments with them. Given that she was planning to spend $200 a week on lessons, she needed to make a careful, calculated choice.

Of course, it didn't work out that way. The first instructor Erin had recommended had moved out of the valley and was replaced by a former PGA Tour player who'd had a brief run inside the ropes in the early '80s. She wasn't comfortable working with someone without a recommendation, so she placed her hopes in the other two. But, being well regarded and extremely popular, they were already booked full with students for the winter. Lena settled on Rich, the former PGA golfer.

To start off on a good foot, she pretended to remember Rich's Tour career when she first met him at the driving range at a course close to her condo on the south edge of Palm Springs. And he pretended to be sober.

The first lesson went well, as Lena did most of the work, showing Rich her full swing, her set-up routine, her chipping and pitching skills, and her putting technique, and talking about what she wanted to get out of the winter's lessons. Later, it occurred to her that he had been able to fake sobriety that first day because he didn't have to say or do much.

By the time they were half-way through her second lesson, though, he was standing too close – when she wasn't swinging the club – and getting too touchy when he readjusted her grip. By the end of the lesson, she deduced that his lack of respect for her personal space was not just a cultural difference between native Californians and the rest of the world. He was not just a lush. He was a lecherous one.

Lena paid him the $80 she owed him for the lesson, and avoided a possibly unpleasant good-bye by rushing off "for a meeting" before he had a chance to ask her when she wanted to take her next lesson.

Unfortunately, as a highly functioning drunk, Rich remembered to call her the next day to try to set up the next appointment, leaving a message on her cell phone. When she didn't call him back, he wasn't deterred, and he left five more messages in the next two days. A week later, she came home after a movie to find him waiting for her on the front step of her condo complex.

"Hey, are you avoiding me?" he shouted to her as she walked up the sidewalk after parking her car at the curb. He stood up, obviously relying on the support of the porch railing. He was finally drunk enough that he couldn't fake sobriety, and for a moment she was afraid that he'd either lunge forward off the porch and fall over, or he'd grab her when she got close to him.

"I am indeed avoiding you. And I am also asking you to leave now." Lena stayed back, far enough from the porch that she would have a fighting chance of getting back to her car if he stumbled down the front steps to catch her.

"But we need to talk," Rich gestured for her to come up and join him on the step, his flailing arm nearly tipping him over.

"We can talk later."

"But you don't return my calls!"

"Really, Rich. Leave now."

"What if I don't. What if I just stay here until you get sick of me." He sat down hard on the step, his long legs splayed across the steps, blocking her path to the door, holding a dented can of Bud at his crotch.

I'm already sick of you, Lena thought, but she held her tongue. She didn't see any upside in making a drunk, 200-pound man with an athlete's – even if it was aging – body mad at her at 11 o'clock at night. Although she'd been in the condo for two weeks, she still didn't know any of her neighbors well enough to want to wake them up with a shouting match on her front step. Being a loner was her thing, but for once, she wished she had at least tried to meet some of the younger residents in the building.

"You don't want me to call the police, do .."

Rich cut her off with a violent wave. "No!" he spat beer with his words. "I just want you to tell me why you think you're so fucking special that you don't have to return my calls. Or talk to me. We had an agreement, you know. We were going to work together all winter."

"Only if it .." Lena stopped. Did it really make sense to try to reason with him? she asked herself. It was clear that he had no sense of what their relationship should be, and she wondered how he had managed to teach for the past year without stepping over the line with a student before. Probably he hadn't.

"How'd you find my apartment?" she suddenly wondered out loud.

"You mean condo. Fucking fancy condo. I Googled you."

"How would you find my address by Googling?"

"I lied. I got it from California Edison. They know where you live."

"But that isn't public, is it?"

"It is if you have friends in high places at California Edison," he replied, in a sing-song voice that sounded like the "nah-nah-na-nah-nah" of kids in a playground.

"Oh Christ."

"And I also found out about your fancy job and your college degree and a lot more shit about you. You're quite the smarty pants, aren't you?"

Lena realized that she wasn't going to talk him into leaving by telling him she had lost her job. Recognizing defeat, she stuck her hand in her shorts pocket where she'd left her car keys and tried to gauge how fast he could follow if she ran to her car. It certainly was a better bet than trying to find her phone in her purse and dialing 911 faster before he could reach her.

Behind Rich, the screen door to the complex's fitness center suddenly opened, and Lena took advantage of the distraction to spin around and run to her car at the curb. Rich had turned to see one of her neighbors step outside for a smoke, and she stabbed the key fob button and quickly slipped behind the wheel. She locked the doors and turned around as she was driving away to see a beer can fly across the front lawn toward her. It fell far short of its target.

Lena wasn't sure where the nearest police station was. When she got a few blocks away, toward the center of town, she pulled into the parking lot of a busy Mexican restaurant and bar and waited for her heart rate to slow down. She decided against going to the police – it would take far more time than she wanted to devote to Rich as a problem, and the police probably wouldn't be much help anyway. She drove to the fancy Renaissance Hotel in the middle of Palm Springs, and checked in for a night. If Rich returned, she'd call the police then and see what they could do. And in the meantime, she'd make sure she always returned home before dark.

A WEEK LATER, Lena found Gary Gussett at Tahquitz Golf Club, a muni only a couple of miles from her condo, and engaged him as her designated mentor for the winter. But she had some trouble settling into a routine. At first, she decided to sleep as long as her body asked her to, going to bed at 9 and getting up as the sun came up, around 7. She walked to the downtown Starbucks, enjoying the quiet streets and cool mornings. She didn't get to the driving range until 10, put in some half-hearted full-swing practice, shot some balls out of the practice bunker and putted. But three hours later, she was home, ready for a nap.

She sat for hours on the patio, staring glassily at the grassy common area encircled by the condos of the complex and at the face of the San Jacinto Mountains that rose steeply out of the valley on the west edge of town. Late in November, the sun sank behind the mountains by 4:00, and it was dark by 5:00. Not wanting to meet Rich on her doorstep again, she was either safely ensconced behind the security fence that guarded the common patio areas, or nestled on her couch with a book and the Golf Channel by then.

After three weeks, she hadn't mastered any of the small tweaks to her swing that Gary had recommended, and the rounds she played on the weekends with strangers weren't impressing anyone, either. Finally, it was Gary who suggested she had better get serious soon, or she might as well consider herself simply on vacation. She certainly wasn't getting ready for a season of amateur tournaments.

"You're wasting your money and you're blowing your chance to do this right," he said. She had dropped her club and collapsed into a crouch with her head in her hands after hitting a dozen poor six-iron shots in a row on the driving range.

"I like you," Gary continued. "I like you a lot, but I don't want to stand here and watch you practice." He shook his head slowly at her, reaching down and helping her stand up. "If you're going to practice only when I'm standing here, you're never going to improve."

Lena liked Gary, too. He had an easy way of explaining her mistakes, and always found a clever metaphor for explaining how to do things right. And he'd been as encouraging as anyone had been when she told him of her plans to play in the USGA Senior Amateur in the fall. "Bravo! I love it when people have real goals we can work toward," he said, echoing Erin when she sat down to interview him after the fiasco with Rich. But now she knew she was not only losing precious time to laziness and lack of focus, but she was also disappointing him.

Gary picked up her clubs and motioned for her to follow him off the driving range and into his tiny office behind the pro shop. He took out a sheet of paper and a pencil, asked one of the assistant pros to brew a new pot of coffee, and together he and Lena made a list of the skills she needed to master over the winter and what practice routines would make it happen.

"Some people just need spreadsheets, and I'm starting to think you're one of them," he said. Lena laughed. How in just a couple of weeks had he come to know her so well?

They settled on a routine that required six hours of hitting full swings, putting, pitching and chipping; an hour of weight lifting in the small weight room at the club; and an hour of walking, bike riding or rollerblading. Lena grimaced at the thought of turning what felt like it should be vacation into a full-time job, but she knew Gary was right. She promised to work on it for the next two weeks, and through the time when he was planning to go home to Atlanta for Christmas. If the routine wasn't working, they'd reconsider the plan in January.

It actually came as a relief to have a plan when she got up the next morning. She walked the mile and a half to Starbucks with more purpose than before, and returned with her one-hour of walking already under her belt. She dressed for the range, packed a tuna sandwich for lunch and was hitting a warm-up bucket of balls before 9. She took it slow and easy and without any concern other than the tempo of her swing. The bucket was empty in a half hour, and she stopped in the clubhouse and filled a Styrofoam cup with thick, lukewarm coffee and headed for the putting green, where Gary was watching a tiny teenaged girl putt, giving her an occasional word of encouragement.

"I hate to admit it, but you hit the nail on the head," Lena told him as he stopped to greet her before walking off the practice green with his young student. "I feel better already. I guess I do need a spreadsheet. Always have, always will."

The plan they developed for Lena started each day with a half-hour warm-up on the range, an hour of putting, an hour pitching and chipping, and a half-hour in the bunker before resting outside the clubhouse with a Diet Coke and her sandwich for lunch. She spent two more hours on the range, starting with the short irons and working up to the driver, focusing on Gary's recommended swing adjustments, and hitting each ball deliberately, with purpose. She changed into her running shoes, and spent most of an hour in the weight room, slowly working through the repetitions she'd learned years ago in Denver, long before she'd married Kurt and had gladly given up her gym membership. Then, she took a break for a glass of wine, and returned to the putting green, leaving just enough time to get home before dark.

For the next two weeks, she followed the same routine every weekday, changing only how she spent the last hour of her practice session. Sometimes she worked on lag putts; sometimes she returned to the bunker to practice hitting out of wet sand. And, sometimes she and Gary spent the last hour playing a couple of holes on the course and discussing course strategy. By the time she returned to the condo, made dinner and turned on a movie or opened a book, she was physically exhausted. She rarely made it through more than an hour of watching TV or reading before she was ready to shuffle off to bed.

She took a break from practice on the weekends, but not from golf. She checked the Desert Sun newspaper ads for special deals and played any course that didn't require a drive of more than 20 minutes from her condo. She moved back to the men's tees as she'd planned to do when she got to the desert.

And although she was far, far, far from reaching the magic 10,000 hours that Gladwell thought she needed to clock before her muscle memory took over and her swing became natural, she could hardly wait to show up for her first lesson with Gary on the third week of her new routine, the Monday before Christmas.

"I putted well, I hit out of the bunkers well and I had fewer miss-hits with my fairway woods than I can ever remember," she reported gleefully to Gary. Her Sunday round at Indian Canyons North had been a joy, and her face showed it.

Gary was pleased, and he congratulated her. But, he said, how had she scored?

"Seventy eight," Lena answered, her voice dropping. She knew exactly what Gary was getting at. A 78 in a friendly weekend round on a friendly resort course would probably be the equivalent of a 90 in a pressure-filled tournament on a championship course. She had a long way to go before she'd be ready for the Senior Amateur. Back to work.

Christmas came and went much as it had for Lena the past dozen years or so. It was a good day to get a tee-time, especially early in the morning when parents and grandparents were busy watching little ones open presents and either screech with delight or whine over their loot. She called Kim and Terry Christmas Eve to wish them a nice holiday, and exchanged text messages with Carly and Brandt. She roasted a duck, and threw out the half she didn't eat the next day, cringing at how fattening the bird had been for her.

While Christmas on the course was quiet and uncrowded, the next week was unbearable. Once-a-year golfers flew down in the desert by the hundreds to visit their parents, grandparents or in-laws, and they took to the links like thirsty drunks. The roads were clogged, and afternoon traffic slowed to a standstill on Highway 111, which ran the length of the Coachella Valley. The pace of play slowed to a crawl as the hackers took four or five shots to get out of every bunker. And they managed to get into as many bunkers as was mathematically possible in every round.

Lena quit trying to play for the week, and concentrated her efforts on the driving range and short-game practice area at Tahquitz. She wanted to show Gary real progress when he got back from his vacation.

ON SATURDAY MORNINGS IN JANUARY, before heading out to play a round, Lena started talking with Kim on the phone. It became his new Saturday routine. He got up early, started a pot of coffee and called her at 6:15. They talked for 15 minutes or so, sometimes a half hour, before he hung up to wake Stacy, help her get into her wheel chair and through her bathroom routine, and then fix her breakfast. He then waited for the caretaker, who came on Saturdays to clean house and keep Stacy company while Kim went out to play a wet round of golf in Seattle or to go shopping. The caretaker also visited Stacy at noon during the workweek, now that Stacy couldn't make herself lunch or use the bathroom alone anymore. One Saturday, he reported that he'd run into Terry at Costco the week before and they'd shared a hot dog and Coke and he caught up on Suncadia gossip. He seemed to enjoy the fact that their threesome was intact, even with Lena in Palm Springs.

Lena described the progress she was making in her golf game and warned him that he might have to move back to the blue tees next summer, if he wanted to preserve his manhood around her improving game. He described his miserably soggy rounds at Newcastle and Willows. They always talked about Stacy, too. He told her that his wife knew they talked on Saturdays before she woke up, and she always asked how Lena was doing. While the news about Stacy was never good, it cheered Lena up to talk to Kim and to have someone who cared about her hear about her steady progress on the golf course. She and Terry talked a couple of times a week about Suncadia gossip and Terry's latest romantic disasters, but they didn't talk much about golf.

8 KIM

About six weeks after she moved to Palm Springs for the winter, Terry flew down to spend a long weekend. Carly, after some major management shakeup at her office, hadn't been able to come along, as she had hoped. But Terry put Rex in a kennel, which told Lena everything she needed to know: this trip was important enough to Terry that she'd even part with her dog for a few days – not something Terry did lightly.

What surprised Lena was how good it was to see Terry come through the sliding glass doors that separated the terminal from the gates. Terry's broad face and long hair was one of the most beautiful sights she had seen in weeks, she realized. They skipped toward each other and hugged like fourth-grade best friends, oblivious of the other travelers who had to wend their way around them. Then, suddenly aware of the scene their enthusiastic reunion was making, they slinked off, arm-in-arm, to retrieve Terry's luggage.

Lena offered to take time away from her new golf routine to show Terry around town, but Terry wouldn't have it. She could drive herself to the tram, to El Paseo to shop, to the airport airplane museum. She wanted Lena to continue to focus and not to lose her concentration that she'd worked to regain.

But Lena cut back her hours on the range to save some energy for her friend, and at night, they made dinner, shared a bottle of wine, and then retired to the comfy chairs in front of the gas fireplace to chill and talk. Lena began to realize how much she had missed Terry since she left Suncadia. The idea was a bit scary: she'd never really needed a close friend before, but then, she'd never had a friend as close as Terry, either.

"How's the shop going?" Lena asked the first night as they sat in the conversation pit and watched the gas flame swirl around the ersatz fireplace logs, twirling the ice cubes around in the white Russians Lena had mixed for them.

"Same," Terry said. "I'm making enough money to pay the bills, but not enough to pay the other artists what they deserve." A starving artist of sorts herself, Terry knew how much work went into the weavings, the pottery, the quilts and the pillows her friends and suppliers made for the shop.

"So you'll be able to hang on?"

"I think so. At least as long as I want to do this."

"Are you thinking of doing something else?"

Terry laughed. "Yeah, either winning the lottery or marrying a prince. But I haven't even kissed any frogs, lately!"

Terry paused and counted on her fingers. "It's been 17 days since I've had a date, so my love drought has been worse than usual. But, I guess it was over Christmas."

"I'm just amazed at how many guys you actually find to date in that town," Lena said. "I'd think that you would have run out of potentials by now."

"Oh, there's always a new guy in town who hasn't figured out how to disappoint me yet," Terry mused. "It's a pretty transient place, you know."

"But how about the guys who are there for good? There have to be firemen and policemen and such. How about a school teacher? I had a really cute biology teacher when I was a sophomore in high school. Have you checked out the science teachers?"

"You know what's weird," Terry answered slowly, pausing to try to make sense of what she wanted to say. "I find it hard to meet the settled-down types. They aren't out at night, and I don't exactly have a reason to attend PTA meetings."

"Yeah, I hear you."

"And the construction and railroad guys are in one week and out the next, always moving on to something that promises them more money – or better looking women," Terry snorted. "Rex and I are getting kind of tired of test runs, you know."

Lena smiled, imagining Rex pouting about ceding his share of Terry's bed to another "test" case every couple of weeks or so. A dog could take only so much abuse and neglect.

"How about you?" Terry turned the tables on Lena. "How's the Palm Springs love life been?"

The pickings were surprisingly slim in Palm Springs as well, Lena answered. In the winter, tens of thousands of snowbirds swelled the population of the Coachella Valley, but far more than half of those were women. Lena figured that was because women outlive men, and therefore, as a given population ages, it becomes more female. It didn't really matter what the reason was, anyway. The fact was she hadn't found many interesting men around, and those that did come down for the winter were either gay or old. And if the old guys wanted to date women 30 years their junior, she didn't care. But she didn't see the attraction in that arrangement for her.

"And, besides, I have absolutely no interest. None whatsoever," Lena concluded flatly.

"You know you have to move on," Terry said. "Kurt is not the only man that you should ever have in your life. And Greg doesn't really count. How long did that last? Three days?"

"Four." Lena knew that didn't move the needle much.

"Okay, four."

"But there have been others," Lena protested. "Just not a lot recently. I thought Ryne was a possibility, but you know what happened there. And now, I've got too much work to do. By the time I finish at the golf course at night, I hardly have enough energy to eat dinner, let alone pay attention to a man or go look for one."

Terry accepted that with a nod, and they sat in silence, watching the gas flames flicker around the fake logs in the fireplace.

"Why don't you sleep in a little later tomorrow, skip your morning putting, and we'll go out tomorrow night and see what this town has to offer in the area of interesting prospects," Terry finally suggested.

THE FIRST BAR LENA AND TERRY decided to check out was called St. Germain. Terry had heard from her seat-mate on the flight down to Palm Springs that it was a hot place to be on Friday nights. They dressed in the nicest golf clothes they could find in their small collection of Palm Springs wear, and Lena put on make-up for the first time since she'd come to the desert. They waited until 9 to venture downtown, not wanting to waste their energy meeting the over-60 early birds who would dominate the scene early in the evening.

The narrow cocktail lounge was filling up when they arrived, and Lena and Terry were lucky to come in just when an older couple wished one of the bartenders a good night and slipped off their bar stools. Lena and Terry each snagged one. It was a perfect setting. If any men were interested in meeting them, the two women were perched in the perfect place – between the patrons and the bartenders. And rather than forcing themselves to approach interesting looking men and risking an uncomfortable rejection, they'd let the men approach them. It was an uncharacteristically passive approach for Lena, but at the moment, having a successful evening with Terry outweighed the need to prove herself.

They ordered wine and before they had a chance to share their impressions of the place, a fortyish man with a buzz-cut and a couple days' of stubble wiggled in between Terry and the heavy-set biker dude sitting next to her at the bar. He wore a long-sleeved tee shirt that was tight enough to expose his chiseled chest and biceps, and while he wasn't particularly handsome, he carried himself as if he thought he was.

Playing coy, he leaned forward against the rail, waiting for the bartender to acknowledge him, pretending not to notice that his arm was making full contact with Terry's on the bar. Terry took the initiative.

"Vintage Scenes," she said, leaning forward and turning her head to read the distorted logo on the chest of his tee shirt. "What is that, a vintage clothing store?"

"No," he smiled, turning to her as if he was surprised at her presence. "I provide vintage automobiles and other things for movies. I know most of the producers and directors in town."

"Oh, you're from Los Angeles."

"Just about everybody in this bar is," he nodded. "Most of these people are friends of mine." He swept the scene behind him with his arm to demonstrate.

"Wow, you have a lot of friends," Terry said, looking around to nod at the full room. Lena could see her friend's mouth twitching to resist the impulse to smirk.

"It comes with the territory," he assured her. Lena didn't know if he was bragging about his occupation, his home town or, perhaps even his physical attributes, which he seemed to find very admirable by the way he stuck out his chest when he leaned sideways against the rail.

"Luke," the man stated, sticking out his hand to Terry for a handshake.

"Terry. And this is my friend Lena," Terry said, taking his hand and then gesturing toward Lena.

"Great," Luke said. He stood silently, waiting for the bartender, apparently having run out of conversation material. Terry forged ahead.

"So do you own those automobiles or how do you get them?" she asked.

"I own many vintage cars – mostly from the 50s," he nodded. "But I have to procure others."

"Wow, that must take a lot of investment capital to have a business like that," Terry noted. Lena surmised that her friend was probably trying to indicate that she understood business. Given the age difference between them and the youth filling the room, Terry's and Lena's brains were probably their greatest competitive asset right then. But, do you want to play your trump card even before you've decided whether to ante up? Lena wondered.

"Where do you get the money?" Terry continued.

"Honey, you'll have to earn that answer," Luke smirked and leaned in toward Terry, nearly touching his forehead to hers. "I don't tell just anyone my secrets without getting something in return."

"Eeeeewwww," Lena spewed involuntarily, quickly turning her head away so that Luke wouldn't see the distaste on her face. Were all of these Angelinos like this?

"Yeah, I have to agree," Terry said, leaning away from Luke's advance and whispering in Lena's ear. "There's no way I'm going to try to 'earn' that information."

Luke had finally earned a bartender's attention, and ordered his drink while Terry and Lena turned their backs to him to survey the clientele that had filled up the tiny space between the bar and the window to the street. The women all looked somewhere between 18 and 30, with the 30-year-olds looking old in the presence of the younger, tighter bodies with their bright, blonde hair. The younger women wore tank tops; the older ones making up for the need to cover fleshier arms and torsos by wearing heavy jewelry and fringe. Footwear, however, seemed to not correspond with age, but with height. The taller women wore flip-flops and the shorter ones favored high-heeled boot-sandals with huge platforms.

The men all looked like they'd stopped shaving on Tuesday, but had continued to slave away at their gyms the rest of the week so as to fill out their near-uniform tee-shirts. The tight shirts contrasted with baggy, knee-length cargo pants, many of which hung precariously below the belt-line, threatening to slip off their slim hips and pile up on the top of sloppy flip-flops. It was fashion for 16-year-olds in most of the country, but perhaps it was just fashion for everyone in L.A., Lena mused.

Whether he had slipped away because he had sensed their rejection or not, Luke had disappeared into the crowd, and Lena suggested they settle with the bartender and mosey up the street to another bar.

Their next stop was the bar at a steak restaurant on the second floor of a building that looked out on the main street. Although the cocktail lounge was situated in the middle of the building, it was only partly covered, which gave patrons the right to smoke cigarettes at the bar. Terry and Lena looked for a couple of bar stools as far from smokers as possible. Lena didn't mind catching a bit of second-hand smoke as she abstained from lighting up her own cigarettes, but smoke really bothered Terry.

The choice of seats left them facing a nearly solid wall, filled with shelves of liquor. They couldn't see who was coming and going. The setting didn't accommodate people-watching or people-meeting, and those customers they could see were all couples, hunched over their drinks, heads together, smooching or sharing intimate conversations.

"Let's not stay here," Lena suggested after they sat down. The bartender had yet to notice them, hidden as they were behind the wall of liquor.

"Agree," said Terry, and they hopped off the seats and descended to the street again.

"I've heard that there's a funky bar up the street where a lot of the locals hang out," Lena said, pointing her friend in the right direction. "You can smoke outside there, but the bar should be smoke-free," she said.

The street was surprisingly crowded, and Lena and Terry were frequently separated as Lena led her friend through the crowd. Well-dressed, high-heeled women strolled arm-in-arm toward their destinations, carelessly swinging baggy, metal-studded purses into the path of on-coming pedestrians. Staggering bums walked head-down, looking for discarded cigarette butts that might yield a pinch of tobacco. Young couples walked down the sidewalks lazily, leaning against each other as if they had lost the ability to walk by themselves. And gaggles of gay men strutted in small groups as if in formation, all dressed exactly like the Angelinos Terry and Lena had just left at St. Germain. Even if Palm Springs wasn't the place for Terry or Lena to find interesting male prospects, it certainly was a great place for people-watching.

They walked two blocks to the corner bar Lena suggested, and walked in past the smoky patio. Immediately, Lena questioned her choice. While the law prohibited smoking in indoor restaurants and bars, nobody had bothered to tell the owners, the bartenders or the patrons inside. Even as an occasional smoker herself, Lena was offended.

The bar wasn't as crowded as the street, and most of the customers were huddled around the bar near the entrance. Lena led the way toward the back half of the bar where they could better distance themselves from the smoke. Immediately, the aging female bartender threw bar napkins in front of them and growled, "What'll it be?" She was dressed in a black tank-top stretched over hefty muffin tops that spilled over her dirty jeans.

Guessing that the wine choices would be unacceptable, if they even existed, Terry asked for a Corona and Lena ordered an Amstel Light.

"We're out of Amstel, honey," the bartender said. "We have Stella."

Lena couldn't see the connection between the two but chose not to argue.

"That'll be fine," she agreed.

Lena squinted in the dim light to size up the regulars congregated at the front of the bar. If these folks were locals, they were a very special subset, she concluded. The women wore low-cut tank tops that bared nearly all of their ample breasts, stopping just above the nipples. The hairstyles and heavy make-up brought to mind a bad '80s Western. Their ubiquitous Daisy Dukes might have been appropriate on their daughters, but only served to expose cellulite-pocked thighs above skinny, nearly muscle-free calves on middle-aged women.

The guys didn't look like catches either. Aging hippies, gnarly bikers and just-plain losers comprised the options. The collective effect was to make Lena shudder involuntarily.

Terry was similarly unimpressed. "If these folks are your local neighbors, you might have to move down to La Quinta," she joked. Lena had told her friend she'd never consider moving "down-valley" to the gated neighborhoods in La Quinta and Indian Wells, as she didn't think she could stand their buttoned-up, conservative conformity.

They didn't have to worry about turning down any offers of companionship from the clientele. The regulars watched them walk in with apparent disdain – it was probably their golf clothes that gave them away – and then the small crowd ignored them for as long as it took them to throw back their beers.

"Maybe Palm Springs is a good place for you to focus on your game," Terry summed up their evening as they drove back to Lena's condo. They mixed themselves a drink and settled down in the conversation pit. They sat for several long minutes in silence.

"You know, I used to think that the older I got, the easier it would be to fit in places," Lena commented, finally breaking the silence. "But I just feel like it's harder and harder to figure out where you fit in."

"You have lots of friends at Suncadia," Terry countered. "Carly, Brandt, Kim, me. You're just away from home."

"But that's kind of the point," Lena said. "I thought as you got older, you just naturally found your ground, gained confidence, felt more at home on earth. It shouldn't just be when you're around your friends."

Terry sat thinking about that, while Lena waited for her perspective. "Your problem isn't the world and what it's really like," Terry finally answered. "Your problem is what you expected it to be. Your problem is that you thought that growing up was going to answer all of your questions and solve all your problems. It doesn't. It just raises more questions and throws more problems at you."

Wow, Lena thought. That is pretty fucking depressing. But true. She had thought at one time that leaving Nebraska and pursuing her own adult life was going to be easier than this. She once thought that leaving Kurt would be the answer to all of her problems. But Terry was right. It just gets harder.

"Gee, Terry. I feel a lot better now," Lena quipped.

"Sorry. I should just shut up sometimes," Terry said.

"No. That's not the answer either," Lena said, getting up to add more vodka to her drink. "You're always honest with me. I don't want you to ever shut up."

She sat back down and the two friends stared at the fire for a long time in silence.

Finally, Terry proposed, "Maybe tomorrow, while you're on the driving range, I'll pick up a nice big jigsaw puzzle for us to work on over the next three nights. At least then, we'll spend our time with people we like."

WHEN HER FRIEND LEFT four days later, Lena felt lonelier than she had before Terry had come. Without co-workers to commiserate with, and without Kim, Ryne, Brandt and Carly around for at least one day of weekend golf, she had become more isolated than she had ever remembered. Watching Terry walk back through the sliding glass doors at the airport left her depressed. It was all she could do to drive home and go to bed without making the rash decision to head back to snowy Roslyn.

Besides her solitude and lack of friends, Lena had started feel her own narcissism grating on her. In Denver and Seattle, she had balanced her pursuit for a good salary and a career with volunteer work – she served on a couple of small non-profit boards, and showed up at the local public radio stations to help man the call centers for pledge drives. But, in her short time in Palm Springs, she didn't want to start something she'd just have to abandon five months down the road.

She had made some casual friends – guys and occasionally couples she'd see regularly on her Saturday morning rounds. But, they never clicked like her friendship with Kim or Ryne back at Suncadia. And so, her weekly calls with Kim took on a larger and larger significance week by week. She looked forward to them more than anything else she did all week long. Kim's Saturday morning voice was the one constant in her life, and other than her random calls to and from Terry, they were the only non-superficial conversations she had while she was in Palm Springs.

Then one Saturday, Kim didn't call at his usual time. She waited 15 minutes and tried to call him. No answer. She dialed Terry's number.

"Hey, it's early!" her friend protested when she picked up the phone.

"I can't reach Kim."

"So? Maybe he's out."

"No we always talk early on Saturday mornings."

"You didn't tell me that."

"Well, it's not a big deal. I was just wondering if you can see if you can find him or figure out what's going on."

"How'm I gonna do that?" Terry sounded like she was flopping back on her pillow. "I am not going to drive down to Issaquah. I don't even know where he lives."

"No. Right," Lena agreed. "I guess I'll keep trying him. I'll talk with you later today."

It was four days later when Kim finally answered the phone.

"Stacy died in her sleep Friday night," he said flatly. He sounded worn out, like he'd been beaten down by sleepless nights and hard, cold, long days.

"I'm so sorry, Kim. Really I am. I know how much you loved each other."

Kim didn't seem to hear her. "I meant to call you," he said. "But, as prepared as I thought I was for this, I just can't accept it. I just can't figure out what it means to go on without her."

"I'm so sorry, I ..."

Kim cut her off. He didn't sound like himself, but how could she have expected him to? "Lena. Look. I love you and I need to talk to you. But give me some time. I'll call you in a couple of days, okay?" He didn't wait for a response before hanging up on her.

He didn't call for two weeks, but Lena did as she promised. He needed some space and she was willing to let him decide when to get back in touch. When he did, she wanted to console him, but he'd clearly made up his mind: Lena was a buddy and a friend, but not a therapist. He didn't want to talk about Stacy with her, or about how he was dealing with it.

"I'm taking some anti-depressants, and I've got a few good people to talk to," he told her when he finally called. "They're good for me, but you're good for me too. You are life going forward. And I need that. Let's not make my pain our subject, okay?"

"But I care..."

"Lena," he cut her off. "I know you do. I really know that. I just need you to be something else for me. I need you to be my golf buddy. Is that okay?"

"Of course."

"Then let's get back to our routine. I'll call you next Saturday."

Lena wondered what they'd talk about then. Wasn't Stacy always a staple of their conversations? And wasn't the most important thing happening to him right now her death?

But, starting the next Saturday, he called with a dozen questions about her game. It was like he had written them down, determined to have plenty of topics to fill up their usual 30-minute phone call without talking about Stacy. At first, Lena tried to think of how to ask him about his feelings – how was it living without Stacy. But before she knew it, they'd filled the half-hour with golf and weather, and they'd said their good-byes and hung up.

It was the same the week after and the week after that. And pretty soon, they'd fallen back into a rhythm and their regular topics didn't include any mention of Stacy. And Lena had begun to look forward to their Saturday morning talks again.

By the end of February, once the days had turned predictably warm and sunny, Lena could see a clear improvement in her game. The biggest difference was the number of miss-hits. Fairway shots, especially with the long fairway woods, had always been a weakness. Gary worked with her to get her more stable over the ball on the fairway, with less sway and more of a strong athletic stance. She also reined in her backswing a bit, and with practice, those two or three 30-yard duffed fairway wood shots that used to inflate her score on every round began to disappear.

And, although it took longer to happen, she also started driving the ball farther. The key was holding the 90-degree angle of the club to her forearms a bit longer in the downswing – not throwing the clubface to the ball at the top of the swing, but releasing it late in the downswing so that the club whooshed through the ball at the bottom of its arc. At first she continually pushed the ball right, as the late release made it hard to square the club face by the time it reached the bottom of her swing. It took three months before it started to happen naturally and until she managed to get it right.

Thanks to those changes, plus her putting and chipping practice, golf started to reward her. And it wasn't just the score. The score is just math. What really started to please her was the consistent and pretty ball flight she was producing. How amateurs love to see the ball sail through the air! she realized. Many of us couldn't care less if it takes five chips and five putts to get in the hole. What we live for is watching the ball fly off of the club face, rise in the air, forming a perfect arc into the distance, she thought.

Finally, late in March, Lena shot par for the first time. It was an easy, tourist-friendly course, but she was playing from the men's tees. She played with a couple of women she'd been paired with before that winter. They were in their mid-twenties and had played golf at Arizona State. Beth, a tall, athletically built blonde, turned men's heads in the pro shop as regularly as she turned tame par fours into birdies. Candy reminded Lena of her younger self: short and a little stout with a self-deprecating sense of humor. She knew where she stood when she stood next to Beth in the company of men, and didn't care.

Playing with better golfers like Beth and Candy helped Lena play better. That day, she made up for her few bogies with an equal amount of birdies, finding herself even par as she walked onto the 18th tee box.

Up to then, the best she'd ever scored on a decently challenging course was three over par. Facing the prospect of recording a scratch score, she stood behind her ball and lined up her last tee shot of the day, pointing her driver across the tee, down toward the target ahead. The driver head bounced lightly up and down, the vibrations from her heavy heartbeat.

"My god," she declared to Beth and Candy, who stood just off the tee-box to watch her. "I can't believe how nervous I am. This could be my first round at par."

"It's a good hole for you," Beth encouraged her. "You can easily get on in two with your length. Just go for it."

All she needed to do on this par 5 was avoid the water along the left side of the fairway down by the green, and avoid the bunkers on the right side and behind the green. The best strategy was to drive up the left side of the fairway. A 150-yard second shot up the right side would get her past the water and give her a clear shot onto the green. Then a chip and a two putt would give her par. Riskier would be a 200-yard second shot past the green-side bunkers, that would give her two putts for a birdie. But with the green sloping away, front to back, a long fairway shot would be hard to stop on the green.

Lena took a deep breath and took her stance on the tee box. "If I can't do it now, how am I ever going to be able to do this under the pressure of a tournament?" she mumbled to herself. There was nothing pressuring her other than her desire to win the admiration of a couple of young women she barely knew and who were rooting for her anyway. It would never be any easier.

She forced the air out of her lungs; one of her tricks for calming her nerves was to exhale right before she took her shot. It was hard to tense up with empty lungs. She swung as fully and yet as smoothly as she could, imagining Ernie Els, and patiently waiting to turn her head to watch the ball fly down the fairway until she was well through the bottom of the swing. She watched her arms lengthen and her right forearm cross slightly over her left forearm in front of her as her body led the club through. She ended solidly on her left foot, belly button pointing at the target. It felt like she was moving in slow motion, but once the ball was flying down the fairway, well past the bunker on the left and rolled within 100 yards of the water, it was clear that she had swung hard enough to get on the green in two.

Lena dropped her arms back to shoulder high and held a pose on her left foot – what Erin had called the "camera finish." The pose only felt right after a full, successful swing, and this one felt just right.

"Well, I guess we can go now," quipped Candy behind her, pulling her out of her pose, making light fun of Lena showing off.

"I'd better sign up for every tournament I can possibly find in Seattle and Suncadia this summer to get used to this pressure," Lena said, dropping her driver into its slot and sliding behind the wheel of her cart. "I was really nervous."

Good drive syndrome was likely – following a particularly great drive with a horrid second shot. But Lena's second shot was fine, staying right of the water and trickling up onto the front of the green. What kept her from scoring her first below-par round was a three-putt. Still, she walked off the 18th green after a quick hug from her two playing companions, feeling for the first time that there really was a chance to play well in the USGA tournament she'd set as her goal.

However well she was playing, by the time the temperatures began to rise above 90 degrees in the middle of April, Lena was ready to return to Roslyn. She was getting tired of the traffic, the sameness of the sunny, dry days. She was ready to trade the swaying palms for swaying fir trees, and the hard, grey mountain-scape that defined the western boundary of Palm Springs for the green ridges and ragged peaks of Suncadia vistas.

Further, she was getting lonely. Independence and self-reliance were two of her strongest qualities, Lena had always thought. She didn't deny the importance of good teachers, a good school, good roads and other public goodies that had helped her on her way. But, she never relied on family or friends. She'd never had the opportunity to borrow money from her parents, or call them for sage advice on career strategy. And she'd enjoyed having friends in the past, but never had thought of them as a necessity.

In spite of all that well-honed self-reliance, Lena now found herself missing her friends in Suncadia. She wanted to get back into her Sunday routine with Kim, and her Saturday day rounds with

Ryne, Brandt and Carly. And, although they talked three times a week, Lena felt that she was missing out on the day-to-day ups and downs of Terry's moods and love life.

LENA'S LAST NIGHT IN PALM SPRINGS was warm and quiet. She packed her old Ford Explorer with her golf clubs and most of her clothes, leaving out a small bag of toiletries and clothes she would need for the two-day trip back to Suncadia. She filled a cardboard box with the two dozen paperbacks she had read over the winter – one benefit of spending all of those evenings alone – and put it in the front seat. She planned to stop at the Revivals thrift store on the way out of town and donate them.

Finished with the packing and cleaning the condo, Lena sat out behind her unit on the patio and sipped a Heineken Light. She propped her tan legs up on a patio chair and sat back so that she could see the San Jacinto Mountains a short distance away. She'd made some progress over the winter, but sitting quietly, listening to the mourning doves coo, she felt anxious.

What was she doing with her life? She was turning 50 in a week, and she had absolutely no career and no career prospects. Once this 18-month golf odyssey was over, she would have to get back into the rhythm of a normal work life. Lena thought back to her high school years. She couldn't remember what her expectations were: what did she think she would do with her life? When she was in junior high – before her parents died – she thought she'd be a lawyer. But what that law career would be like, she'd never been able to imagine -- not having TV at home to watch Perry Mason, and not knowing any real lawyers. Certainly, she hadn't thought she'd be a corporate lawyer – she didn't even know what a corporation was at that time. When she graduated from high school, her imagination hadn't grown much in sophistication. She just knew that she wanted to get out of her small town and find a way to be happier than her parents had been. That was it.

Now that she'd spent more than 25 years in journalism and corporate work, she was both surprised and disappointed in where she had ended up. She'd been more successful than she had imagined – but only because that imagination had been so limited. But, as she had moved up at the newspaper and then in her speech writing job, she'd missed many opportunities to do more. Again, she thought of the women who had risen to run corporations. She hadn't even risen up the ranks enough to run important projects or divisions.

Lena sighed. She leaned her head back and watched the sky turn dark and the stars start to burn through the atmosphere. This wasn't a new anxiety. And Terry had put her finger on the fallacy – that getting older answered all of your questions. But, as every year passed, she had done nothing to change the flat trajectory of her work life. Getting fired had seemed at first like an opportunity to change things. She might never make it to Davos, but she could turn her back on an ungrateful CEO and an incompetent boss, and find something more challenging. Something that defined her as a professional with value to add.

But now, she was nearly a year into a golf sabbatical, and she'd done nothing about figuring out what's next. The practice and focus required to get ready and qualify for the senior tournament gave her a short-term excuse for putting off career decisions, and she'd embraced it. But now she wondered: what difference would it really make to get into the amateur competition?

A door slammed next door and she overheard an angry exchange between a husband and wife she'd not met in her five months in Palm Springs. Apparently, a disagreement over dinner had blossomed into examination of their entire marriage, and someone had decided to resolve the argument by squealing car tires and leaving the scene. At least she didn't have to deal with that problem, she thought.

Lena got up from her patio chair and went inside. She tossed the empty beer bottle into the trash and grabbed another from the refrigerator. She popped the cap with a bottle opener and returned to her patio chair, letting the door slam behind her in solidarity with her neighbors.

9 OPENER

The return to Suncadia was sweet, if chilly. Spring was taking its time returning to the mountains, and it didn't look like it would come anytime soon. If anything, it was even later than ever. The elk were hanging around on the fairways longer than usual, as the snow up in the higher elevations was still deep, and the dirty patches of snow that lingered down the center of the fairways stubbornly refused to recede. The slow start to the golf season was going to push back the work she still needed to do on her game, but Lena busied herself at the wine shop, helping Terry make some improvements in the shelving and re-doing her snack menu.

In spite of the chilly wind blowing off the mountain snowpack in the distance, Lena found herself happy to be back with Terry and her golf friends instead of having to return to dreary, grey Seattle. When she first left Denver and moved to the Puget Sound, Seattle was in some ways the perfect spot for a loner looking to be as unnoticed and unknown as possible. No one seemed to care who she was or even whether she lived or died, for that matter.

Lena thought it was a little lame for people to blame the city's Scandinavian roots for the infamous "Seattle freeze" that characterized how difficult it was for people to get to know each other in the city. After all, thousands of people had migrated from other parts of the country over the past decade to take advantage of the boom in high-tech jobs, Microsoft's growth and the flowering of its many start-up offspring, and they weren't all Scandinavian. What made people distant, Lena thought, was the insecurity brought on by so much sudden, serendipitous wealth, and by the worship of left-brained, unemotional, 20-somthing techies who had crowded out Boeing workers and part-time fishermen in the city's bars.

Or maybe it was the eight months of persistent rain and drizzle that pretty much guaranteed that no one would ever stop to talk to a stranger on the street.

In any case, even with its chilly mountain air, Suncadia felt warm in comparison. And, two weeks after her return, the weather had warmed enough for the course to open, and Lena pushed herself to settle back down into a practice routine. She spent the first couple of days on the driving range and the putting green, letting the spring melt drain off the fairways before making her first tee-time. She decided to play a couple of rounds before she and Kim started back on their Sunday routine. On a chilly, but dry Wednesday late in April, she signed up for her first 8:30 tee time.

Like the good golfer she wanted to become, Lena showed up an hour early at the course, and spent 30 chilly minutes at the driving range, running through her clubs. The irons were a bit recalcitrant – she was not getting the club face square, and pushed her shots to the right. She made a mental note to work on that in the coming week. She moved over to the chipping area, hit a few out of the sand and chipped a few short shots, sinking a couple, to get a feeling for the wet softness of the greens. Returning to the starter desk, she greeted Bill, the usual weekday starter, and relaxed, waiting for her playing companions to arrive.

At the starter desk, she was pleased to recognize Jim. She'd played with him a couple of times the summer before, and he seemed genuinely glad to see her again as well. And now that she had started playing from the whites, instead of the forward tees, she expected that most men would be happy to play with her – she was playing their game.

The starter introduced them to the other half of their foursome. They shook hands, but Bob and Larry didn't look her in the eye or verbalize any kind of greeting. They quickly jumped in their cart and headed down to the first tee. As she walked toward the tee box with Jim, Bob turned to Larry and said, in a voice that was clearly meant to be heard, "I've never played with a woman who could make contact with the ball." What a way to start the season in Suncadia!

Lena glanced at Jim. If he had heard the insult, he wasn't showing it. They walked up to the first tee behind Bob and Larry and Jim asked them what tee box they intended to play from that day.

"What do you play?" Bob asked Jim.

"The whites. With her."

Bob looked at Larry, and Lena could see their reaction – they weren't impressed; they were irritated. "I'll play the blues then," Bob announced. "This must be an easy course."

"Me too," Larry concurred quickly.

Lena and Jim waited while the two men teed off. They hit decent drives, but both landed nearly 200 yards short of the hole. If they were really suited for the blue tees, they probably would have little problem reaching the striped barber pole in the middle of the fairway. Still, both Lena and Jim declared "nice ball" to both drives. It seemed nicer than "that didn't suck," if not more accurate.

Jim let Lena tee off first from the white tee box, and she hit her drive to about 120 yards from the hole. "Maybe that will shut them up," she thought, hearing nothing from their playing companions behind them. It wasn't a great drive, but it would do. Jim drove his ball close behind hers, and without a comment from the other two players, they walked off toward their balls.

There were two things that keep women from playing golf, Lena believed: slow play and sexism. Women seem to have more things to do on an average day than men – too much to do to waste time on a six-hour round of golf. She remembered a drawing of hunter-gatherers in one of her high school textbooks. The men were lounging under a tree after a returning from a hunt while the women, babies on their backs or at their breasts, continued to forage and cook, and herd toddlers. In 100,000 years, things hadn't changed much. Men still didn't mind hanging around, swinging clubs and telling jokes for four, five or six hours; perhaps these days they deserve it after the tiring and gruesome "hunt" of their workdays (at their desks with lattes delivered by underpaid assistants or unpaid interns).

The other thing that kept women off the course: sexism. It was endemic, it seemed. Even the enlightened media were drenched with it: Golf Digest had once illustrated the embarrassment of short drives by dressing a man up in pink, photographing him putting on lipstick. Private clubs all around the country lamented the downturn in membership while at the same time they built Taj Mahals for men's locker rooms – complete with weight rooms and plunge pools and special sports bars – while constructing windowless 12x12 card rooms for the women, furnished only with high-school metal lockers. They expected women to accept the disparity, even while they expected them to pay the same membership fees as men.

Lena's first day out on the course for the season wasn't jovial, but their foursome finished in under four hours – a good pace at Suncadia, and Lena ended with a 76, well outscoring the three men.

"Better than usual," she said to Jim, downplaying her success.

"No, it was great. Let's have a beer. My wife is joining me at the Inn. You should meet her," Jim said. Bob and Larry brusquely declined their offer to join them, blaming the long drive over the pass and down the west side of the Cascades to Issaquah.

"They can't face the fact that you beat them," Jim said, waiting for her to catch up to him as they headed up the stairs to the Inn deck that overlooked the 9th and 18th greens.

Jim's wife looked young – no more than 38 or 40, but given the camouflage of her fancy coif and obvious plastic surgery, she could easily have been 45 or 50. Tiff, as she called herself, didn't seem to appreciate the fact that Jim had brought Lena to the bar. As they sat in awkward silence waiting for their drinks, Lena remembered that 20 years ago, stay-at-home wives suspected that women who had entered the professional - not pink-collar - workplace had done so to steal their husbands. In Lena's experience, the husbands were usually stolen by secretaries, not by women like herself in management. Did Tiff think she was playing golf to steal her husband?

Lena and Jim tried to engage Tiff in some quick review of their round, but Tiff resisted, and after one beer for him and a glass of wine for Lena, they gave up. Jim and Tiff headed back to Tumble Creek, the private community across the river from Suncadia where they lived. Lena imagined that the short drive wouldn't be short enough for Jim.

THE SUNCADIA CLUB OPENER, the first tournament of the year, was the first weekend in May. Lena was looking forward to her first competition of the year and a chance to start getting used to playing under more pressure than her usual weekend rounds with her friends. She figured that she'd never get to the point where she wasn't anxious on the first tee, but her goal for the first couple of tournaments of the year was to get over that anxiousness earlier in the round.

Lena and Carly were assigned to the same foursome with Ann, a very good golfer from Tumble, and Karen, a perennial last-place finisher whose only saving grace was that she kept all of the other women in the tournament from ending up at the bottom of the day's leaderboard.

Lena loved playing with Ann, and was pleased when the tee sheet put them in the same cart. The tempo of her swing was mesmerizingly smooth, and every shot was at least good, if not great. She'd played since college, and generally won the gross award for the lowest women's score in Suncadia tournaments, not counting handicap. Playing with a better golfers should help Lena bring her game up a notch, and she looked forward to a good round.

Carly, however, wasn't so lucky, ending up with Karen. But, she rarely complained about things to the club management, even when she had good cause. When Carly read the tee sheet taped on the club house door, she lowered her head, walked over to Lena, and grumbled under her breath, "Shit, I got Karen."

"I know," Lena winced. "I'm sorry. Do you want to switch?" she asked, knowing that Carly would never accept the gesture.

"No, I'll just drink a lot," Carly attempted a little laugh, but it fell flat.

"You could talk with Will," Lena suggested. Will was the head pro, and he usually ran the tournaments, although it was fairly clear to everyone in the club that he detested the chaos that went with a club tournament, especially one run on a budget. Since the recession had started, the clubhouse staff had been cut a couple of times, and Will was not only working longer hours than he liked, he was having to spend a lot more time with members than he cared for as well.

"Will would make too big of a deal out of it," Carly predicted. "I'll just hope Karen has improved since last year and is learning to keep her mouth shut a bit."

Lena snickered and Carly rolled her eyes in hopelessness. Lena patted her friend on the back and walked to the practice green to get a few putts in before the tournament started.

Both Lena and Ann started off the round well. It was a shotgun start, and their foursome started on the fourth hole, which somehow helped Lena skip right over the first tee jitters, and she parred the long, downhill par 5. Ann's drive was much shorter, and it took her four shots to reach the green, but her approach shot was beautiful, and she had a tap-in for par.

The day was surprisingly warm for early in May on the east slope of the Cascades, and Lena got absorbed in her game and the joy of the day. She parred the next hole, bogeyed the easy par-three and then got back to par on the long par-four seventh hole, which she had always found difficult the year before. She wasn't paying much attention to Carly and Karen, until Carly walked up behind her on the eighth tee box.

"I'm going to strangle her!" Carly growled in a loud whisper.

"What's the matter?"

"She won't shut up. And have you seen how many frickin' practice swings she's taking? It takes her 15 minutes to get off a shot. I can't stand it!"

Lena had noticed that Karen was playing slowly, but she and Ann had been cheerfully talking about their winters in the desert – Ann's in Phoenix, not Palm Springs – and that had distracted them from Karen's irritating multi-swing practice routine.

"Do you want me to say something to her?"

"No. I'm not sure that's a good idea. She'll just get pissy and then we'll have to deal with her temper on top of her blabbing and her slow play."

"What can we do?"

"I don't know, but this is driving me nuts," Carly said, walking away and shaking out her arms as if to shake out the bad vibes she was getting from her cartmate.

Ann watched their quick exchange and raised an eyebrow at Lena. "What's going on?" she asked her as Carly walked away.

Lena turned her back so that Karen wouldn't hear and relayed Carly's frustrations.

"Yes, she's awfully slow," said Ann, as if she were commenting on the color of her golf cart. Part of Ann's success stemmed from her ability to let nothing on the golf course bother her. Then, she stepped up the tee markers and got ready for her attack on the long par-five.

As they played the hole, Lena watched Karen. Oblivious to the fact that she was absorbing about half of the foursome's time on each hole, Karen blithely sauntered along, lining up her shot, stepping up for three or four practice swings, stepping back to read her line again, taking another three or four practice swings, and finally addressing the ball ... only to back up and start the excruciating routine all over again.

"Who does she think she is? Keegan Bradley?" Lena quipped to Ann, referring to the PGA pro known for his belabored pre-shot routine.

"Yeah, but without the result," Ann said as they watched Karen's ball skitter forward about 40 yards after the long wait.

For the next few holes, Lena could tell that Carly was trying to encourage Karen to play faster, largely by trying to set an example of fast play. She moved up to her ball on the fairway quickly, and most times, didn't even take a practice swing. Tacitly conspiring with her, Lena tried to pick up her pre-shot routine a bit too. But it made little difference.

By the time they reached the 12th hole, they were a full hole behind the group in front of them. Lena kept expecting a marshal to come by and hurry them along – that might give Karen a hint – but Suncadia was notoriously cheap when it came to hiring marshals to keep the pace moving on the course, and Will didn't see a tournament any excuse for improving service.

After teeing off on 13, Carly grabbed three clubs out of her bag and walked down the side of the fairway toward her ball. It kept Karen behind her and out of her sight. From then, she walked the 50 or so yards between Karen's poorer shots and hers, sized up her shot, took a practice swing and made her shot before Karen had even addressed the ball.

On the 14th hole, Carly gave up on Karen, and pulled her bag off the cart and started walking the course, abandoning the cart. She strode up to the green after Lena and Ann, dropped her bag off the fringe, and yanked her putter out of the side pocket.

"I'm going to kill Will for doing this to me," she grouched, as they stood and waited for Karen to hit her approach shot.

"I don't blame you," Lena said, as they watched Karen hit three more shots to the green.

"Don't you like playing with me?" Karen screamed at Carly when she finally parked the cart behind the green, and strode up to them.

Carly stood still, leaning against her putter, as if she hadn't heard Karen.

"Karen, it would be nice if you could keep up a little better," Ann said calmly.

"But I'm not as good as you guys," Karen cried. "You can't expect me to get here in the same number of shots."

"No, but you've got to speed up your routine a bit," Lena said, a little less diplomatically than Ann would have.

Karen turned on her, now red-faced with embarrassment and from the exertion that came with taking 10 shots to get to the green.

"I don't have to do anything! I don't even have to play in this damned tournament!" she yelled. "This is not fun. Do you guys think this is fun for me? Well, you're wrong. I don't have to do this! Fuck all of you!" She stomped off the green to her cart, slammed her putter into its holder, and jammed her foot down on the accelerator. She squealed the tires as she pulled a risky u-turn on a side hill next to the cart path and took off in the wrong direction to the clubhouse.

"Well, she could have left the cart for you," Lena said quietly, once she was out of earshot.

"Do you suppose we'll get in trouble for this?" Carly wondered out loud.

"Who cares?" Ann said, and bent down to mark her ball on the putting surface. "Let's play."

At the end of the round, Lena had beat Ann by a stroke, Carly had redeemed a respectable score, and with the three of them sharing one cart, they returned to the clubhouse in first, second and third place. Will met them at the cart return, as they expected he would.

"What happened out there?" he asked.

"Lena shot a 76, I shot 77 and Carly, what did you get?" Ann said, pretending to not understand the question.

"No, you know what I mean," Will cut her off. "Karen came in bawling and screaming, and none of us could figure out what happened."

"Well, it would have been nice if you'd sent a marshal out, or maybe another cart for Carly," Lena observed. "She had to walk the last five holes, by the way. Then maybe we could have told you what was happening."

Ann chimed in quickly, trying to diffuse the heat of the argument. "Karen wasn't playing well, and she took my request to speed up her play very badly. I'm sorry."

"Ann didn't call her on it, I did," Lena jumped in. "She was taking a dozen practice swings and taking 15 minutes on each shot."

"Well, she obviously feels hurt," Will retorted. "Couldn't you just give her a break? She's trying, and we need all of the participants we can get in this tournament."

Lena looked at Ann and Carly and shrugged. "I don't think we need her all that bad. Let's go get a drink."

The three pulled their bags onto their shoulders and walked up the hill to the parking lot, leaving Will behind, still sputtering, but not really forming sentences anymore.

They met Ryne and Brandt at the bar in the Inn, and talked over each other, trying to tell the story. The other players were gathering for the awards ceremony, which was set to be a very low-key affair with guacamole, chips and beer. After a half hour, Will had still not appeared to present the pro-shop gift certificates to the winners.

"Wow, he must be pissed," Brandt said. "He usually loves the little stage he gets to strut on at these events." The awards ceremony never did happen, and eventually, everyone drifted away. Lena got her first-place award in the mail a week later – a $100 gift certificate to the pro shop – with no note from Will.

A week later, news filtered through the club that Will had quit and taken a job at a sister resort in Oregon.

THE FRIDAY AFTER the tournament, Lena woke to bright sunshine. The mountain air smelled of pine and spring mud, and she decided to skip her usual Friday practice routine and play a round instead. Erin frowned at her when she rushed by her office and out of the clubhouse after securing a tee-time. Lena decided to ignore it. Life is too short, she mumbled to herself.

Out at the starter desk, Lena found herself paired up with Jim again, and after the round, he invited her to dinner at the Lodge restaurant. Tiff, he explained, was busy that evening, and Lena imagined that meant she had some social function over in Tumble Creek or back in Issaquah. Lena quickly accepted. Living fairly frugally to preserve her funds through her work hiatus – who knew how long it would be – she rarely got a chance to dine in a nice restaurant.

To be polite and show her gratitude, Lena dressed nicely in a short, simple linen shift, and put on make-up. She knew it wasn't a real date – the guy was married and his wife was just busy for the night – but she didn't want to show up for dinner looking like she just walked off the golf course, either. As planned, they met in the condo in the Lodge that Jim and Tiff owned as a rental property. It was empty for the weekend, so they decided to have a drink there before heading down to Portals for dinner.

"Wow! You look gorgeous!" Jim exclaimed as he opened the door. Maybe she overdid it, she thought immediately.

"Oh, you've just never seen me in make-up before," she said, trying to brush off the compliment. For the first time since his invitation, a quick suspicious thought crossed Lena's mind. This is on the up-and up, isn't it? she silently asked herself, and then quickly pushed her suspicions out of her mind.

"No, you look usually healthy and athletic and competent," he said, "but tonight you look beautiful."

Lena nodded demurely, not wanting to prolong the discussion. She sat in the comfortable divan and watched Jim open an Abeja red from the Columbia Valley. He used the same old-fashioned wine opener she preferred – the simple one with a cork screw and a lever for pulling the cork up out of the bottle, not the "rabbit" used by amateurs.

She glanced around the room, looking for something familiar or interesting about which to start a conversation. Three or four books on the end table held some promise. "I see you are reading Christopher Hitchens," she said as he handed her a healthy pour of the red. It was nice to think that perhaps Jim shared her political and economic worldview, but she waited to hear his comment before assuming that was true.

"Yes, I loved his book before this, and couldn't wait to start this one," Jim said, settling down in the oversized chair across from her. From there, the conversation flowed easily, eventually leading to his grandchildren, which allowed him to move onto the divan next to her to show her pictures of his extended family. He sat a little bit closer to her than she thought necessary, but looking at his grandchildren's photos, while a bit dull to her, seemed innocent enough, and she let it slide.

An hour and two glasses of wine after she had knocked on his door, Jim stood. "We'd better slip downstairs. Our reservation is in five minutes."

Lena and Jim were seated at a table on the far end of the restaurant, near the windows that overlooked the river and the two Tumble Creek fairways that peaked through the trees on the other side of the river canyon. It was getting dark, and red and orange tints in the clouds over the western horizon absorbed Lena's attention. She sat and took in the view.

"Hey!" Jim finally elbowed her. "Pretend you're not alone for once!"

"Ha. Sorry. I'm quite used to having freedom to let my mind wander. Usually, there's no one around to notice," she said.

Sticking with Washington reds, Jim ordered a bottle of Syncline Cuvee Elena, one of Lena's favorites, and she began to think that cultivating more wealthy, bored husbands as friends might not be such a bad idea.

"What's Tiff doing tonight?" she asked after he offered a toast to her "vastly improved golf game." "Is she doing something at Tumble Creek?"

"No she's in New York, visiting her mother," Jim said. Noticing Lena's raised eyebrow, he continued. "Oh, she grew up there. Actually, on Long Island. Her father worked for Manufacturers Hanover in the city, and we met when she was at Barnard and I was at Allen & Co. She came to work for us as an intern one summer."

"Ol' Manny Hanny." Lena recalled. She hadn't heard anyone mention the bank in years. "I don't suppose he had anything to do with all of that bad Latin American debt in the mid '80s, did he?" she said, really meaning the comment as a joke rather than an inquiry.

"I think he actually did," admitted Jim with a shake of his head. "I'm not sure."

"But, you're a banker, didn't you ever talk about it?"

"Not really. He was quite a bit older and he had pretty advanced Alzheimer's by the time I met him. He died shortly after we were married."

"Oh, I'm sorry."

Jim waved off her sympathy. "Tiff spent a lot of time back East those days. I'd say we probably missed a big part of our early lives together." He paused in a way that made Lena think he was trying to make a bigger point. "That was time we've never really gotten back."

Jim didn't look up at her, which struck Lena as being surprisingly coy. He was sharing something personal – something about his marriage that she really didn't want to know, while his body language communicated a shyness. It seemed disingenuous, like he was acting a part. She decided to change the subject.

"Your golf game is better than I'd expect from a full-time CEO," she said. "You played very well today."

Jim looked up at that, and met her eyes. "Well, I'm not exactly working 40 hours a week anymore, let alone the 60 hours a week I used to work," he admitted. "But your game is excellent. Do you think you're on track for the amateur?"

Lena had told him about her quest, and she began to describe where she thought she had made progress and where she was still looking for improvement in her game. The waiter brought their food, and they continued to talk while the plates were arranged around them.

"I probably won't go far in the tournament, of course, but I'm feeling good about my game," Lena said. "I worry that I'll find that playing golf feels completely different once I'm in with real competition."

They focused on their entrees and continued to talk about her golf game and who her competition was likely to be. The subject made Lena feel a bit narcissistic, but oddly, it also seemed safe – like it had nothing to do with her personally, just with her golf game.

Over coffee after refusing dessert, Jim stopped responding to her monologue, and when she realized he was only half listening, Lena stopped. She sipped her coffee and waited for him to pick the conversation up again.

"So, tell me about Lena," he said, stirring a second spoon of sugar into his coffee.

"Oh, it's actually Magdalena," Lena answered, thinking he was asking about her name. "My mother got it from some old movie. She thought I'd go by Maggie, but my father preferred Lena – you know, like Lena Horne – so that's where it came from."

"Nice. But really, what I was asking was about you. What about you? Once the tournament is over, what are you planning to do next?" Jim asked.

"I haven't thought much about it. At my age, I'm not sure how easy it will be to find another job, but, of course, that's probably what's next." Since her return from Palm Springs, Lena hadn't thought much about it. "Maybe I'll just try to pick up some free-lance writing jobs until I figure it out."

"Well, one of the reasons I wanted to have dinner with you tonight was to ask you what you would think about coming to work for me," Jim said.

Lena was surprised. She looked away from him, and tried to focus her suddenly blurry vision on her coffee cup. What did he mean? If she had been suspicious of Jim's invitation tonight, it was because she anticipated a sexual pass, not a job offer. And he might actually have a good job offer that could solve a lot of problems for her – although she had no idea what he had in mind. It was so unexpected.

"I'm thinking you'd be great at investor relations," Jim continued, ignoring her obvious discomfort. "You write well, which is about a third of the job, and the rest is pretty standard business fare."

"But, I don't know anything about finance or accounting," Lena said. She didn't want to dissuade him from giving her a job –

however far into the future – but she didn't want to get in over her head either. "Yeah, I can read an income statement, and I know financial reporting well enough to write conference call scripts and newspaper stories about earnings, but not well enough to interpret them for analysts."

"We have lots of folks in accounting who can help you with that," Jim countered. "I think your skill set is perfect. You're personable, not shy, which is evident on the golf course, and you write well, which is usually the hardest thing to find in an IR person."

"Well, I don't know what to say. I'd have to think about it."

"And I'd get to see more of you." That sentence fell like a lead weight at the table. Then it bounced off the table and landed with a thud at the bottom of Lena's stomach. She was totally unprepared to handle a job offer and sexual pass at the same time. Usually, older men were more sophisticated and subtle – get the woman in the door first and then make the pass. Was she reading what she feared into his comment, instead of what he meant by it? Was she flattering herself by interpreting it as an interest in a personal relationship? She certainly didn't want one. But, she was also afraid of overreacting and turning his simple comment into something he didn't mean to say.

"You mean professionally, of course," she finally managed to respond.

Jim sat back in his chair and looked her in the eye sternly for a long minute. She held his gaze, not wanting him to think she was embarrassed or being coy. But, the heat rose in her face, and Lena had to concentrate on breathing evenly.

Finally, Jim's expression softened as if he'd reached a decision. He looked away, across the room.

"Of course that's what I meant," he said. "Whatever else would you think?"

The heat burned her cheeks, and Lena was pissed. He was acting like she was the one who had made an inappropriate advance. Sure, she thought. Act all innocent, make a pass, and then retreat and feign surprise and disdain. She wasn't going to fall for it, but she didn't know how to move on. The evening was clearly over. What had been a pleasant outing had been a simple cliché of a set-up.

Picking up her purse from the side of the table, Lena downed the swallow of wine left in her glass and pushed her chair back. Jim reached out to catch her arm, but she was already too far away. Walking slowly and as casually as she could, she slipped past the other tables and the hostess stand and out of Jim's line of sight. She knew he wouldn't risk making scene by trying to follow.

In the elevator, Lena berated herself for being so unsophisticated, so naïve – such a Nebraska girl. She quickly played the evening over again in her head. The way he sat close, showing her pictures of his grandchildren. His compliments. Then the creepy "I'd get to see more of you." It now seemed so obvious. And, yet, the way he bristled at her question – was she was right to assume the worst? Yes, she decided, she was. But why didn't he wait until they were actually working together and then make his pass? He'd be so much more in control and she would have been stuck. She was lucky it hadn't worked out that way.

When she reached her condo, Lena went immediately to the bathroom and scrubbed off her makeup. She stripped off her clothes and pulled a long, unflattering nightshirt over her head, turned on the TV to the Golf Channel and poured a glass of wine. She fell asleep on the couch with her head propped up on a pillow at a bad angle and woke the next morning with a stiff neck.

10 TERRY

Meeting Kim for golf the next Sunday, Lena was already well on the way to sequestering the awkward evening with Jim in a part of her memory she chose not to access much, and she didn't mention it to her friend. She and Kim had settled back into their easy relationship that she appreciated for its simplicity and Kim seemed to appreciate for its warmth. Lena had a feeling that Kim didn't have many close female friends – how many married men or widowers really did?

After golf, Kim headed east to Yakima for the afternoon to take care of some business with Stacy's estate. They agreed to meet that evening back in Suncadia at the winery for dinner with Terry.

Terry was in rare form when she skipped past the hostess desk to meet Lena at the bar that evening. She'd obviously already had a few glasses of wine, and although she looked put-together in new leggings, over-the-knee leather boots and a long, soft cashmere sweater, Lena wondered how she had managed to drive the two miles from her Roslyn to the winery without running off the road or into a telephone pole.

"Any more word from that asshole Jim?" was the first thing out of Terry's mouth as she pulled her short frame up onto a bar stool and dropped her huge artsy, quilted bag at her feet. Lena cringed. She wished she hadn't told Terry about that evening at the Lodge, but who else was going to listen to her work out her confusion and distress?

"No, thank god. Perhaps he'll avoid the golf course for a while."

"I doubt it. That kind never feels regret. He probably has no idea how uncomfortable that made you. It was all about whether he could get some young ass to help him feel youthful again."

Lena laughed. Her friend had such a wonderful, if vulgar, way of simplifying complex human interactions. It was one of her charms.

"Mine isn't that young anymore!" Lena laughed. "But what's with you? You don't seem particularly sober tonight."

"Nah. I probably shouldn't have driven, but it's only two miles."

"What's the occasion?"

"That asshole Sam."

Sam was a chemistry teacher at Cle Elum High School, and he and Terry had been dating now for all of two weeks – nearly a record for Terry. Saturday morning, when Lena had called Terry to talk about Jim, it seemed that things were going well with Sam.

"Oh, no." Lena was disappointed for her friend. She really had hoped Terry had found the stable relationship she craved, and she felt guilty for having recommended a science teacher as an option.

"Oh, yes."

"What?"

"He has been screwing that skinny special ed assistant all along."

"How did you find out?"

"She called me. Told me their relationship was something special that I shouldn't butt in on. I got the pleasure of telling her what I thought of his little dick and his short attention span – if you get my drift." Terry's tone got louder as she warmed up to her story.

"Oh, sheesh, Terry, keep your voice down. You really said that?"

"What did I have to lose? The jerk." Terry threw her hand up in the air to wave at the winery's regular bartender. "Bret! I'm not here for my health!"

Bret pulled himself away from what appeared to be a torturous monologue of a middle-aged man dressed in argyle golf togs. He was recounting every stroke he'd taken on Prospector that day, and expected Bret to be just as fascinated by the tale as he was. "The usual?" Bret asked, not waiting for her answer before pulling the cork from a bottle of red wine and pouring a very large portion for Terry.

"Does a bear shit in the woods?" Terry repeated the same line she always used in place of a simple "yes." Lena cringed. Terry definitely needed some new material.

"Kim's joining us when he gets up the hill from Yakima," Lena told the amused bartender, in part to change the subject.

"You two doing anything other than golf yet?" he asked

"You mean shopping? Watching TV? Walking the dog?"

"No, you know what he means," Terry interjected. Lena was not pleased by the way Suncadia acted like a small town sometimes. Everyone knew what everyone else was doing, especially who was or wasn't sleeping with whom, or who should be.

"Sex you mean?" Lena decided to not try to concoct a metaphor that had no chance of obfuscating what they were talking about anyway. "No, Kim's still struggling with Stacy's death. And, I am really not attracted to him, to be honest." Suddenly uncomfortable with the topic he'd broached, Bret quickly moved down to the other end of the bar to polish the stainless steel top of the dishwasher.

"Are you ever attracted to anyone?" Terry laughed.

"Don't you remember Gary?"

"I guess I mean anyone you actually know. Not some guy you pulled off the golf course and into bed."

"Not fair. Not fair. How about Ryne? I know him pretty well, and I was attracted to him, although that didn't work out too great."

"I know. But what about Kim? You guys seem to have a lot in common. And, even widowers must get horny now and then."

"I'd like to change the subject," Lena said.

"Consider it changed," Terry quickly obliged. She wasn't sober enough to hold much of a train of thought anyway. "How's the golf game coming?"

Kim reached Lena on her cell phone an hour later, apologizing. He wasn't going to be able to make it back to Suncadia for dinner. He was staying with Stacy's parents in Yakima, feeling like he couldn't refuse their invitation to dinner.

"That's a really jerky thing to do to you," Terry reacted to the news.

"No it isn't," Lena insisted. "It's perfectly reasonable. Even nice. He told me today he was feeling a little guilty for not spending more time with her folks since the funeral."

Terry shrugged. She was definitely in a foul mood. While they had waited for Kim to arrive, Terry had been on a rant about her latest string of troubles – all minor but irritating – at the wine store. She looked great, though, and Lena caught several men looking her friend over from a few seats away at the bar and from tables across the restaurant. If her friend drank a little less, she might actually find a decent guy and hold onto him for a while. Terry had many great qualities – the guts to be an entrepreneur, the brains to run the business, the charisma to charm and keep customers, the looks to garner far more amorous glances from strangers than Lena would ever get. But, her biggest faults were her poor judgment in men and drinking.

"You should really eat something to help soak up some of that wine you've had today," Lena suggested. They signaled for menus from Bret and ordered at the bar.

Another hour later, Terry's meal seemed to have sobered her up enough that Lena wasn't worried about her friend driving the two miles back into Roslyn. They exchanged hugs at the door, and Lena walked to the parking lot and unlocked her car. But before she closed her door, she heard a crash of metal and glass against something hard, dull and unmovable. She left her purse in the car and ran back to the front of the building. Terry had backed her car up too far, and knocked several stones off the façade of the winery building, in the corner by the golf shop. She was standing outside of her car, hands on her hips, furious that the building had gotten in her way.

"Oh, my god, Terry, what the hell did you do?"

"Shit. What does it look like? I hope I'm sober enough to pass a breath test."

"Fat chance. Your best hope is that the sheriff is on the other side of the county and will take a while to get here."

They stood and surveyed the damage to her car and the building as Don, the stocky, balding winery owner, was walking toward them, cell phone at his ear. He hung up and stuck his phone in his pocket as he reached them.

"Oh, Terry! What did you do to my pretty building?" he asked, expressing far more humor and far less anger than Lena would have expected from herself in that situation. He put his arm around Terry. "Don't worry. It's not a big deal. The worst you have to fear is that Tom is inside. If he sees this, he's going to be pissed."

Lena was relieved for her friend that Don was taking the damage to his fake stone wall as well as he was. "Who's Tom?" she asked, letting Don give her a quick hug.

Lena's relationship with Don was peculiar. It took him months before he began to recognize her. One wintery Saturday, a week after she'd been re-introduced to Don a dozen times, Lena had gone over to the winery, feeling cabin fever brought on by her tiny condo and thinking that the tall windows of the winery would make her feel better. She spotted Don talking with a couple – rich, she could tell from their clothes and their posture – and she settled down with her Kindle and a glass of wine near the big windows that faced out on the snow-covered Rope Rider golf course. Perhaps, she thought at the time, he'd finally come over to chat. But, when he finished his conversation with the rich people, he hurried by her as usual, without so much as a nod of hello. Eventually, after two years of regular patronage of his winery, Don at least recognized her now, even if he never remembered her name.

"Tom built this wall. He's quite the perfectionist," Don said. And, then, as if called by telepathy, one of the men Lena had witnessed inspecting Terry from across the bar earlier walked out of the winery, trailed by his two friends. Seeing the accident, he broke into a sprint toward the small pile of debris behind Terry's Subaru.

Tom ran his hand over the wounded wall and picked up one of the dislocated stones, bouncing it in his hand as if to weigh its effectiveness as a weapon against whoever had done this horrible thing to his art.

"Who?" Tom looked right at Terry. He knew who. He tried to look angry, but even in the dim starlight of the late evening, Lena could see a smirk playing at the corner of his mouth. He'd been watching Terry all night, and seemed to be amused that he'd not only come upon an excuse to meet her, but he was clearly starting out the relationship from a position of power.

"Well, maybe if you'd built the wall out of stone instead of just pasting these pieces on the outside, it would have held," Terry sputtered. The criticism didn't seem to dent Tom's humor. He laughed and nodded in agreement.

Lena felt her side for her purse and then remembered she'd left it in the car. "Anyone have a cigarette?" she asked the assembling group, trying to dispel the tension. One of Tom's friends reached into his pocket and pulled two from a pack of Marlboro reds. He lit them both, and handed one to Lena.

"I'm Brad," he said, standing next to her while the other friend knelt down by the corner of the building to inspect the damage with Don.

"You girls need a ride?" Brad asked, exhaling a cloud of smoke.

"No, I'll be able to drive this home. It's just a flesh wound," Terry laughed. "Don, I'm so sorry. I'll pay for the damage."

Don waved her off without turning away from his inspection.

"It'll be no problem," Tom assured Terry, putting his arm around her shoulders. "I'll be able to fix it very easily. Why don't we go inside and talk about how you can help me repair this on Monday?" Terry glanced over to Lena, who shrugged and shook her head.

"I'm going home. You go ahead," Lena said. "Just try to behave yourself for a change. Thanks for the cigarette, Brad." She gave her friend a quick hug and walked back toward her car.

"I'd better move my car first," Lena heard Terry tell Tom. "But, then I'd be glad to let you buy me a club soda. I don't think I need any more wine tonight."

LENA RETURNED to her practice routine on Monday – the routine she'd honed in Palm Springs. She'd checked in with Erin, to be polite and not appear dismissive, but she didn't feel she needed the instructor's constant coaching at this point. She started the morning with an hour of putting, an hour pitching and chipping, and a half-hour in the bunker. She spent two hours on the range, starting with the short irons and working up to the driver, changed into her running shoes, and ran up to the fitness center across the road from the driving range, slowly working through the same repetitions she'd worked on in the desert. She stopped for a quick lunch at home. Each day that week, she followed the same morning routine. After that, it depended on her mood. If she felt like it, she went back to the range for another 100 balls, and if not, she ended her day back at the putting green. Afterwards, she hoisted her club bag on her back and walked back to the Lodge for an early dinner, some mindless TV and bedtime.

Halfway through the week, it felt tiresome, this relentless work on her game, and at times she thought it would be easier to go back to work, if she could. But that was a big "if." The prospect of facing rejection after rejection on the job market got her out of bed the next few days, and she trudged to the range and the practice green. If she hadn't had weekend rounds with her friends to look forward to, she still might have waved the white flag of surrender.

Friday, she was happy to wake up to the soft patter of rain on her condo deck. She spent the day reading a trashy novel in front of her condo fireplace, taking an hour out mid-day to walk over to the fitness center for a half-hearted workout. She invited Terry to come over for dinner at her condo, and they ended the work week with a couple bottles of wine and a Netflix movie they both forgot by the next day.

CARLY AND LENA HAD ALREADY grown close – at least as golf buddies – but the incident with Karen at the club opener had created a different kind of bond – the kind forged by having weathered a very uncomfortable situation together.

So, when Carly lost her job early in June, it was a blessing for Lena. Carly started staying up at her home in Suncadia most weekdays, letting Brandt return to Seattle for work alone, and she and Lena began to practice together. With Carly's attention, Lena started to take her practice routines seriously again. Having someone else to talk to and work out swing problems with – even if they didn't play at exactly the same level – relieved the tedium of the repetitive routine. They incorporated contests into various drills, and while lacking the nerve-racking seriousness of real competition, the games helped Lena focus.

As the summer wore on, the Roslyn twosome of Terry and Lena became a threesome including Carly, and Terry didn't mind a bit. She and Tom had fallen in love – or at least the closest proximity to it that Terry could remember. The relationship started with his demand that she return to the winery the day after her accident to help him repair the damage she'd caused. They had gone from mixing concrete and setting stone together to mixing pancakes and settling in together in Terry's cramped one-bedroom cabin in less than a week. Lena was glad for Rex – finally some stability in his life too – and Terry said she was glad that Carly was able to stay around more. That way her new relationship with Tom didn't leave Lena alone without a pal who could drink and play pool on weeknights with her.

Up to that summer, the only people in her current life who knew about her past with Kurt was Terry. Everyone else who knew her story was back in Denver. Otherwise, she'd told no one. But now, she decided to tell Carly, and over pizza in Roslyn one night, with the rest of the Village Pizza café tables empty, she'd told the whole ugly tale. It didn't take too long; the distance between the last telling and this one editing out much of the superfluous material.

But the real punch line in the new Suncadia equation was Carly's impact on Lena's game. Carly improved through their practice rounds, too, but for Lena, the constant prodding to keep up the routine and the cheerful encouragement she got for the yards she was adding to her drives worked magic.

Oddly, the improvement in her game seemed to soften up Ryne, too. They'd always enjoyed their rounds together, but her new proficiency drew a different kind of attention to her, and he started to get possessive. It was in little ways at first. When they went to the bar after a round, he secured a spot that left an empty seat at the end of the bar next to him, where he could monopolize her attention. And at the driving range before their rounds, he spent as much time watching her practice as he did at his own lackadaisical warm up.

At first, she pretended not to notice, but eventually, it was so obvious she had to comment. "What?" she asked turning around to confront him, standing 20 paces behind her on the driving range. "You don't need to warm up anymore?"

"I like to watch," he deadpanned. Lena laughed and turned back to her bucket of balls. The fact was that the attention was helping her get used to an audience, which would surely come in handy when she entered the qualifying rounds for the amateur tournament that fall. While Ryne didn't have much swing advice, having him watch her helped her concentrate on every swing – setting her stance, taking her time to relax her shoulders, and finishing her swing with a complete turn and perfect balance – the camera finish.

Lena mentioned his growing attention to Carly during one of their weekday practice sessions, admitting that she was somewhat embarrassed to have even noticed.

"Yeah, well if you hadn't noticed you'd be the only one," Carly said. "Don't you think there's something going on there?"

"What?" Lena asked innocently.

"Oh, come on. If it's not obvious to you, like it is to the rest of us, why don't you ask him?"

"Ask him?"

"Yeah, why not?"

"Well, for starters, I'm still embarrassed about the encounter with his girlfriend at his house. I don't want to make the same mistake again."

"Well, you don't have to show up with a dozen roses in your hand."

"I didn't…"

"Yeah, I know. I meant you don't have to ask him to sleep with you. Just ask him about his girlfriend sometime. You two spend enough time together, he shouldn't mind talking to you about her."

"But, you'd think if he were really interested in me, he'd have said something."

"He's probably just as embarrassed as you are. You know how when you were a kid, the guy who was your best pal could never admit it if he ended up having a crush on you?"

"No. I don't think that ever happened to me."

"Well, it probably did. You just had your head in a book and didn't notice. But the point is, he might just not know how to get things started down a different path."

Ryne hadn't become any less attractive to Lena, and in fact, it was the opposite. As they got closer, he let his shy guard down and talked more, and she liked the things he cared about – politics, books and wine. Not a bad list. She'd dated guys who were into local bands, TV shows and the NBA, and found their conversations inane and unbearable. Ryne was interesting and clever.

But the next Saturday, after their round, Lena decided to follow Carly's advice and ask Ryne about the girlfriend. Lena had shot under par, and she was feeling a little frisky anyway. The four friends were watching the end of a golf tournament on the TV above the bar, sipping beer and tossing around snarky comments about Tiger's latest new swing. During a commercial, Lena, as she had planned, casually turned to Ryne and asked, "how's that love life of yours?" It was an open question that could be answered quite generally or quite specifically, depending on the inclination of the respondent. She'd thought about the right approach for a couple of days, and decided the best thing to do was to not beat around the bush and ask him like it was just another regular conversation.

Ryne looked at her, put down his beer and answered flatly, "I am sick of it."

She was surprised at his blunt answer. "Sick of what?"

"I feel bad about this, but I've been bored with it for a long time. I just don't know how to get out of it."

"Are you talking about the same relationship you were in last year? I thought you told me last fall you had ended it."

"Yeah, I thought so too. Turns out it wasn't that easy. She has me over a barrel. If I break up with her, and she gets pissed, she can file a sexual harassment suit. I'm not her boss, you know, but I might as well be. And I don't think she wants out of it like I do."

"You don't think? You mean you can't tell?"

"Okay, I'm pretty sure she doesn't. She has it made, after all. I can't criticize her work, I can't ask her to move out, I can't end it."

"Is she in love with you?"

"I don't think so. She doesn't want sex anymore, and we talk about nothing. We're like an old married couple that has nothing in common after 50 years but stay together out of habit. Only for her, it's not a habit, it's a lunch ticket."

"It doesn't sound like much of a habit for you either."

"No. You're right. Bad analogy. But the point is, I am stuck."

The tournament was back on TV, and Ryne seemed relieved to be able to turn back to the golf game. But after watching Ryan Moore tee off, he turned back to Lena.

"So, how about your love life?"

"I don't have one. Or if I do, my partner is my golf bag," Lena laughed. She hadn't really expected him to turn the conversation around. Oddly, the surprise emboldened her. "You know, the last time I reached out to someone, it was when I brought you those Pro-V1s for your birthday last year. And we both know how that went."

Ryne grimaced and turned to answer a comment Brandt had just made about the tournament. Quickly, though, he faced Lena again. "I'm sorry about that. I should have been more upfront with you, but we've already been through that."

"Yeah, water under the bridge."

"Something like that," he nodded. "Look, I'd really like it if you would try again."

Lena blinked and swallowed a mouthful of beer hard. "But, you still have a girlfriend."

"Nominally."

"So you think. She doesn't think so. You can't date other women if she isn't ready to move out or move on."

"She doesn't have to be ready. I don't have a ring. I have made no vows. I don't see why we can't see each other on the side."

Lena pushed her bangs back with one hand, leaning her elbow on the bar and steadied herself with the other hand, clutching the railing.

"That is absurd. And you know it. No. The answer is no. I don't want to see you 'on the side,'" she answered firmly.

Ryne looked sheepish, even embarrassed. He looked down at his beer.

"God, that was stupid. Forget I said it. Must have been a bad week at work."

Lena shook her head and looked over his head at the TV. What could she say that would preserve their friendship, which she did care about, and yet hold her position on the girlfriend?

"Okay, let's forget it. And, just for the record, if you didn't have a live-in girlfriend, yes, I do still find you interesting, and I would like to try again. But, that's just not possible right now."

"Well, I guess that makes me feel a little better. What jerks men are, huh?"

"Yup," Lena said. She finished her beer with a quick gulp and gathered her stuff to leave.

"Hey guys," she called out to Carly and Brandt. "See you Monday, Carly. See you next weekend, Brandt." She turned to leave, and then decided, what the hell. She turned around and stood on her tiptoes, and gave Ryne a platonic peck on the cheek.

But when she went to bed that night, she reached over to her bed table and pulled out her vibrator, and imagined him inside of her. I'm not going to make a habit of this, she admonished herself, although she was surprised how well it worked.

IT DIDN'T COME AS ANY surprise to Lena when she woke up a week later, a Sunday morning, with Ryne in her bed. She looked over at him sleeping – my god, she thought, he's good looking even when he's sleeping. She thought about the sex of the night before and involuntarily let out a little whimper. She was glad that it didn't wake him up. In spite of its erotic success, she was already starting to regret her willingness to let him come home with her. It was a night of great fun, she admitted to herself quickly. But, nothing good could come of a relationship with a man who couldn't commit to his girlfriend or to her.

Lena pulled back the covers and turned her legs over the side of the bed. Her feet found her slippers – at least something was where it should have been – and slipped into the bathroom. She brushed her teeth and her hair, and leaned forward to look at herself in the mirror.

"You aren't getting any younger," she mumbled to herself, pulling at the skin next to her eyes to stretch out the crow's feet. "And sleeping with a lost cause isn't going to help."

The evening before, when Carly, Brandt, Ryne and Lena had uncharacteristically taken their camaraderie on the golf course into an evening at the Brick in Roslyn, Ryne had seemed anything but a trapped man. She put off asking him where Kimberly was and if he shouldn't be getting home until it was too late for the subject to be relevant. He flirted incessantly with her, leaning over her back as she lined up her pool shots and celebrating her bank shots with quick pecks on her lips. She had enough beer to let his public displays of emotion slide, and eventually, when they walked to their cars, she didn't protest when he demanded he follow her home to make sure she'd get back to the Lodge safely. After they arrived at her door, she'd lost any pretense of not wanting him to stay. Now, she faced the outcome of that decision with a mixture of satisfaction and regret.

She opened the bathroom door quietly and peeked out at the bed. Ryne was awake, and he looked at her nakedness with a self-satisfied smile. It wasn't a lecherous grin, thank god. But it definitely signaled that he wasn't regretting what happened.

"Nice morning," he summed up his feelings. Her face must have quickly communicated her chagrin, and he sighed deeply. "I don't suppose you're going to let me stay for breakfast."

"Oh, hell, why not?" she said, grabbing robe she left on the hook outside the bathroom door and quickly covering up. "Do you like French toast?"

"Love it!" He jumped out of bed like a 12-year-old and, then, suddenly showing his age, lumbered like a man of 50 into the bathroom and closed the door.

Lena went into the kitchen, made two quick cups of coffee on her Kuerig machine, and sat one on the breakfast bar for Ryne. She turned back to the refrigerator and pulled out eggs, milk, bacon, butter, syrup and a half-loaf of week-old French bread. She pulled a frying pan down from the overhead rack, pulled apart the bacon slices and layered them in the heating skillet. She broke four eggs into a glass bowl and turned to grab a whisk under the bar. Ryne was standing on the other side, dressed, watching her. She stopped. He was grinning.

"This is more like it," he said.

"More like what?"

"Just more like it."

"What?"

"A great night of sex followed by a breakfast that includes bacon," he said, grinning like he'd just discovered the secret to happiness.

Lena shook her head and turned back to the stove to turn the bacon. She really wished they could get through breakfast pleasantly, and then she could go on with her life as if this hadn't happened. But she doubted that was going to be possible. Even if Ryne left right now, the night before was going to haunt her – both for the mistake it was and for the mistake it wasn't.

She poured a bit of milk into the eggs and whisked them with a fury they didn't deserve. She set the bowl to the side, bent down to pull her cast iron griddle out of the cupboard below, and placed it across two burners. She lit the burners and reached up for the Pam in the cupboard above. She moved with the assuredness of a cook who knew how to time every step in the preparation of a meal, because, in fact, she did. Suddenly, she was aware of how graceful it must all look to Ryne. A woman who knows her way around the kitchen. She wasn't at all happy at the cliché.

She stopped and turned around. He was watching approvingly. But, as if he read and needed to dispute her thoughts, he shook his head.

"I'm not admiring your kitchen skills," he assured her. "I'm watching your body move under that robe."

"What? Are you Superman?" she laughed.

"What do you think?" His raised eyebrow communicated that he was thinking more about his abilities in bed, as demonstrated overnight, than his possible x-ray vision. She pantomimed throwing the spatula in her hand at him and turned back to the stove. "You could help, you know."

"Okay, what can I do?"

"Set the table."

"Where are the dishes?"

"Find them," she ordered. She opened the bread bag and cut the bread into thick slices. She heard Ryne open and shut cupboard doors behind her, but she didn't turn to help him navigate his way around her tiny kitchen. She feared that she'd find herself face-to-face with him in close proximity, and she knew what would happen then. Sex at night under the cover of alcohol was one thing, but leaving a half-cooked meal on the stove and diving back into bed in the daylight was quite another. There would be no excuses for the latter.

Ryne managed to find plates and silverware, and even located the paper napkins, which he folded and placed under the forks, where they should be. He took the initiative to find orange juice and glasses, and moved the salt and pepper shakers off the counter next to the stove onto the bar, where he'd laid out their place settings.

"I don't think we'll need those," she commented on the shakers, watching out of the corner of her eye. "But you could make me another cup of coffee."

She grilled the egg-battered bread and drained the bacon on a paper towel, and they sat down to eat. They ate in silence as Lena tried to decide how to discuss the night before and how to get Ryne to agree that it was a mistake. Not an irreversible mistake, but one that would be acknowledged jointly.

But she couldn't find the right way to start the discussion, and she reluctantly admitted to herself that she wasn't really convinced of what she wanted. Maybe they did have a future as a clandestine couple, operating under the guise of golf buddies and never letting others in on their new relationship.

Whoa! she suddenly thought. What about Kimberly? Where they hell was she last night? Wasn't she expecting Ryne to come home?

The questions demanded she break the silence.

"What are you going to tell Kimberly?" she asked bluntly, putting her fork down and pushing her plate away, signaling it was time to face the music. "What's your excuse for not coming home last night?"

"What makes you think she noticed?" he smirked. But her unsmiling gaze stopped his humor.

He pushed his plate to the edge other side of the breakfast bar, too, and pulled his coffee cup under his chin. He stared down at the dark liquid as if trying to figure out if he could have both of them – the best of all worlds. What was he going to do next?

"Look," she interrupted his thoughts. "Let's just stop this right here. We aren't going to do this again."

Ryne said nothing. He pushed his stool back with a loud scrape and walked around to the kitchen. He pulled their dishes down from the bar and pushed the remaining breakfast crumbs into the garbage disposal. He rinsed the plates off under the faucet and set them down next to the sink. Finally, he looked up at her and met her eyes.

"I don't want to."

"Don't want to what?"

"I don't want to not let this happen again. I really want you." He stood with his hands on the counter, resting his weight on his arms. "I don't want to be with her."

Lena held his eyes and considered her response. She wasn't sure. Right now, she wanted Ryne too, as much as he wanted her, she thought, but she didn't know for how long. She didn't want to share him with a young 30-something, and she didn't want to fight the battle that taking him away from Kimberly was likely to entail. She wanted to focus on golf. She certainly didn't want a protracted romantic drama that would leave her in limbo – who knew for how long – and distract her from what she'd set out to accomplish this year on the golf course. But how could a long-shot like getting to the amateur golf tournament be more important than having a relationship that might turn out to be the best one she'd ever have?

"No." she said, finally.

"No?"

"No. Let's do the dishes and then you go back to Kimberly and decide what you want to do. Until that's over, I think 'no' is the best answer."

"Oh, Christ. It's more complicated than that."

"I know. You've got yourself into a relationship that you don't want. But you have to figure out how to get out of it, or settle for it. I won't be your number two."

Ryne leaned against the counter and looked down at the floor between his feet. As he stood there, Lena got up and brought their cold coffee cups around to the sink. She reached around his arms, dumped the dregs into the sink and bumped him aside with her hip.

"Now move or do something useful."

Ryne moved to the side and stood for a minute, mute. Then he walked into the living room, picked up the jacket he'd left on the arm of the couch the night before, and wordlessly walked out the door.

Lena stood in front of the sink, listening to the elevator bell ding, the doors open and close, and the whirr of the elevator take Ryne down.

She washed the dishes and wiped down the counters. She walked down the stairs to the coffee shop on the first floor to buy the Sunday New York Times Sunday and then walked back up. Her guilt was slightly alleviated by taking the stairs and by reading the paper – at least she was keeping up on the tragedies of the world, even if she was doing nothing to solve them.

But even with her favorite jazz station playing in the background and a dozen sections of the paper in front of her, she couldn't settle down. She read the same paragraph of an op-ed piece in the Sunday Review before giving up and throwing it on the pile on the coffee table. It often took her the entire week to finish the Book Review, the Travel Section, the Magazine and the Business section. But she was usually able to get through the front section and the op-ed section before her attention span ran out on Sunday mornings. Now, Ryne kept interrupting her thoughts.

Giving up on the paper, she showered and got ready for her 9:30 round with Kim.

11 QUALIFYING

Carly, Brandt and Lena didn't see Ryne again for the rest of the summer. He didn't show up for their regular foursomes and his name never appeared on the tee sheet. Lena told Terry about the night with Ryne the next week, and she tried to mute her emotions as she filled in the details. For Lena, it was like getting a pony for Christmas, but only for a day. And then, realizing that the pony – however missed – wouldn't really fit in a condo anyway. His disappearance from their foursome would leave a void, but Lena was dead set against asking him to come back.

"Where's Ryne?" Carly asked as they gathered at the starter's desk the next Saturday.

Lena grimaced. "I'll explain later." Carly rolled her eyes.

On the second tee, while they waited for the group ahead to clear the middle of the fairway, Lena told her what had happened with Ryne.

"I'm thinking the soundtrack to my life should be 'Let's Get Drunk and Screw,'" she said, summing up the evening. "Screw it up, anyway."

"Or maybe it should be 'Let's play golf and screw and let's get drunk and screw, and ...'"

"Yeah, okay. I get it. Why can't I have a normal relationship? You know, have dinner, watch a little TV, go to bed and have decent sex?"

"Is that normal?" Carly laughed. "Do you know anyone like that?"

"How about you and Brandt?"

"Well, kind of. We get along, and I can't say I'm unhappy. But, was it like that with you and Kirk?"

"Kurt. Not Kirk. But, hell no. We had sex for the first month or so, and then he spent the next year falling asleep on the couch with a beer in his hand."

"I hate to say it, but that's probably more like normal."

"Yeah. Something to tell your grandkids when you have that birds-and-bees talk."

"It would probably be healthier for them," Carly admitted. "But you and I are not going to have kids, let alone grandkids, so I guess we don't have to worry about it."

"Yeah. I'm sorry I screwed up our foursome. It just seemed like such a good idea at the time."

Lena's golf went downhill for a couple of weeks, even though she was loath to attribute it to the one-night stand. Everyone had slumps in their games, and the key to getting over them was figuring out where the swing had gone bad, or figuring out how to set new goals that looked beyond the shanks and yips, and moving on.

It didn't help that their foursome had now become a threesome, which meant they were usually joined by a single golfer, and, of course, it was always a man. Very few women go out to the course by themselves as a single. It is too intimidating. And the men who come out as singles are either playing alone because they're jerks on the course, have no friends, or because their wives or girlfriends don't play, or all of the above.. And if their significant other doesn't play golf, many of them carry an attitude about women on the course: they can't play.

Having a playing partner once a week who expected her to play badly didn't help. Lena swung too hard and abandoned the smart, strategic game she'd crafted over the past year, trying to prove herself with long drives and risky shots. Even though she still nearly always outscored her stranger-partners, her scores regularly crept up into the low 80s. Lena had a tough time reconciling her pursuit of the senior women's tournament with how she was playing. She had to pull it together and start playing her own game pretty soon or she'd have to give up the quest. This game was so damn hard.

Not having anything but golf to focus on meant she didn't have the usual golfer's answer to a slump – put it in perspective; a bad day on the golf course is better than a good day at the office. Nothing else distracted her from her poor play, and she lived with it eight hours a day every day for nearly three weeks.

The fact that Terry was so obviously and madly in love with Tom didn't help Lena put things in perspective either, but the fact that Terry's relationship had settled down into a predictable and comfortable regularity was a blessing in another way. Terry had more time for Lena again, and now that she didn't need to be with Tom every night, she had started to call Lena for chick nights out.

Carly, Terry and Lena started to make a routine of Tuesday and Friday nights at the Brick, shooting pool and drinking beer. Tom would pick Terry up at the bar about 10 on Tuesdays nights and he joined them after work on Fridays. Brandt would meet them at the bar as he returned from Seattle on Friday nights, and Lena would slip quietly into her role as the fifth – but not unwelcome – wheel in the group.

Lena's rounds with Kim on Sunday mornings served as a cool break from having to watch the happy couples cavort around her. Then, one Sunday in July, Kim showed up at the starter desk without his clubs.

"Where are your sticks?" she asked.

"I'm going to caddie for you," he said. "It's time we start getting ready for your tournaments."

"You're going to caddie for me in my tournaments? Is that legal?"

"Yeah. I checked. I did some research. You can walk with a caddie or you can take a cart in those tournaments. You can even ride a cart AND have a caddie. It's up to you. I know how much you like to walk, and I can be your caddie."

Lena looked at Kim for a long minute. He was serious.

"Okay. Let's give it a shot."

For the next few weeks, they alternated. One week, Kim walked with her and worked as her caddie; the next week he played along with her, and they took a cart. It started to make a difference, and Lena put her non-Ryne-induced slump behind her. Walking the course again also helped. She started playing better and more consistently, and as she and Kim worked out a routine, she found it helped her relax and play better to have him at her side. He reminded her to slow her pace and swing in tempo. He helped her choose her clubs, cautioning her against over- or under-estimating her ability, plot her strategy on each hole, and decide when to lay up and when to go for the green. The joint decisions weren't much different from the ones she would have made herself, but they gave her more confidence in each swing.

Together with her weekday practice sessions with Carly, her Sundays with Kim drove her game forward. The slump ended. Her handicap started to inch down again, and by the end of August, she was playing to a solid two – two strokes over par. She had a few more sub-par rounds. And when she didn't play to par or better, she was still playing better golf than she had ever expected of herself. It was still a hard game, but she had clearly started to meet its challenge.

THE CLOSEST QUALIFYING ROUND for the Women's Senior Amateur tournament turned out to be closer than she could have hoped. It was held at Tumble Creek, where the ex-banker Jim lived and just across the Cle Elum River, only two miles down the highway from Suncadia.

Lena had played Tumble a couple of times with Ann, and she didn't particularly like the course, but the fact that it was familiar made her first qualifying tournament seem a little less scary. The pro at the private club was happy to let her have a couple of practice rounds the month before the tournament, and she and Kim played them on two Sundays in August. Kim played with her the first round, and he caddied the second.

The morning of the qualifying tournament, she and Kim met early at the Lodge for breakfast with Terry, avoiding the tournament breakfast at Tumble Creek's clubhouse. Lena didn't want to join in on the sizing up that would take place prior to the shotgun start. She really didn't care whom she was paired up with in the round. What mattered was her own focus and her own ability to stay with her own game plan.

When they arrived at the bag drop in front of the clubhouse, most of the other competitors were still inside, finishing their breakfast, but a couple of women huddled over their putts on the practice green, and a couple more were already on the driving range warming up. It was a cool late August morning, and the driving range and fairways were covered with dew. The wind, which was expected to pick up later in the day, was still just a breeze, and Lena was pleased to see that she was scheduled to start on the second hole, which meant that the most wind-affected holes on the front nine would be behind her before the breeze picked up mid-day.

But still, starting with a par-three hole was a bit tricky. It meant that instead of having a wide, forgiving fairway to hit with the first nerve-racking tee shot, she'd have to start with a narrow target. But then, her playing partners would too.

Lena's psychological advantage was showing up with a caddie and an intention to walk the course. Everyone had a choice – share a cart with a competitor or walk, and Lena was one of only two women who had come to the qualifier planning to walk the course. It was a sign that she took the game seriously.

The spectators were few – only Terry had shown up to watch her round, and a handful of relatives and club-mates of her opponents sauntered along the cart paths, keeping up with them.

After birdieing the first hole, Lena thought she might relax a bit, now at a one-stroke advantage over two of her foursome and a two-stroke advantage over the fourth. But, as she and Kim strolled to the next tee box, she struggled to stop her hands from shaking.

"Chill," Kim said in a slightly harsh tone. It was probably what she needed – a bit of tough love. But, it wasn't going to work like magic. Still, when she lined up her next tee shot, taking her grip on the club felt so familiar it calmed her down. A great drive, a decent approach shot up the hill to the green, a good chip from just off the fringe and a one-putt gave her a par, and she retained a one-shot lead over the other three.

The tough par 5 that came up next was not easy for any of them, though. Lena hadn't parred it in either of her two practice rounds, but at least she knew what was coming: a long uphill drive to the target landing, and an even harsher uphill second shot to a fairway that tilted sharply to the left. Anything but a perfect shot onto the second landing would roll 100 yards or more down into the thick rough and deep bunkers on the left side of the fairway. Hitting their third shot from there, the golfers faced two more dastardly deep bunkers in front of the hole, and a huge sloping green.

Her opponents all thought they'd nailed their second shots, but Lena and Kim shook their heads with local knowledge and pity, and walked up the hill. All three of them had landed in the middle of the fairway and were perplexed to not find their balls anywhere in the short grass. She and Kim watched them finally accept their fate and begin the search for their balls in the tall fescue down the hill to the left. Lena had hit her ball far enough to avoid the left-ward roll, but she'd bounced off into the rough on the right. Her next shot landed short of the green, and she chipped and two putted for a bogie. Still, the others came in with a bogie, a double bogie and a triple, and she hadn't lost any ground.

"We call this the clown hole," she sympathized aloud with her opponents as she walked off the green toward the next tee box.

"Have you played here before?" the tall, slender Kylie asked, heading toward the cart she had to herself because Lena was walking.

"Twice. How about you?"

"Never. We're from Portland. I couldn't get a chance to get up here. Are all of the par fives this hard?"

"Not if the wind isn't blowing too hard," Lena assured her, not terribly encouragingly.

Kylie tied her with a birdie on the next par four with an amazingly long drive. Lena settled for par. After that, the two played neck and neck over the next 10 holes, with Lena finally pulling ahead by two on the back nine to post an even par by the end of the round. The other two players quickly fell back and ended up well over par and out of the competition.

By the final two holes – numbers 18 and 1 for her foursome – the wind had picked up. It helped Lena par the uphill and generally tough 18th, and with a hefty tailwind gust timed just perfectly, her drive on number 1 was the longest she'd ever produced on the hole. Again, her local knowledge helped her avoid mistaking the false front as the green on her uphill approach shot, while the other three left their balls 30 and 40 yards short of the pin.

By the time they backtracked down No. 1 and reached the clubhouse to turn in her card, she and Kim knew they had a pretty good chance of qualifying for the tournament in Georgia. Terry's cheerful greeting as they walked past the cart barn and over the practice green confirmed their suspicion, and it hit Lena that all of the work of the past 15 months had come to this: she was indeed going to compete in the Women's Senior Amateur Tournament three weeks away.

They mingled politely with the other contestants in the clubhouse, saving the noisy celebration for later that afternoon at the Brick. Two or three of the top scorers were likely to go to the finals, but as the outright winner of the qualifier – the only one with an even par, Lena was guaranteed a spot at the tournament.

She wasn't particularly proud of it, but she knew that her elation about making the cut was a big part of why she and Kim ended up sleeping together for the first time that night.

"OH, NO! What happened?"

Lena picked up the phone a week later to hear a sobbing, blubbering Terry on the other end.

"I blew it. I knew I couldn't make it work."

"What? Tom?"

Lena didn't really have to ask. She knew Terry well enough to tell a lovesick sob from a financial-trouble moan.

"He packed up last night and left. I blew it. I blew it again!"

"Are you sure it's over? What did he say?"

The story came out in spurts of broken sentences and nose-blowing, but it was far from an unusual tale from her best friend. The argument had started the Saturday before with Terry's decision to paint her bathroom a bright orange, and Tom's indiscretion in suggesting he should have a say in something she wanted to do with her own home. The disagreement spilled over into the following week, with heretofore unstated grudges and complaints tumbling out from both of them. The final straw, apparently, had been Tom's accusation that Terry tried far too hard to be "quirky," and Terry's retort that Tom tried far too hard to be boring. The fact that they needed each other to balance out both of those true, if exaggerated, tendencies got lost in the fight.

Even though she needed to concentrate on practicing for the tournament, Lena invited Terry and Rex to come over and stay with her a couple of nights, putting the half-painted bathroom out of sight. Lena also wanted Terry to have a safe place to self-medicate without drinking alone or having to drive home drunk. She knew Terry well enough to predict that a lot of alcohol would be commissioned in her battle turn the heartache into anger and finally acceptance. For Terry, break-up grief never involved more than those three steps – sadness, anger and acceptance – all lubricated with expensive wine.

It turned out to be a blessing. Having her friend retell Tom stories and mull "I should-have-knowns" aloud every evening over the next week kept Lena calm and kept her from obsessing about the coming tournament. It also kept her from having to share the story of sex with Kim.

"You know, I'm really envious of you," Terry mused through her tears and the influence of a couple of glasses of wine the first night while Lena cleaned up from their dinner. "You've really re-invented yourself and I just seem stuck in the same old rut. Or worse. It's like I've scraped the bottom of my oil pan and I'm stuck in one spot. "

"Re-invented? Hardly. I'm just avoiding reality for a while," Lena countered. "I'm playing golf and not looking for a job."

"But it's something new and different," Terry sniffed, staring into the dark red liquid of her wine glass as she slouched on Lena's couch.

"Something different would be taking up yoga, going vegan, moving into a 300-square-foot apartment on Eastlake and tearing up my driver's license. That's re-invention," Lena asserted. "I hate the whole 're-invention' concept anyway. I can't imagine a person can really change who they are on purpose. Change comes slowly or in spurts, as a reaction to things. You don't plan it."

"Wow. I was just trying to give you a compliment," Terry seemed close to tears at Lena's pedantic reaction.

"Oh, honey. I'm sorry," Lena said, dropping the dish towel in her hand and plopping down next to her friend. She put her arm around the sobbing woman's shoulders and gave her a big hug. "I didn't mean to be disagreeable. I just think I'm probably not any better off than you are when it comes to figuring out what to do with this silly life of mine. You at least have a business of your own. You're your own boss. There's a lot to be said for that."

"But I really don't want to do this alone," sniffed Terry, burying her head in Lena's arm. "I really wanted to move forward with my life with someone."

For the rest of the evening, Lena let Terry sniffle and sputter her way through a wandering re-examination of her past 10 love-starved years without much interruption or disagreement. Finally her friend dropped off to a drunken sleep and Lena pulled her legs over onto the couch and tucked a warm throw around her.

During the day, Lena practiced religiously that week, sticking to a rigorous routine and continuing her workouts while Terry slowly worked her way out of her slobbery depression. Lena planned to take the next week – the final week before the tournament – easy, and she and Kim planned to arrive at the tournament hotel two days early to adjust to the three-hour time change and get in a couple of practice rounds at the tournament course – an option for all of the qualifying players.

As the results from the other qualifying tournaments around the country were posted on the USGA website, Lena and Kim discussed her opponents over the phone. Even though women with handicaps as high as 18.6 were eligible to play in the qualifying tournaments, all of the qualifiers were single-digit handicappers, according to their official Golf Handicap Index Network postings, and most were in their early 50s. But Lena was surprised at the number of older veterans who were qualifying or otherwise making the cut. Some were clearly not contenders anymore, but they were granted a pass by virtue of having won the tournament in earlier years.

Kylie, her opponent in the qualifier, was an alternate who wouldn't know if she would be playing in the tournament until commitments from all of the qualifiers had been secured. A week before Lena left for Georgia, she opened up the USGA website and saw that Kylie would not get to play.

"Good luck, friend," Kylie said graciously, when Lena called her to offer her condolences. "I hope you kick their butts like you kicked mine."

"I didn't kick your butt," Lena laughed. "I only had you by two strokes, and I had a little local knowledge that helped at the end. I won't have that in Georgia."

But she and Kim had studied the Georgia course online, reviewing the layout on the country club's website the last weekend before they left for the tournament, trying to get as much course wisdom as they could from the virtual experience of the flyover videos posted on the website. They worked on it late into the night before they flopped into bed, both begging off sex with excuses of exhaustion. Lena knew that was a pretty good sign that she had not been terribly attracted to Kim in the first place. It had been sex of convenience. Yup, another relationship without real commitment, Lena mused. But, it was also a bit different: the first time in her adult life when sex with a new partner had cooled so significantly so quickly.

TWO DAYS BEFORE Lena's flight to Atlanta, Terry decided to come along to cheer her on. She'd made the flight reservations and had booked a room at the tournament hotel.

"But, we can stay together," Lena protested. "Cancel your reservation and stay with me."

"Don't you want to keep your options open?" Terry asked, still oblivious to the recent complication in Lena's relationship with Kim. "Maybe you'll meet someone interesting enough to invite 'home.'" She wrote quote marks in the air with her fingers.

"Terry, even if I did, I'm not going to mess up my tournament with some one-night or two-night stand," Lena bluffed. The truth was that she was glad to have an excuse to keep Kim in his own room.

"Okay, I'll cancel my room. But are you sure I won't distract you?"

12 GEORGIA

The ceremonial opening of the tournament in Georgia both exceeded her expectations and disappointed them at the same time.

They had arrived at the hotel mid-afternoon the Wednesday before the tournament so Lena could play a couple of practice rounds before the Saturday start of competition. Lodging at the tournament's headquarters was a large and exquisite Renaissance Hotel with a mid-sized conference center that would also hold the players' dinner the night before the first round. After they checked in, they left Terry, who declared the need for a nap, and Lena and Kim went to the driving range under dark skies. A front had passed through earlier in the afternoon, making their landing at the airport a bumpy one, but it promised to move east and leave clear skies and warm temperatures in its wake. Lena hit a dozen shots with each of her clubs with Kim watching. He made a couple of gentle suggestions on her pace and her set up, but seemed content just to watch. It was best not try to change much in her swing at the last minute before the tournament. They putted a while, playing a golf-version of the old basketball standby, horse. The game helped her calm down and concentrate on each putt rather than think about the coming days.

During the first practice round the next day, Terry followed along the side of the course, generally sticking to the cart paths but occasionally slipping closer to get a better angle on Lena's shots down the fairway. After nine holes, she decided to retire to the hotel pool for a nap and a cheap novel, leaving Lena and Kim to finish alone.

Most of the other competitors were getting in practice rounds as well, and Lena noticed how the pairs and foursomes in front and behind her seemed to be amazingly friendly and chatty for soon-to-be competitors who came from all over the country. The two women she'd been scheduled to practice with were old friends from back when they'd played the USGA Women's Amateur when they were in college.

"Do you think they all know each other?" she asked Kim, a couple of holes into the round.

"I'm sure many of them do. There's only four of you rookies on the roster," he said.

It hadn't occurred to Lena to check that out – to find out how many of the 132 women in the tournament had been in either the senior or mid-amateur tournament before. She had checked out the qualifiers' handicaps, but she hadn't drilled into the USGA archives to see who the veterans were. Apparently, Kim had looked at a press release that detailed the golf accomplishments of about four dozen of the competitors. In fact, he said, one woman was playing in her 17th senior amateur tournament in a row. Many had played in a half-dozen or more USGA tournaments at all levels from the juniors to the seniors. It was clear that Lena was up against a field of women who were very accustomed to the pressure of the competition and had made good friends along the way.

The condition of the course they were going to play also surprised her. She was used to the public, resort courses at Suncadia, which were often indifferently maintained and at times an embarrassment to Lena. The courses were owned by a resort chain and a private equity firm, for whom sales of lots and condos were more important than the happiness of the club members. They flooded the fairways with enough water to ensure that the course looked green and pretty for visiting tourists and potential home-builders, without any concern for the flooded, soggy acres the golfers had to endure, or the hard, pock-marked greens.

But this Georgia course was delightful. The tee boxes and fairways were perfect carpets of Bermuda grass, and the bent-grass greens looked like they'd never received a ball before. The rough along the fairways was tended and fair and stretched from one hole to the adjoining one. There wasn't any matted, foot-high fescue, knockweed, Canadian thistles and mahonia that hid errant balls off the fairways back in Suncadia.

At dinner that night in the hotel's Mexican restaurant, she and Kim shared their impressions with Terry. But, when they'd finished their entrees and Terry started in on her dessert, Kim turned serious.

"I really wish we'd had a chance for you to play in some serious tournaments before this," he said. "I think it's going to be hard for us to adjust to the atmosphere here."

"You mean the humidity?" Terry asked, her mouth full of peach pie and ice cream.

"No," Kim frowned. He didn't give Terry the thumb – as in "out of here" – but she got the message anyway. It was clear he didn't want Terry to be part of the conversation.

"I think I'll visit the ladies room," she said, abandoning her pie and sliding out of the booth with her purse.

After she was out of earshot, Kim started again. "It's a totally different gestalt here."

"You mean the fact that they all seem to know each other?" Lena asked.

"No. The fact that they're all so focused. I don't think you've really had a chance to practice that kind of focus."

"How about the qualifier?"

"Yes, that was a little more serious than most of our rounds. But even that seemed more casual than what we saw out there today."

Lena thought back over the day's round. She and Kim had been shushed several times by her playing partners – not so much verbally as with dirty looks. They were used to laughing and joking about the game in front of them, and about the world in general. The women at this tournament seemed to be maniacally focused on each shot.

"I saw that too," she said. "I figured they're just still working on their games."

"Oh, no. I think their games are pretty solid. I think they just play this way. They're probably just as focused in their club championships," Kim shook his head. He looked concerned. "I'm not sure either of us is ready for the kind of game these women play."

Lena had trusted Kim to help her get ready for this tournament, and now he was making her more insecure – not less.

HER INSECURITY GOT WORSE at the opening dinner on Thursday night. As a caddie, Kim wasn't invited to the opening ceremony, and she found herself at the cocktail hour before dinner standing alone while gaggles of women chatted amiably in tight circles all around her. God, it feels like junior high all over again, she thought.

Seating at the tables wasn't assigned, and Lena had no way to seek out the other rookies at the tournament – the better to commiserate and feel less alone. As she sat at her table, silently listening to old friends recall prior battles, mishaps and controversies at earlier tournaments, she wished she'd skipped the dinner and gone out again with Kim and Terry.

While the food was slightly cold and uninspired, she was impressed with the presentations at the podium. The prior year's winner was introduced and gave a short but articulate and heart-felt speech, and the USGA Women's Tournament Chairperson welcomed them all with an address that made the contestants feel as if they had just been chosen as finalists for a Nobel Peace Prize. Thank-you gifts were presented to a few contestants who'd participated in USGA charitable events or raised money for USGA causes through the prior year. And the USGA staff had spent considerable effort in pulling together a professional and entertaining slide show and video of earlier years' tournaments.

Next came an introduction of the town's bigwigs, who bragged about their small community's history, as well as its fine golf courses. The tournament was being held in Gleason, Georgia, a town that had the good fortune of being the chosen landing spot in the mid-19th Century of Marvin Harrison Gleason. The young Gleason had fled England and his extended family's feud over control of the family's furniture factory there, and he started a furniture factory here in the thick woods of Eastern Georgia.

He hired workers from all over three counties – largely lumberjacks who had experience in felling the large timbers of the region, but who were eager to learn the skills that led to much higher paying jobs in manufacturing. Gleason and his children reinvested their profits in other businesses in the community and in charitable institutions, like a hospital and the schools. The town grew and changed its name to Gleason. The prosperity had continued right up to the present.

Recently, Marvin's descendants realized that they had other opportunities to build their own fortunes – mostly in hedge funds managed on Wall Street – and had better things to do than run a factory – like flying their private jets to exotic resorts around the world. Not only was building furniture in the humid backwater Southern town of Marvin's choosing hard and unglamorous, it was also getting harder and harder to compete against cheap Chinese imports – especially in the middle of the recession. They sold their family business to a private equity firm out of Memphis, which had announced only two weeks before the tournament that they would be moving the Gleason furniture factory to Indonesia.

The announcement had rattled the company's unions and some local – mostly Democratic – politicians, but it didn't seem to have phased the town bigwigs, who huffed and puffed about the town's heritage and success before the tired women seated at the banquet. Finally, the lights were turned up and the evening reached an end. The women at Lena's table resumed their exclusionary chit-chat and although no one was paying attention, Lena excused herself.

She wasn't ready to go back to her room and face Terry's eager questions. Instead, she rode up the elevator and knocked on Kim's door.

"Hey, can I come in? I'm suffering a little bit of anxiety and regret at being here," she said when he appeared. "I'm not sure Terry would understand. If she's even awake. Or alone."

"Sure. Come on in. Do I need to get dressed?" He stood at the open door in a bathrobe, smelling like soap and hair conditioner.

"Hell, no. I'll just be a minute."

Lena walked in and surveyed the room. It looked like no one had checked in yet. His suitcase and clothes were out of sight, and he hadn't so much as mussed the bedspread or pillows on the bed.

"Wow, you are neat!" she said, slightly suspiciously. "Are you really staying in here?"

"Well, yes. I haven't received any other offers," he chuckled. "Would you like to move in?" He raised an eyebrow and looked at her sideways gesturing at the immaculate room.

Without taking the time to discern if it was joke or serious, she answered. "No!" a little too emphatically.

"Well, I was just kidding," Kim said quickly, backing away from her a step. "Yow! You could give a guy a complex, you know."

"No, I'm sorry," she said, shaking her head. "I didn't mean to snap." She pulled out the desk chair from under the desk and slumped down in exhaustion. "I'm just a little tired and a lot intimidated."

"How did the dinner go?"

"I've been in friendlier TSA lines," she said. "It was like being in seventh grade all over again. No one talks to you, no one even sees you. They all act like they've known each other forever and don't need any more friends. Or even enemies."

"Yuck. I'm sorry." Kim sat down on the edge of the bed and discretely pulled the robe across his legs, ensuring that he wouldn't make another mistake by baring his thighs – or more. "Women can be so cliquish, can't they?"

Lena nodded and studied the geometric shapes in the carpet at her feet. "I suppose guys would be the same way, except with a little added bravado and trash talk. I'm not sure it's really cliques. I'm afraid it's just me. I don't really make new friends that quickly. As loud and pushy as I can be, I'm still the shy girl who lived in the country with a dog and a mom and dad who didn't talk."

"Probably," Kim agreed. They fell into silence. Their ability to sit there quietly, neither of them needing to say anything else, was reassuring to Lena. She took a deep breath, slumped back in the chair and relaxed a little.

The Golf Channel was on TV, but Kim had been watching on mute. They watched in silence for a few minutes. Kim rose and pulled a couple of Stella lagers from the bar refrigerator and opened them. He handed one to Lena, and flopped back down on the bed, fluffing the pillows up against the headboard and settling back.

"Are you comfy?" he asked Lena. She nodded without looking away from the TV. The rerun of an episode of the Big Break was almost palatable with the sound off. Lena didn't follow the series; she hated the snarky comments and the hyped-up competition. But with the sound off, it was fine. She slowly sipped the beer and started to relax.

"Well, I just needed to commiserate," Lena said, rising once she'd finished her beer. She reached over to pat Kim's slightly wet hair. "Thanks for letting me come by."

She moved to the door and Kim followed her.

"Get some sleep and I'll meet you at 7 downstairs in the breakfast room," he said, holding the door open. Lena turned and stood on her tip-toes to touch his cheek with a quick peck of her lips.

"Thanks, buddy. You know, I wouldn't even be here if it weren't for you. And I'm glad I don't have to be here without you." She turned and walked down the hall.

She felt Kim watching her for a few steps before he quietly closed the door behind her.

THE TOURNAMENT comprised the usual set of competitions for the USGA: two days of stroke play to whittle the field in half, followed by match play in which the top 64 stroke-play finishers competed in six rounds over three days.

Lena and her two playing mates started off their first round on the tenth hole at 9:30 with no spectators other than Terry and their assigned USGA rules official. Lena had been assigned to have the last tee shot on that first hole, and she watched as her two competitors drove their balls straight down the middle of the fairway, the shortest 210 yards away.

It was clear this was going to be the best all-woman threesome she'd played in so far in her life, but rather than be intimidated by the good drives, she was exhilarated. It was a relief not to have to think of some nice platitude that was meant to make a poor player feel better about her mediocre play.

Lena stepped up to the tee at her turn, and focused on the rhythm of her own routine: picking her target, lining up beside her ball, taking a slow, deliberate practice swing, relaxing her shoulders, exhaling, and swinging smoothly but aggressively through the ball.

It ended up right in the middle, farther down the fairway than either of her competitors' drives. It was a respectable start, and she smiled at Kim as she handed him her driver.

The course was in immaculate shape. A nice soaking rain the night before was enough to soften up the greens slightly without leaving any standing water. Even the low areas were well drained and playable. A typical Georgia course, its fairways were flat and straight, especially compared with Prospector at Suncadia, where a perfectly centered drive was required – but not guaranteed – to find a flat lie. A few slight doglegs gave the players opportunities to show off their ability to fade or draw the ball on command, and the tall cypress trees between the fairways were far enough apart to leave plenty of room for slightly wayward drives. From the white tees where the tournament was played, the rating was 73.1 and the slope 130 for women. Tough, but not ridiculous. The biggest challenge for the women was the length – at more than 6,600 yards.

Lena tipped her head back to catch the warm sun on her face as they walked down the fairway to their balls. It was already rainy and cloudy back in Suncadia nearly every day, and the chance to play in warm and sunny weather was alone worth the trip.

The three women in her pairing played fairly evenly through the first nine holes, but Lena and a woman from Ohio, Jane Dayne, pulled ahead by three strokes over the third player – an older woman from Alabama – by the time they reached their 12th tee box. Water on the right had caught the Southerner's drive on the No. 1 hole – where they started their back nine – and a duffed shot out of the heavy Bermuda rough had cost her another stroke on No. 2. Lena wondered if the heat of the day was bothering the older woman, but she couldn't tell from her demeanor. She was just as chipper after two bogies in a row as she had seemed when she parred the first nine holes.

Halfway through the round, it occurred to Lena that her choice of walking with a caddie gave her a certain cache amongst the contestants, but it also meant that she was unlikely to make friends the way the women who shared a cart would. On the other hand, there was no irritating small talk to distract her, and she could bounce her club choices off of Kim, even if he didn't make the final decision. She and Kim discussed her target for each shot before she slipped into her pre-shot routine.

Walking up to the green on the last hole of the day, Lena was happy. She was coming in with a chance to two-putt for a two-over-par 74, likely good enough to make the cut if she didn't totally blow the second round. She glanced over and Kim was grinning. He caught her eye and she reached over and slugged his arm in solidarity.

"We did okay today, caddie," she said. "Thanks."

"You did the work, dear," he said. "Nice game."

The women finished up and gave each other a warm hug. Lena pulled off her visor and shook her hair to dry off the sweat that had collected under it. She and Kim took their time walking up to the clubhouse to drop off her clubs, wending their way around small groups of competitors who stood in the shade and discussed their rounds.

Dropping off the clubs, they stopped for a glass of water at the water dispenser and walked toward the big scoreboard erected next to the clubhouse. As they approached, Lena stopped short. A tall and dark-haired man with broad shoulders stood in front of the scoring desk. From the rear, he looked just like Kurt.

Lena ducked behind Kim, who looked confused at her sudden disappearance. As the tall man turned around and walked past them, Lena flushed with relief and stepped back beside Kim. From the front, the tall stranger didn't look at all like her ex-husband, and he didn't even glance her way. But her heart was pounding, and she realized the power Kurt still held over her – the power to inflict anger and fear. For a minute, she stood, hearing nothing and seeing nothing, her thoughts swirling.

"Are you okay?" Kim bent his tall torso around to study her face, and her vision came back into focus.

"Yeah, just a dizzy moment. Probably menopause," she lied. She breathed deeply and slowly and wiped the sweat from her forehead with the back of her hand.

She hadn't thought about Kurt for a long time and hadn't dreamed about him in months. He'd receded into the dark past as if he were dead, and she'd successfully moved on – a new city, a new job, and now golf and new friends. But, confronted with his doppelganger – at least from the back – he leapt back to life, as if he was standing right next to her instead of Kim.

Kim put his hand on her back protectively and steered her toward the chairs under the patio of the clubhouse. She didn't protest. Any other time, she would have waved away his concern.

"So what happened back there?" Kim asked. Other women were gathering their clubs and heading to the driving range for post-round effort at fixing whatever swing problem they'd encountered on the course, but she was ready for a shower and a strong margarita.

Lena considered lying again. She could tell Kim that she was just tired and not used to the heat. But, looking at his open, sympathetic face, she decided to let him in on the dark history of her marriage. "I'll tell you about it when we get back to the hotel and get a drink in front of us."

THE AMATEURS AT THE SENIOR TOURNAMENT weren't young and lithe as the young women who dominated the LPGA tour these days, but they were still athletic, strong and by-and-large no-nonsense kinds of middle-aged women.

It surprised Lena that the LPGA women – the ones on the top of the best professional women's golf tour in the world – could slam their drives more than 250 yards every time and still so many of them threw a flirty girly wave when they walked by fans along the course. So, it pleased her that this group of mature and tough women displayed none of that silliness. It wasn't all business, as some of them cheered each other's good chips and long putts. But they truly acted like grown-ups. Compared with some of the ill-mannered, club-throwing, verbally abusive men she'd played with over the past few years on public golf courses, these women seemed like the true professionals they'd decided not to become in sticking to their amateur status.

Their games were astoundingly mature as well. They didn't top their fairway woods the way Lena did only a year ago, and most of her friends still did. They landed their chips where they intended to, and second shots out of the sand were as common as holes in one. But it was clear that these things required concentration, and the women approached their games with a focus and stoicism that seemed almost cheerless at times.

The seriousness that came to her as a surprise and a relief on the first day started to wear on her by the second round. It made golf feel like work.

The second day of the tournament had turned hot and humid early, and Lena felt discouraged by the possibility of long days ahead of them. This tournament had been her goal for the past 16 months, but now she wondered why. She longed for a funny, obscenity-filled, recreational round with her friends on Prospector – her favorite course in the world, despite its flaws.

Was this fun? The constant pressure to perfect every shot was exhausting. Golf had always been recreational – even in the tournaments back at Suncadia – and not a matter of life or death. Now that she was hovering on the cut-off line for the final match play rounds, every shot and every swing required focus.

On the other hand, she found that the pressure was working, even if it didn't seem fun; she'd had no miss-hits between tee and green. But the nerves did affect her putting. If she had been putting as well as usual, and, in fact, as well as she was striking the ball, she would have been well in the front of the pack on the second day of stroke play, not just hoping to make the cut.

And while she hadn't expected to strike up a bunch of lifelong friendships at the tournament, she was disheartened at her own insularity. She had acquiesced and showed up for the social hour at the hotel after the second round. As with the opening dinner, the women had quickly huddled in groups of well-established friends. She retreated after only 15 minutes of a solitary glass of wine, and went to dinner at an Italian restaurant down the street with Kim and Terry.

"Great game today," Kim raised his Scotch for a toast after they'd ordered and the waiter placed their round of drinks in front of them. "Congratulations on making the cut." Lena lifted her Diet Coke and met his glass; she had decided to limit her alcohol intake to one drink per evening during the tournament, as much to preserve hydration as to reduce the possibility of a hangover.

"Yeah, but I'm afraid that I'm likely to be playing a pretty high seed in match play," Lena mused. "I just can't seem to putt. And putting has always been my strongest suit."

"Putting probably cost you five strokes today," Kim agreed. "But you are driving really, really well."

"Funny, but I've always loved an audience on the tee box," Lena admitted. "It seems to help me concentrate on form."

"I would never be like that," Terry giggled. "My motto is: 'The first tee is the worst tee' I just made that up. It rhymes. Did you notice?" Terry had started drinking right after the day's play ended, and had managed to make a half-dozen friends at the bar before they pulled her away to join them for dinner. In a way, her silliness was a relief after the intensity of the day.

"Thanks for that, Terry. I'll try not to think that way tomorrow when I tee off," she chided her friend. She turned to Kim. "How much farther do you think I can go?"

"There were about 30 players between you and the cut line," Kim predicted. "So, I think you are wrong about your seed. Your opponent will probably have a similar seed, if that counts for anything. I think you can do it, but tomorrow, let's spend less time on the range warming up and a bit more on the putting green and work on your breathing," he suggested.

Lena nodded, and looked at Kim. He met her eyes, and she didn't turn away. He had turned out to be a very good caddie and friend. She'd never expected their friendship would have become so important to her back when they first started playing golf together. And she appreciated the way it had turned back to platonic without any long, difficult discussion. Now she wondered if she had given him the chance he deserved at a romantic relationship.

"What are you thinking?" Kim asked, his blue eyes not leaving hers.

"Just what a great guy you are," she said. "Thanks so much for doing this. I don't know how I can ever repay you."

"There is no balance sheet," he said, nudging her with his elbow, seeming a little embarrassed at her sincerity. "And Terry's here for you, too."

"Yeah, what am I? Chopped liver?" her friend whined.

"No, thanks to you too. You're just not lugging my bag around in this awful humidity," Lena said. "But, no really. Thanks. It's so nice to have someone in the gallery who's there just for me."

13 TOURNAMENT

When Lena was a senior in college, she had moved out of the dorms and shared a small house off campus with three wild women. They partied so many nights of every week and smoked so much pot it was a wonder that she ever graduated. But the best part of their living arrangement was that her roommates knew so many guys.

In her first three years at school, she lived in the dorm, studied at the library, worked in the cafeteria, took a once-a-week job filing in the admissions office and slept. There were plenty of men in her classes, but except for the occasional group project, she didn't find much opportunity to meet any of them. Finally, in her last year, she decided to load up on student loans, drop her campus jobs and have some fun. She figured it was her last chance to be a kid before she graduated, started work and chipped away at her debt.

And what fun it had been! In the first three months, she slept with six different men, the first six sexual relationships of her life, and all of whom she earlier would have considered too handsome for her. She got a prescription for birth control pills at the student health service, which she'd only visited once in her first three years, and that had been for an ear infection.

By Christmas, she got a little pickier about her romantic partners. If they weren't going to be picky enough to reject her, then she could start to differentiate between the easy, good-looking hunks and the guys with something going on between the ears as well as between their legs. And, by February, she had narrowed her choices down to Pete.

Pete wasn't the most handsome of the men who frequented their parties at the messy, off-campus house. But he was witty and smart. He worked at the campus dairy farm, which kept him in great shape. He was more muscled than any of the handsome guys who went to the gym every day that she'd slept with in the past semester. But more than all of that, what attracted her to him was – amidst all of that partying – his seriousness.

Like Lena, he'd grown up on a farm outside of a small town, and to him, this education was a chance to get out of that life and explore the rest of the world. She respected that. He was there for a reason that went beyond pot, parties and easy sex, although he wasn't above enjoying them. Most of the other guys might have been there for the education, too, but they were not about to admit it or act like it. There was a kind of one-upsmanship played amongst them – who could discount their education the most; they actually wanted people to believe they were still children, there at college just for the temporary highs and to get away from the parents for four years. Many of them had rich families – Creighton being a pricy, private institution. For them, success was assured – if nowhere else, back at daddy's law firm or dental practice.

When she graduated and took a job at the local newspaper, Lena and Pete stayed together – they even considered moving in together at one point. But Lena didn't want to stick around for long. While they had a lot in common, she didn't want to be that person – that person who was a lot like Pete – forever. She wanted to travel and be a foreign correspondent, live a bohemian life for a change, try on some different cultures and gather fodder for the novels she planned to write at the end of her career. So she turned him down when he asked her to move into his little house not far from the campus. And she turned him down when he asked her to marry him.

Pete hung around for a while, working at a law firm as a paralegal, and they continued to date and sleep together on occasion. They both worked hard, but over time, they invested less and less in the relationship, although Lena pulled away the most.

After a couple of years, Pete applied for law school in Chicago, and when he was accepted, he left. Lena kept working, and eventually faced the reality that moving up to the Denver Post was probably as far away from Kansas as she was ever going to get in journalism since she had no well-placed family or college connections to speed up a transfer to the New York Times or the Wall Street Journal. Her dreams of being a foreign correspondent died quite some time before she met Kurt.

In a way, Kim reminded her of Pete. He was kind and supportive. He was serious about life. He accepted and even seemed to like monogamy. So far, Kim hadn't asked her to move in with him or get married. But, if she let her imagination dwell on the subject, she could see them setting up housekeeping together. But, she also knew that as soon as she got bored with him, and as soon as she wanted another change in her life, she would move on. She wouldn't make the same mistake this time that she had made with Kurt – accepting a mediocre relationship. Eventually, Kim wouldn't be right anymore and she'd leave him the same way she did Pete. And the way she abandoned Pete still nagged at her with guilt – even some 25 years later.

After that first round in Georgia and the shock at seeing Kurt's doppelganger, she and Kim had met at the bar in the hotel and waited for Terry to meet them for dinner. It gave Lena a chance to tell Kim an abbreviated version of Kurt's story. He took it calmly, almost as if it weren't very surprising.

"I'm glad you told me," was his response after she'd finished the story with her divorce and the move to Seattle. But his eyes were sympathetic as he reached an arm around her shoulders and gave her a gentle squeeze. "But don't let that past be a part of who you are now, especially this week," he said.

ALIENATION MAY BE the most common experience for all humans. But then, why did Lena always feel like she was the only one wandering this world alone?

Even with Kim and Terry in tow, Lena realized she was very alone at the tournament. First, they'd made a mistake by moving to a cheap hotel near the course instead of staying at the designated hotel for the whole week, where all of the other women gathered after their rounds for drinks and for dinner in the Key-West themed bar. It had made sense at the time she booked the room – less than half the rate of the Renaissance, and yet closer to the golf course.

She heard some of the threesomes across the fairways the first two days of stroke play, chattering and congratulating each other on good shots or good escapes. But the two women in her group were stoic. They played as if they had a bubble around them, and they didn't want anyone to puncture that delicate surface with a stray, unnecessary word. The woman from Ohio even complained to the rules official on the fifth green in the second round because one of the volunteer marshals on the fairway had the audacity to say, "Nice drive," when she pulled up to her ball. How dare he shatter her concentration! And, neither of them appreciated her jokes and increasing silliness as the second round progressed.

As she warmed up on the putting green under Kim's watchful eye before her first match-play round, Lena tried to emulate the concentration she was witnessing around her. Maybe she'd gotten by with her casual attitude so far, but in match play, she was more likely to get intimidated by her opponent's focus than her opponent was by her giggles.

Lena and Kim gave themselves plenty of time to get to the tee box for her match, and arrived in time to see the two-some ahead of hers tee off. Both women hit beautiful drives, down the middle and long. Watching such consistently strong players could have been intimidating, but Lena was starting to believe their smooth, efficient strokes were rubbing off on her.

Lena's opponent for the day was Linda, a three-time mid-amateur champion from Texas. She smiled pleasantly, if not warmly, as they shook hands on the tee box. With the No. 32 seed to Linda's No. 33, Lena was introduced by the USGA official first.

"Welcome to the 9:50 tee time at the USGA Senior Women's Amateur tournament," the grey-haired official read from her clipboard to the six people within earshot – Terry, Lena, Kim, Linda, Linda's husband and caddie Joe, and the USGA official who would accompany them in the round. "Today is the first day of match play, and this match is between Lena Bettencourt of Cle Elum, Washington, and Linda Canton of Longview, Texas. Ms. Bettencourt has honors. Ladies, show each other what ball you are playing."

Kim handed Lena a bright new Pro-V1, and she held it out for Linda to see while glancing at Linda's TaylorMade Penta. Then, she walked up to the tee markers, set her ball on a tee, went through her pre-shot routine and lined up to the ball. Without hesitation, she swung smoothly and fully, sending the ball far down the left side of the fairway. A decent start.

Other than the USGA official, Terry was the only audience that Lena and Linda were going to have that day, and Terry clapped a respectful golf clap. Lena smiled at her standing on the cart path, and moved out of the way for Linda's drive.

The round went quickly, as the twosome ahead of them kept pace and didn't take extra time to find lost balls or debate a rule. Lena played steadily and solidly, getting on the green in regulation on the first 14 holes, and three-putting only once. And even though she led at that point by three holes, Lena thought Linda may be the better player. She sure seemed to have the shots. On the short par-four fifth hole, Linda had hit her drive into the left rough. With low-hanging branches and a long-shallow bunker between her and the green, her chances of getting on the green in two seemed limited. She couldn't deliver a high lob over the bunker for a soft landing on the slippery putting surface without hitting the branches. Neither could she hit a low stinger under the tree without either plugging the ball in the lip of the bunker or firing it over the green, well past the hole. But after a few lazy practice swings, Linda hit a soft, low sand wedge that carried the perfect distance over the bunker and under the tree, landing it precisely on the slim fringe of rough between the sand and the green. The ball skidded softly and rolled up to a foot from the hole.

"My god," Lena turned to Kim, watching beside her. "Is there a shot that she doesn't have?"

"I haven't seen one," said Kim. "How do you think she's won all of those tournaments?"

But then, Linda started hitting sand traps instead of the middle of the fairway on the back nine, and before she knew it, Lena was 3-up with four holes to play. Desperately, Linda tried to hit the green on her second shot of the long par-5 15th hole, put the ball in a nasty tangle of bushes where no one could find it. She had to replay the shot, and trying even harder to make the green, she put her second attempt in a deep greenside bunker on the right. After it took her two shots to get out, she conceded the hole and the match. Lena's ball was sitting only three feet from the pin after her safe lay-up and her easy, risk-averse approach shot onto the elevated green.

A sweet, efficient volunteer helped Lena load her clubs onto a cart, and gave her a ride back to the clubhouse to store her clubs. Kim waved off an offer from another volunteer for a ride, and walked in. As she waited for Kim to get back, she walked over to the big scoreboard that had been erected for the tournament. She gave Linda a quick conciliatory hug and Linda introduced her to a couple of other players she'd met in previous tournaments.

But Lena couldn't help staring over their shoulders at the scoreboard where her day's scores, hole-by-hole, were being read off and posted in neat calligraphy by a USGA volunteer and an official. Suddenly, it seemed surreal. Here, 18 months since losing her job, she was, playing at a level that she'd never even dreamed of, surviving the first three days of the most intense competition a woman golfer her age could take on.

By the time Kim arrived at her side to see her victory posted, she was ready for a nap and a quiet dinner with her friends.

On the second day of match play, the 32 survivors of the first matches started early in the morning, and Lena's opponent seemed oddly out of sorts. She was the eighth-seeded player, and Lena had braced herself for a tough match and the probability of a loss and an early flight home. But, as a fellow rookie, Beth seemed unprepared for the physical endurance required for a sixth day of golf – counting the two practice rounds – in a row. She hit bunker after bunker. Her drives sliced farther and farther right as she tried to make up for her physical exhaustion with a faster, harder swing. The match ended after only the 13th hole, with Lena up seven with five holes left.

Lena started to feel Beth's pain after lunch, as she lined up for her first tee shot of the second match of the day. It was the first time she had to play two rounds in one day in competition, and she wasn't excited about the possibility. She was tired. She didn't confess it to Kim, but she was ambivalent about winning the match; it would have made her just as happy to be getting on a plane and heading home as teeing up the next day for another round.

Diane, her afternoon opponent, outdrove her on every hole, but Lena didn't make any unrecoverable errors, managing either to get to the green in regulation, or chipping close to the hole for pars on 10 of the first 11 holes. Diane's long drives set her up for short-iron approaches on most holes, but she struggled with her putter, and didn't record a birdie all day. After 18 holes, they were even. It seemed cruel to have to go back to the first tee and start over for the sudden-death extra holes, but as she and Kim trudged down the hill from the 18th green to the first tee box, Lena decided she'd worked too hard that day to accept a loss.

She watched Diane launch another long drive down the first fairway. Lena turned to Kim and standing on tip-toes, whispered defiantly in his ear. "I'm going to end this now."

She knew she could drive 280 yards. She didn't usually try to do it, because the faster swing speed increased the chance of a slice or a duck hook, but it was time to stop being intimidated by Diane's length.

Taking in a deep breath, and relaxing her shoulders, Lena said out loud to herself, "Grip it and rip it." She swung hard, concentrating on a complete turn and strong finish. The ball launched as if shot out of cannon, and her Pro-V1 landed about even with Diane's shot, and rolled another 30 yards. Finally, advantage Lena.

"I don't ever want to see you do that again," Kim said to her as they walked back to the clubhouse after she won the hole and the match. "Stay within your own game," he scolded her. "This turned out okay, but I think it was foolish."

Lena simply smiled an exhausted agreement and nodded. She couldn't wait to get to the hotel, order pizza delivery and go to bed.

THE THIRD DAY OF MATCH PLAY dawned bright and sunny again.

"Doesn't it ever rain here?" she asked Terry as she looked out of the window at the parking lot of the Best Western and started to get dressed for her seventh day of golf in Georgia. Terry had graciously agreed to do laundry for the three of them the night before, as they all had run out of clean underwear and Lena was out of good golf shirts. Tacitly, the chore was an acknowledgement that none of them had expected she was going to get to the round of eight.

The holes and the opponents all started to blur undifferentiated in her mind as she plugged along through the day's two matches. She felt uninspired, but oddly calm and methodical in her play. After nearly 500 shots over the previous six days, her swing started to feel as automatic as driving a car. She made more mistakes than she had in stroke play or the first three matches, but her opponents made even more. Feeling a bit like a zombie going through the motions at the tee box and on the greens, she survived her rounds, and qualified for the championship round.

At the end of the day, she emerged from a long semi-somnambulant daydream on the course to face a small crowd of golf journalists, USGA officials and volunteers. They were obviously as surprised as she was to find her headed for the final match the next day. Never had a rookie with no previous collegiate, professional or USGA amateur wins made it to the final round.

"Did you have any hopes of getting this far?" the official USGA blogger asked her as a Golf Channel cameraman moved his video camera uncomfortably close to her face. Now, she understood why LPGA player Christie Kerr got testy at times in similar interview situations.

"I had no idea where I would end up," she tried to answer honestly. "I really don't believe it yet."

"What's your strategy for tomorrow?" asked the Golf Channel reporter standing next to his cameraman.

"I have no idea," she shook her head. "I will just try to hit good shots, keep it in the fairway, avoid the bunkers and never three-putt." She realized it wasn't clever, but she was too tired to try to come up with anything better. "I really need to go rest, if you guys don't mind," she said, reaching for Kim's arm and making her escape. "Maybe a glass of wine to celebrate," she suggested to Kim.

14 AWARDS

When Lena was in the fifth grade, a teacher recommended her to represent her elementary school in a county speech competition.

Skinny and practically friendless, thanks to her family's home far out in the country, she was shy on the playground and in line for lunch at school. But she was strangely calm around older people and in front of an audience, something her teacher saw in the way she answered questions in class and spoke confidently to the other mothers who occasionally visited the classroom.

Lena memorized the speech that she was assigned for the competition easily. She practiced in front of her mother every night for two weeks before the Saturday morning competition. Her mother listened patiently, but absent-mindedly, giving her no significant feedback other than "that was nice" at the end of each rendition.

On the day of the competition in the high school in the nearby town that served as the county seat, she and her mother sat and listened to a dozen other fifth-graders deliver the same speech over and over. They all stood confidently in very nice, stylish outfits and delivered the words and sentences with dramatic flair, apparently having been coached on expression and carriage. She realized she hadn't thought of anything except saying the words in the right order. She certainly hadn't considered how her simple, out-of-style skirt and blouse would look.

"Magdalena Bettencourt." Lena cringed at hearing her full name called. She was thankful that none of her classmates were there, as they certainly would have giggled at it. She rose from the folding chair in the audience, smoothed her damp cotton skirt behind her legs, and walked a bit shakily to the front of the room. She turned around and looked at the three judges sitting at a folding table in the front, waiting for the nod to begin.

"Although the history of the region was well known to…," Lena started speaking, and then gasped. Having heard all of the other children recite the full speech, she had started in the middle, not the beginning, of the prescribed text. Her face flushed and tears gathered in her eyes. She swallowed hard, not daring to look at her mother. She blinked a heavy load of tears down her cheeks and turned to the judges.

"Can I start over?" she asked.

Sympathetically, the judges all nodded and said "sure" in unison.

Speaking through a steady flow of hot tears, Lena started over and recited the speech without even hearing the words coming out of her mouth. When she was finished, she nodded at the judges, whispered a quick thank you and headed back to her seat next to her mother.

Lena's mother rose to meet her daughter, and hustled her to the back of the room and out of the door. "Let's get out of here" were her only words. They retrieved their coats from the coat rack by the big front doors of the schoolhouse, and rode home silently. Lena didn't tell anyone at school what had happened. Her teacher was a little disappointed with the "fine," which was the only response Lena offered to her question about how the competition went.

A week later, a fat envelope arrived in the mail from the state political group that had sponsored the competition, and inside was a red ribbon and a letter congratulating Lena on her second-place finish in the speech competition. Lena opened it and dumbfounded, showed it to her mother.

"They must have felt sorry for you," was all her mother said before turning back to the soup she was cooking on the stove.

WALKING UP TO THE 17TH TEE BOX in the final match of the USGA Senior Women's Amateur, Lena found it odd to suddenly remember that big fifth-grade mistake and the sting of tears that day in front of a room full of strangers in a strange school. And, with the memory came the suspicion that once again, she had prevailed in a competition because someone felt sorry for her. Someone noticed how poorly she fit in. They had noticed her lack of experience in this kind of event. They could see all the way through to her unsophisticated rural roots, and decided she could have this chance, not because she deserved it, but because she was a little pitiful.

As she and Jan negotiated their way around each other on the 17th tee, Lena shook her head to clear the bizarre thought. There was no truth to it. No one cared who she was or where she came from or what she wore or how many friends she had. All that had mattered was how she had played over the past five days.

The match was tied 5 to 5, but Jan had lost the last two holes, and Lena had honors on the tee again. She had momentum on her side, but she knew she had to win at least one of the last two holes and at least tie the other to win the tournament. Old insecurities from her childhood had no place in this competition. She smiled and snorted a little laugh meant only for herself and stepped up to the tee box.

Her hand was shaking as she placed the ball on the tee. She stepped back and closed her eyes. She was back in the present. She swung her driver a couple of times with her eyes closed, trying to relax. Then she took a deep breath and took up her usual pre-shot routine.

For the first time in six matches, she pulled her drive into the deep left rough. It didn't appear to be in big trouble, but it was short and given the thick rough, it was likely that Lena wouldn't be able to reach the green on her second shot. Disgusted with herself, she hit the ground with her driver and turned around to walk to the back of the tee box with Kim.

"Where the fuck did that come from?" she whispered angrily at him while Jan lined up for her drive.

"I don't know. You're tired," Kim said, not too helpfully. He cleaned off the driver with a towel and dropped it into the bag. He had no way of knowing the weird historical detour her mind had just taken. "Take a deep breath. Think about the next shot, not the last shot."

Jan strode up to the tee box a bit stiffly and swung jerkily. Her shot wasn't much better than Lena's. It was longer, but sliced off into a patch of small pine trees. Lena hated to benefit from anyone else's misfortune, but she couldn't help but feel relieved. Neither of them was likely to make the green in regulation. And, if the hole came down to good putting, she had an advantage there.

As Jan stepped back from her drive, Kim and Lena started down the left side of the fairway. Terry was standing next to where her ball landed, keeping the ball in sight so they wouldn't lose it.

"Thanks, friend," Lena nodded to back her friend away. She was relieved that no tree branches or bunkers blocked her access back to the fairway.

"I think five wood," she said, holding out her hand to Kim for her club.

"I think you should maybe just punch it back in the fairway with your seven iron," he said. "This rough is pretty juicy. You can make up the stroke on the green."

"I can make it to the green in reg with my five wood, though," she argued. "The ball is sitting up nicely."

Kim sighed. Lena ignored the sigh and grabbed the five wood out of her bag. This was not the time for him to begin second-guessing her. She needed to hit this shot with confidence.

"Concentrate!" Lena scolded herself, and then swung too fast. The ball squirted only 50 yards forward into the fairway. That one bad shot could end up costing her the match, Lena realized. And the tournament. She bent over for a long minute, and swore at herself.

Before Lena straightened up, Jan hit her ball crisply out of the rough with an iron, and it landed a decent distance up the fairway, leaving only a 50-yard chip to the pin.

"That was a good shot," said Kim absent-mindedly. He turned to Lena. "Sorry, but it was."

Lena had to laugh. She looked at her friend and saw the innocence and decency that made him who he was. How could she be mad at him if he stated the simple truth. She'd made a bad call, her opponent made a good one, and she had no one to blame but herself.

She stopped at her ball, quickly hit a good five-wood shot a little beyond Jan's ball, and tossed her club back to Kim in relief. As they started walking up the fairway, two carts sped by with USGA officials yelling into their squawking radios. They headed directly for Jan and her caddie in front of them.

"What the hell?" Lena asked.

"It looks like a rules question," Kim said, hiking the bag onto his shoulder. They walked quickly down the fairway toward the group gathering at Jan's ball. One of the officials met them before they reached Jan.

"What's happening?" Lena asked.

"It appears that the caddie accidentally kicked Jan's ball in the rough with her foot, and they didn't replace it," the official said, holding her walkie-talkie at the ready to hear the latest discussion among officials. "Jan probably didn't see it happen."

"Oh, shit," said Kim. "How could that happen?"

"I don't know, but the spotter saw it and tried to warn her, but didn't get there in time," the official said, turning down the static on her radio.

"This would mean loss of hole, right?" Lena asked, trying not to sound like that would make her happy. Obviously, if Jan did lose the hole, Lena would only have to halve the final hole to win the match and the tournament. It was hard to keep the optimism out of her voice. "That would be horrid," she added quickly, sounding as grave as possible.

Then, she did feel bad. This would be no way to win the tournament, she realized. She wanted the match to be a true test of the better player on this, the eighth round of a long tournament, not the result of a rules violation by a caddie that her opponent barely knew. Not because someone, somewhere felt sorry for her.

Kim and Lena stayed back, letting the group at Jan's ball deliberate. Jan looked as if she'd been hit with a five iron. She bent over and put her hands on her knees as her caddie and an official argued. But it was clear that the decision had been made and now it was just a question of getting Jan to accept it, and move on to the 18th.

By the time they gathered at the 18th tee box, Jan had recovered enough from her misfortune to smile weakly at Lena. "Good luck," she said. "It's been a great match, whatever happens."

Lena was surprised by Jan's magnanimity. She wasn't sure she would be so nice, given similar circumstances.

"Thanks," Lena said, nodding in agreement. "I'm really sorry about what happened back there. That's no way to lose a hole." She stopped short of saying "lose a tournament," as it was still possible, if Jan won this hole, they would go into sudden death and Jan would win the tournament. It wasn't over yet.

But, then it started to look like it was. Lena lined up and drove one of her best shots of the tournament long and down the middle of the fairway.

"Great drive," Jan said, passing her on the way to the tee. She took a couple of practice swings that looked half-hearted. And, then she lined up to the ball and duffed her shot about 100 yards down the left side. It was one of the worst shots that Lena had seen from any of the competitors all week. Both women were tired, but it was clear that the wheels had come off Jan's game.

Jan took two more shots to get within chipping distance of the green, while Lena hit a solid approach to make it in two. She had a 16-foot putt for birdie, and Jan was going to be on the green in four. Still she hoped Jan would at least chip before conceding the hole.

With all of the fortitude of a wounded bull nearing the ugly end of a bullfight, Jan stepped up and chipped onto the green, close to the hole.

Lena waited for Kim to pull the flag and stand aside for her lag putt. Despite what had happened in the second round of the tournament, Lena knew that putting was still her strength. It was what convinced her that she could get to this tournament in the first place, and it was why she was standing on the 18th green in the final match with a chance to win.

But, now, thinking of the possibility of winning the whole thing, Lena saw the world swimming around her. Nothing was standing still. Her ball seemed to wobble at her feet. Her putter swayed unsteadily in her hands. She bent over and imagined the "plunk" of the ball falling into the hole. With confidence gained from those hours of practice before the tournament, she pulled the putter back and swung it solidly through the ball.

She knew not to turn her head and watch the ball roll to the hole. She stayed still, keeping her eyes on the green ball illusion that remained after the white ball moved out of sight. Then she heard it. The ball spun around inside the cup and rattled to a stop.

Lena looked up to be sure she wasn't imagining things. The ball was nowhere in sight. And Kim was beaming at her. Terry was running toward the green. The world hadn't stopped spinning around yet, but the tournament was over.

THE AWARDS CEREMONY was brief. The crowd facing the podium in front of the scoreboard had swelled to 50 or 60, hanging around to watch her receive the trophy. Lena didn't know if she had expected a crowd or not – she'd never thought that far ahead, and certainly didn't think she'd be the one receiving the championship trophy and kudos at the end. The USGA Women's Tournament Chairperson presented the semifinalists and Jan with their medals. Jan gave a brief thank you speech, ending on a thank-you to God, whom she seemed to believe had favored her over 130 others in helping her become the runner-up.

Then Lena was presented with the big silver cup, and – as a gift from the Gleason community and furniture company – a nice wooden stand to place it on over the next year that she got to keep it in her possession.

She stepped up to the podium and hesitated. She hadn't known she'd be asked to speak, and she didn't know what people generally said in times like this. Taking a cue from Jan, she thanked Kim, Terry and her friends back in Suncadia for supporting her quest. She thanked the volunteers and the USGA staff for their help. She thanked her competitors for being friendly. Finally, she admitted that she was as incredulous as anyone else at her victory, and then, with nothing left to say, raised the trophy and said a final "Thanks to all of you."

The town fathers and the golf course pro each received a plaque from the tournament committee, and the ceremony was over. She was immediately surrounded by the golf media. The Golf Channel reporter was there again, as well as the USGA blogger and a local newspaper reporter and photographer. She granted the photographers' requests for holding the cup, kneeling behind the cup, and shaking the tournament chairperson's hand. She tried to focus on the questions from reporters, but finally, she became irritated with their unrelenting theme – how unexpected her victory was. She knew she could get burned for it, but she cut them off with a plea of exhaustion.

And then it was over.

Sixteen months of practice, focus and competition had ended with a 15-minute ceremony, and then suddenly, she stood in the parking lot next to the clubhouse with Kim and Terry. She thought she was happy, but more than that, she wanted to sleep. And to go home to Suncadia and sleep some more. She wanted to play a friendly round of golf that meant nothing with Kim, Carly, Ryne and Brandt. Well, maybe not Ryne. And then she wanted to do nothing for a couple of weeks. Just chill.

First, though, Kim and Terry convinced her they had to go out for a big steak dinner to celebrate. They went back to the hotel, took a shower and a nap, and drove the 15 miles to the nearest Ruth's Chris steakhouse. She'd always loved the steaks there – charred to a salty crisp on the outside, moist and red inside.

"To our hero," Terry said, raising her wine glass across the table to Lena once they'd ordered a round of filet mignons. "May this just be the start of great things in golf for you."

"Thanks, Terry," Lena rose her glass to clink edges with Terry and Kim. "But, I think this is the end of great things in golf for me. I really am looking forward to not having any pressure, and just playing for fun for the rest of my life."

She took a sip of wine and added, "Actually, I think I'm looking forward to not playing golf at all for a while."

She noticed that Kim took a sip from his glass, set it down, shifted in his chair next to her and busied himself, rearranging his silverware. He didn't look up at her when she tried to meet his eyes. Lena looked from Terry, who fidgeted as if she had big news, and then back to Kim, who was staring at his silverware. They seemed to be conspiring in some pact that Kim wasn't so sure about, but Terry couldn't wait to tell Lena.

"We think you should bring the trophy home and play in the Pacific Northwest Women's Amateur later this month!" Terry blurted out, as if she'd just solved the mysteries of the universe.

"It'll be so much fun. All of our friends can come and watch. It's by Walla Walla, and I've already talked with Brandt and Carly and they can't wait to see you ..."

Lena stopped her. As if the look on her face – that of pure horror – didn't convey her thoughts, she slapped her hand on the table, startling not only Terry and Kim but also the women seated at the table next to them.

. "Sorry," Lena nodded to the startled women on her right. They stiffened and returned to their soup, not trying to shield their disgust at her poor table manners.

"Terry! Are you out of your fucking mind?" she hissed low enough to keep the stiff women next to them from hearing. "I just got through the most stressful 16 months I've ever experienced in my life, and you don't want it to end?"

"It hasn't been that stressful," Terry asserted. "You have enjoyed an awful lot of this time since you quit your job." She paused, and Lena realized that Terry had a good reason to convince herself of that; she'd been the one who talked Lena into this 16-month ordeal in the first place.

Lena stared at her wine glass and thought about that. She looked over at Kim, who was now sheepishly looking at her out of the corner of his eye, while keeping his head bent toward the perfectly aligned forks and knives in front of him.

"Alright, it wasn't that stressful. It certainly wasn't any worse than work. Or living through Kurt's trial," Lena admitted. "But enough is enough. I really want to move on and figure out what I'm going to do next.."

LENA DIDN'T KNOW HOW IT HAPPENED, but by the end of the next week, she had lost the argument, and shortly after she returned to Suncadia, she downloaded the application for the PNGA tournament and sent it in online. She had two weeks to prepare, which shouldn't be hard, given that she had been preparing for the past 16 months. But the tournament would not just be for old broads like herself. It was open to any woman who had either won a slot in a qualifying tournament or had won another USGA event, as she just had. That meant there would be college players in the group, and young women trying to work their way into the Symetra Tour or LPGA. The competition would be much, much tougher.

Part of what encouraged her to try another tournament was the nice recognition she got from her win. GolfWeek ran her picture and short blurb about her victory in its "Bunkers" section. Her mug shot and a brief description of her victory ran in Sports Illustrated's "Faces in the Crowd." The Seattle Times interviewed her by phone and sent a photographer up to Suncadia for a photo. Even seeing her picture and accompanying article in the Northern Kittitas County Tribune in Cle Elum was fun.

And, when she had first returned back to her condo in Suncadia from Georgia, she opened her door to find a huge bouquet of red roses waiting in the foyer. They were from Ryne. *You did it! Congratulations!* the card read. Lena surmised that he had dictated that message over the phone to the FTD florist, who had added the exclamation points on his or her own. Ryne was undoubtedly averse to using the most overused punctuation mark in the English language – as were most journalists.

At least the florist hadn't put the congratulations in quotation marks.

15 WALLA WALLA

Back in Suncadia, Lena tried to return to her pre-Georgia practice schedule, but her heart wasn't in it. She wasn't surprised. She had agreed to go to the PNGA tournament, but she'd already proven all she wanted to prove to herself by winning the Senior Amateur. She knew she was a good golfer – one of the top amateurs at her age. She stood up to competitive pressure for six days in row. She had the perseverance to practice hard and long enough to make up for not starting to play the game until she was in her forties. She really didn't care to prove anything more, and she found herself bored with the driving range, and with the hours of putting she would need if she was going to handle the slick greens she'd face in Walla Walla.

And oddly, now that her single-minded focus was wavering, she started to worry about her next move. She tried to postpone questions about her next job, her next goals, but they kept intruding, particularly at night. And, worse, her nightmares about Kurt had returned.

She'd had the dreams nearly every night when she was still in Denver, waiting for Kurt's trial. Usually, she and Kurt were in their old house together and the tension was stifling. She wanted to leave him. She knew she should leave him, but she couldn't summon up the energy to move. She seemed stuck on the couch, or stuck at the dining room table, staring across at his scowling face, unable to get up and walk, let alone pack up and leave for good.

By the time she, Kim and Terry arrived in Walla Walla for the PNGA tournament, she was 10 pounds heavier for the lack of practice and play, and her muscles and joints were stiff to the point of painful from her irregular workouts. Her back was threatening to spasm again, and she feared that swinging in the cool air would only make it worse.

She attended the pre-tournament cocktail hour with Kim, meeting a handful of women who had played in the qualifying tournament at Tumble Creek with her. She distractedly accepted their congratulations on her win, knowing that those who didn't know her very well were likely to think she was aloof. She was disheartened by her own lack of interest; of all of the talents she'd cultivated over the past 50 years, social skills weren't highest among them. But, she was flattered at being introduced at the dinner as the reigning women's senior amateur champion to a nice, polite applause.

As she and Kim left the ballroom, she decided to do her best to rally and get up the next morning ready to play her best.

THE WALLA WALLA PUBLIC COURSE where the tournament was held was surprisingly beautiful, given the barren, treeless Palouse region where it lay. The first tee box faced east at long, low loess hills that rose and fell for a hundred miles toward a faded purple ridge on the horizon. Brilliant green fairways contrasted sharply with the bright gold wheat fields that surrounded them like green ribbons on honey-blonde hair.

Through her first round, she and Kim took turns pointing out pairs of coyotes frolicking in the wheat stubble or chasing a jackrabbit across the fairway. The sun shone brightly in a cloudless sky, but a light breeze kept the dry air from getting too warm. Without a single tree or bush in sight, Lena imagined how difficult the course would play with a normal, prevailing westerly wind blowing down from the Cascades 200 miles away, nothing but a few windmills in the way to slow it down. The Palouse was created over the millennia by a persistent wind that blew silt into mounds and ridges, and Lena felt lucky to have a rare calm day to play the sparkling golf course.

Although the temperature rose above the dew point quickly once the sun rose, a frost delay postponed the start of play, and she and Kim milled around the putting green and driving range with the other players for more than an hour. Taking some practice swings with her driver, Lena tried to focus on her tempo but she couldn't concentrate. The long, uninterrupted vistas lulled her into staring off into the distance, daydreaming about nothing in particular.

Finally, when she was called to take her stance on the first tee, Lena felt uncomfortable. Her skort felt tight and too short. She felt the extra pounds she carried to the tournament around her waist as she rotated her shoulders on her drive. The first shot wasn't a disaster, but it didn't look like the drive of a national amateur champion, either.

From the beginning of the round, Lena felt she had let Brandt and Carly down. They'd travelled five hours across the state to watch her play, and she wasn't playing her best. By the middle of the round, she had started to warm to the competition and scored a couple of birdies, but it was too late. She turned in a middle-of-the-pack, mediocre score in the clubhouse and joined her friends for a beer on the unadorned clubhouse patio afterwards.

The conversation drifted around her, and once again she found herself staring off into the depth of the hills, unable to sustain a train of thought. I'm tired, she finally decided. It was a mistake to allow her friends to talk her into this tournament when what she wanted to do more than anything was hang up the clubs for a while, read a few good novels and sleep 12 hours a day.

Returning an hour later to the downtown hotel with her entourage, Lena begged off another cocktail, promised to meet the gang for dinner and plodded up the stairs to the room she was sharing with Terry. She unbuttoned the tight waistband of her golf skort and let it fall to the ground. She turned on the shower and finished undressing while she waited for the water to heat up, and then stepped into the spray. She stood with her eyes closed and let the water pour over her head and down the length of her arms and legs. She wasn't sure she had the energy to shave her legs, but she had to wash her hair. She smeared on some smelly hotel-issue shampoo and gave herself a good scalp massage.

The phone on the bathroom wall shocked her out of her reverie, and Lena was relieved to hear Terry had returned to the room in time to answer it. She closed her eyes again and took a deep breath. She hoped the call was Tom. Before she left for Walla Walla, Terry and Tom had a couple of tentative conversations over the phone about trying to get back together, and Lena hoped they would figure it out.

But, Terry stuck her head through the door into the foggy bathroom and startled Lena again.

"I think you should take this call," she said in a very serious voice.

"I've got shampoo in my hair. I'll call them back."

"It's about Kurt. He's out."

Lena felt the blood leave her head, and she quickly sat down in the shower, pulling the faucet off on her way to the floor. Her heart pounded. She heard Terry ask for a phone number in the next room and hang up the phone before she quietly opened the door to the steamy bathroom again.

"Do you need some help?" she asked, concern in her voice.

"No. I'll be fine. Just give me a minute."

"Here's a towel," Terry helpfully pulled a towel down from the rack and draped it over the top of the glass shower so Lena could reach it.

Once she had stood back up, rinsed her hair, dried off and tied a towel turban-style around her head, Lena stopped at the sink and stared at her face in the mirror. The last time she had to face with the mistake she'd made with Kurt was when she signed the divorce papers in her attorney's office in Denver. Since then, she had felt she had turned her back on that part of her life, and except for the nightmares where she was trapped in her old bungalow with him and the brief encounter with his doppelganger in Georgia, she had not had to waste any psychic or physical energy avoiding him.

She leaned up against the bathroom counter and studied her face in the mirror, lifting a finger to trace the fine lines radiating diagonally down her cheeks from the outer corners of her eyes. When she left Kurt and her life in Denver 10 years ago, she didn't have them. She pulled at a tuft of hair at her widow's peak. A little grey showed at the roots; it hadn't been there when she left Denver either.

If it had exhausted her to work through Kurt's trial and her divorce 10 years ago, she wondered, how could she possibly find the energy to face him and the threat he posed now? She was tired and unfocused. She wasn't sure who she was. She wasn't an insecure, lonely kid on the plains of Nebraska anymore. She wasn't a journalist. She had tried to become extraordinary, but had ended up as normal as a person can be: a middle-aged lackey at one of the most mediocre companies in America. Then, she tried to become an exceptional golfer, but couldn't hold onto that either.

And what's next? Fate, she thought is not a story about the future, it's the story of your past. No matter what hip, liberal, urban center she moved to, she'd always be a farm girl from Nebraska. No escaping it. No matter what job she took next, what enterprise she found that could use her, the invitation from Davos wasn't coming; the Science Times wasn't going to call her for an interview. No matter how hard she practiced and dedicated herself, she was never going to be a great golfer or earn a living at it. She'd started too late; she probably never had enough talent in the first place. And, no matter how far she ran from Kurt, she'd never get away from the mistake she'd made marrying him.

It was time to stop carrying that "poor rural Nebraska girl" chip on her shoulder; it wasn't doing her any good. And it was also time to stop hoping for something good to happen to her. Hope is not a strategy. She'd heard that a million times, yet she was awkwardly aware that she was still hoping.

She shook her head at herself and stepped back from the mirror. Suddenly she shivered violently, losing the towel she'd wrapped around her torso, and what it revealed wasn't any more comforting than what she'd just examined in her head. She reached down to pick up the towel, and tossed it in the corner. She pulled the hotel-issue bathrobe off the hook behind the door and slipped it on. Taking a deep breath and straightening her shoulders, she walked out of the hot, steamy bathroom into the cool bedroom and picked up the phone.

KURT HAD BEEN released in a court-ordered prison de-crowding, and Jan, the detective who worked on the murder case, had called to warn her. No, Jan assured her, there was no reason to believe that Kurt knew where she was. Jan had figured it out because she had followed Lena's golf adventure, and as a golfer herself, she'd considered playing in the PNGA tournament in Walla Walla – at least seriously enough to notice who had registered for the event.

There was no reason to believe that Kurt was interested in finding her, Jan assured Lena. He'd said nothing to anyone, as far as she knew, about his intentions. But still, she wanted to let Lena know he was free. "Call me if you need anything. Anything at all," she said as they hung up.

Even if he did know where she was, Lena said to Terry once she got off the phone, she figured that Kurt couldn't afford a plane ticket to Walla Walla from Denver. He would have to drive or hitch a ride. The soonest he could get there would be the middle of the next day.

They decided to keep their plans for dinner with Kim, Carly and Brandt so that they could tell them what had happened, and then get a good night's sleep. The news meant they had to bring Brandt up to speed with a Readers' Digest version of the story of Kurt, but he didn't seem shocked or worried. Lena suspected that Carly had already told him about it. Unanimously, they agreed there was no reason for Lena to quit the tournament. She couldn't stop living the rest of her life just because Kurt was no longer behind bars.

All of that confidence should have helped Lena sleep, but it didn't. She tossed fitfully and glanced at the clock every 15 minutes between midnight and six. Finally, relieved to be done with trying to sleep, she rose and showered and slipped out of the room to let Terry sleep in. She was surprised to run into Kim in the hotel dining room; they hadn't made plans to share breakfast. But she was glad for the company. Given the pressure Lena was already under, Carly and Brandt had decided the night before that they would let her play in peace, and they left early to drive into Idaho to play Circling Raven.

From the first tee box onward through the day, Lena felt anxious. She reasoned with herself – and with Kim, when he was within earshot – that there was no reason to believe that Kurt knew where she was or would find her. He obviously cared nothing for her, and her decision to leave him fit nicely into his view of how things were supposed to turn out. On the other hand, thanks to a decent divorce attorney, she had managed get to keep her house and all of the money she'd saved in her 401(k), so he could be pissed that she had left him with nothing but the measly $2,000 he'd saved in 10 years for his own retirement. But, for all of his faults, Kurt had never appeared to crave material things.

Lena tried to find motivation in the idea that she had something special now to play for – to show herself, her friends and maybe even Kurt that he held no power over her. Even his potential appearance wouldn't affect her play. She had successfully erased that big mistake from her life, gaining more control over her future.

But, by the third hole, it was clear that she was kidding herself. She wasn't going to play any better. To her credit, she told herself, she didn't play any worse, either. She ended the day in the middle of the pack – far below where an amateur champ should be. But by the time the five-hour round was over, she was so exhausted from anxiety and lack of sleep that she was glad to simply be standing.

She, Kim and Terry skipped the event's closing ceremony, and phoned Carly and Brandt to schedule an early dinner at a downtown bistro that advertised 100 different wines by the glass. Lena wondered how many she could get through before passing out, which didn't seem to be an unreasonable way to end the weekend.

But first, she wanted a shower and a quick nap.

TERRY LED THE WAY INTO THEIR ROOM, chatting energetically in a way that indicated she had not lost any sleep the night before thinking about Kurt. As Lena closed the door behind them, Terry screeched. It was so unexpected and extraordinary that Lena paused, puzzled before following her into their room.

And there he was. Kurt was sitting on the bed, his stocking feet propped up on a pillow and a beer in his hand, watching TV.

"How the hell did you get in?" Terry screamed at him, far more rationally than anything Lena, in her shock, could have done. She had wrestled with the mental image of him showing up all night long, but she still wasn't prepared.

Before she had gathered her wits enough to say anything, Kurt jumped up and pushed between them and the door and threw the deadbolt. The TV was still blaring an NFL game, which added to Lena's confusion. Roughly, Kurt pushed the two women farther into the room, and Lena turned around to face him.

Kurt was dressed sloppily in a tee shirt that looked a couple of days from a wash, the short sleeves revealing a complicated web of tattoos on his arms. He didn't have them the last time she saw him. Seven years of working out in the gym at Canon City had obviously been good for him, though. He was much broader and his arms were thicker than she remembered. His bushy hair was gone, replaced by a close buzz-cut and a big tattoo on the side of his head. It was obvious that neither woman could defend herself against him alone, and even together, they were no match for the tall, bulky man standing behind them.

Lena said nothing. She was afraid that anything she might say would trigger a violent response, and apparently Terry felt the same. The two women held his eyes as he sneered, looking from one mute woman to the other. Finally, he nodded at Lena and gesturing toward Terry, he chuckled. "You a lesbian now?"

"No, we're ..." Terry started to answer, but Lena slapped her with her elbow. There was no benefit in answering. They needed to get out of there. To do that, they needed to focus.

Again, Kurt pushed the women backwards, and Lena tripped over his boots, catching herself by grabbing Terry's arm.

"What do you want?" she blurted out, losing some composure as she stumbled.

"Well, maybe you could demonstrate a little bit of your lesbian sex for me," he said with a nasty grin, pointing toward the bed.

"No, I mean, what do you think you're accomplishing by being here? How do you think this ends?"

Kurt looked at her with amusement, a wry smile spreading over his face. "Do you think I care?" he asked calmly. Then, suddenly, he lost the cool composure he'd maintained since they walked in. His face reddened, and he shouted. "Do you think I care how this ends? What the fuck do I care how this ends? Ends? What makes you think it ends?"

Kurt was sputtering, spit flying far enough to reach Lena's chest.

"Maybe there is no end, sweetie," he sneered. "Maybe I'm here in your precious little life forever."

Reaching back, he angrily pulled the pillows off the chair behind him and threw them at Lena and Terry.

"Fuck you! Fuck you!" he shouted. He'd obviously crossed over some boundary between mean composure and uncontrollable anger. His moved jerkily and unsteadily.

He reached out to slap Lena, but she ducked, avoiding the swipe and steadying herself by putting her hand down on the bed behind them. His sudden anger didn't surprise her. It wasn't out of character. But she had no idea how to respond. Back when they were married, she would get up and walk out of the room – sometimes out of the house – when he started ranting like this. It didn't resolve anything, but it allowed her to end the confrontation.

But, she didn't have the option of leaving now. He was blocking the path to the door.

Kurt threw himself against them, pushing them down on the bed. Lena's suddenly feared for Terry more than herself. She deserved this; she'd married Kurt. She married him without caring whether she loved him or not. She married him for the convenience of it all. Because it seemed easy. Because it didn't involve any commitment.

But Terry hadn't done anything to Kurt. She didn't deserve any of this. Lena glanced over and saw the fear on her friend's face. She gripped the bedspread in both hands as if hanging above an abyss. Lena felt her heart pounding, and she suddenly felt sick.

"I have to throw up," she said, and with the element of surprise, slipped past Kurt and ran into the bathroom. She bent over the toilet seat, not having time to lock the door behind her before the vomit erupted from her stomach and splashed into the toilet bowl.

Behind her, she heard Terry shriek, but she couldn't move away from the toilet. The sour vomit erupted again and again, and her eyes, full of tears, lost focus. Then, just as she was starting to feel the physical relief of the end of her vomiting spell, she felt Kurt directly behind her.

Sweating and crying, Lena tilted her wracked frame toward the sink and cupped some water in her hand to rinse her mouth. She reached for a towel to wipe her face.

"Ouch," she heard Terry complain behind her, and turned to see Terry grimacing at the clutch that Kurt had on her friend's arm. Kurt's eyes were hard on Lena, and he pushed Terry out the bathroom onto the floor of the bedroom, slamming and locking the bathroom door behind her.

Lena clutched the towel to her face. Kurt had to know that this could only end badly for him; there was nothing to keep Terry from running for help. She heard the door to the hallway open and imagined Terry running down the two flights of stairs to the lobby.

Kurt didn't seem to care. Lena realized that he didn't expect this drama to end up any better than anything else in his life ever had. His entire life was much less about winning than about forcing the bad result that met his expectations.

Kurt grabbed the towel from her face and pushed her against the bathroom cabinet, smacking the small of her back against the porcelain. He grabbed her hair and twisted her around, pushing her down over the sink. Pulling her hair with one hand, he yanked at her skort, forcing it down to her knees.

Lena didn't even think to yell for help. All of her energy was focused on fighting back, but she couldn't escape his grasp. He tore her panties down and pushed her head down into the sink. Holding her with one hand, he fought with his own zipper. She squirmed against his hold, and he slugged her between the shoulder blades.

"What, you don't like it from men anymore now that you're a lesbo?" he bent over and whispered hoarsely in her ear. He tightened the grip on her hair, and pushed her head farther into the sink. With one arm around her stomach, he pulled her up against his crotch and slammed his hips against hers.

Crash! The hallway door to the hotel room swung open against the entry wall, and heavy footsteps rushed into the bedroom. Yet Kurt still struggled to push between her legs.

"Where?!" a man yelled.

"In there!" Terry screamed behind the closed bathroom door. Unphased by the interruption, Kurt again pushed Lena hard against the edge of the sink.

Three hard kicks rammed against the bathroom door and it crashed open. Someone ripped Kurt's arms back, but he scratched Lena violently, trying to hold on. Finally, Kurt fell away, nearly pulling her back with him. She grabbed the sink to regain her balance as she heard him slammed to the floor. Lena slumped to her knees, and for the second time in her life, she found herself on the floor, staring at a huge pair of black boots.

16 AUTUMN

Looking back on it later, Lena realized the 16 months she spent working on her golf game, avoiding the work world, avoiding politics and engagement with virtually any institution other than golf, was a kind of self-imposed purgatory. Unlike traditional purgatory, though, from which one emerges into heaven and the only question is how long the wait will be, hers was less certain. She didn't know where she would end up at the end of her suspension in time.

For 16 months, the rent checks for her condo in Seattle were automatically deposited, the mortgage and utilities for her condo at Suncadia were handled by automatic online bill pay, and money automatically moved each week from her savings account into her checking account so she could pay for greens fees, golf lessons, gas and food and get an occasional massage.

She didn't look up old friends, volunteer, send birthday cards or buy Christmas presents. It was a relief to float above the messiness of real life. She thought this is what it must be like being rich and untouchable. Worry if you want to or if you're neurotic, but you really don't have to.

So, when her amateur golf career was over, she struggled with re-entry. Suddenly, there seemed so much to manage: finding work, planning dinner with friends, re-engaging with one community or another, financial planning.

The worst part of her return to real life was the realization that unless Kurt was executed for his crimes, which was impossible, she'd never really be free of him. His return to jail pending trial for assault – unfortunately now closer in proximity to her than before –would keep him at bay only until the trial began in a few months. And even assuming he would be convicted and sentenced to prison again, she knew the justice system would not be able to keep him behind bars for the rest of his life.

"Some mistakes you are bound to live with forever," she mused to Terry.

"It doesn't seem fair," Terry responded. "You did nothing, and yet you have to be afraid of him the rest of your life."

The two girlfriends sat up late into the night in Walla Walla after Kurt was taken away. Lena and Terry had spent an hour with a young, but kind detective who came to the scene to gather evidence, as Kim, Carly and Brandt sat on the bed and listened. The policemen at the scene had offered to take her to a hospital, but she insisted that she'd only suffered bruises and a sore neck. Kim begged Lena and Terry to let him stay in the room all night, but Lena insisted he leave. She was in no danger from anyone else, and Kurt was clearly not escaping the grasp of the tough swat team crew that had manhandled him to the floor of the bathroom.

Once alone, the two women pulled on their nightgowns, opened a mini-bar bottle of wine and sat against the headboard of the bed with their knees tucked up to their chests and every blanket they could find tucked around them. At first, they said little, just shaking their heads occasionally in relief and in remembering the violence of Kurt's intrusion. Then, moved by the deep bond forged between them in surviving Kurt's attack, Lena began sharing with Terry things she hadn't told anyone in decades. First, she described the recurring nightmares she had about Kurt. And then she moved on.

Another story was this: her mother was pregnant with a son when she died in that car crash 36 years ago. He would have been Lena's brother. Lena didn't know about him until several years later when her aunt had too much to drink on a visit to Denver, and couldn't hold the juicy secret inside anymore. There was obviously no reason to tell Lena at that point, but for her aunt, it was like an itch that needed scratching; she needed to tell someone. Lena, who was already in her mid-twenties at the time, didn't know whether having a brother 16 years younger would have made her feel less alone. In fact, she thought that it probably would not have made a difference. But, she thought, it might have given her a little practice at investing some emotion in someone else's life.

Now, Lena theorized to her friend, at 50, trying to learn to do that with any man would be like trying to learn a foreign language as an adult: she'd never cleared a neural pathway for those kinds of feelings for other humans. She wondered if it was something she could ever learn to do.

"But you seem to have plenty of room to accommodate other people," Lena said, trying to turn the monologue into a dialogue with Terry. "I'm surprised, given you were nearly an orphan and an only child like me."

"But, I had two older brothers who were perfect because I only saw them long-distance," Terry countered. "I think that makes me intolerant of real men – the ones with faults and selfishness and their own agendas."

"Yes, men are a lot more acceptable in the theoretical," Lena agreed.

"With Tom, I just couldn't accept that he had any right to judge me. That bathroom thing, that was about a lot more than color. That was about my right to do what I want to do with every aspect of my life. And be totally accepted for every bit of it. My brothers never criticized a thing I did; I was a perfect little girl to them. What horrid training for marriage!"

The two fell into silence and drank their wine in big gulps. As her mind wandered through her past and considered what shaped her as an adult, Lena thought about Stripe. She described him to Terry.

Stripe was a funny name for her childhood dog because he had none. He was all yellow and all ears. His ears stood up like a German Shepherd's, except bigger. Otherwise, he looked no breed known to the AKC. He'd been abandoned by the side of the road by some city folks who didn't have any better answer for an animal they'd either tired of or who no longer fit their "lifestyle." He came with a thin webbed collar and a small heart-shaped tag that simply said "Stripe." He was a 50-pound mutt, probably as close to proto-dog as a creature could come in the era of careful breeding by dog fanciers and rampant euthanasia of so many mutts of the world.

He chased rodents in the woods while she walked with him. He wasn't tall, but he could jump over logs suspended four feet above the ground. He growled at mysterious noises at night, and stood between her and her father when things got ugly between them. When Lena went to bed at night, they spooned in her slender bed together, and in the morning, Stripe was curled up at the foot of her bed in a perfect donut.

Lena believed that after the earth was devoured by the sun, and the galaxies have reversed their outward movement and started to collapse back into the primordial black nugget that contained everything, that love between Stripe and her would still exist. It would be eternal.

After the news that her parents had died reached her via an inelegant policeman and a local social worker, her uncle came to hurry her along to pack her clothes and a box full of personal things so that she could move in with her friend Linda in town. He promised he would return the next day and bring Stripe to town. But, the next day, her uncle put the house on the market, and called to tell her that when he went back to clean the house out for sale, Stripe had run away. She tried for a month to sneak back to the farm to look for him, but she had no way to get there.

Her school teachers and Linda's mom, a single woman who'd had Linda when she was only 16 and had never married, chalked Lena's two-year depression up to her parents' death. Lena was the only one who knew that her pain was more about Stripe than her distant and unhappy parents. It was the intense sorrow that she expressed in an essay she wrote about Stripe that had won first place in a state-wide writing contest and garnered her a partial scholarship to attend pricey Creighton. Thirty-four years later, she still felt the sting of new tears in her eyes when she thought of Stripe.

ON A SUNDAY NIGHT, a week and a half after the tournament and a week after their return to Suncadia from Walla

Walla, Lena and Kim sat at the restaurant in the winery. Kim planned to go back to work the next morning, heading over the pass in time be at his desk in Redmond by 9. Lena would do something other than play golf. That was as far as she had progressed in her plans.

The attack had brought them closer. But, she didn't get that sense of a connection that would last into eternity like she'd had with Stripe. Or the sense of sexual excitement she'd had with Greg and Ryne.

Still, following her brutal attack in the bathroom in Walla Walla, Terry and Kim had been constant friends like no one had since Stripe. But there wasn't time for Terry to sit with Lena while catching up at the wine shop and trying to patch things up with Tom – a project that seemed to be going well – all at once. Finally, Lena convinced Terry that she should get her own life in order first, and Lena would let her know if she needed anything. Terry seemed relieved and had, since then, reported that she and Tom were doing much better.

Kim took a week of vacation after the PNGA to stay with her at Suncadia. He slept on the couch in her condo, shopped for groceries and cooked. He'd become protective in a way that bordered on cloying at first, but as Lena tried to move beyond the nightmares that haunted her for the next month, she was grateful for his attention and company. And his housekeeping.

Now she was looking forward to having the condo to herself and some time to sit and think without anyone worrying about her from across the room. She figured she'd miss Kim, but she couldn't really move forward and figure out what she would do next as long as she was leaning on someone else. Even if it was just for company.

But Kim was clearly struggling with the idea of leaving. On Sunday evening, he hadn't started packing. His suitcase was still at the bottom of the coat closet and his clothes were in the bottom drawer of her dresser. When she suggested they go to the winery for dinner, he hesitated. Why not dinner alone at her condo? Wouldn't that be a more comfortable way to wrap up the crazy month they'd had?

But Lena prevailed.

"Aha! Prime rib," she exclaimed as her entre arrived at the winery table. "That's what I wanted tonight," Lena snapped open her napkin and rearranged her silverware in preparation for her attack on the big slab of red meat on her plate. The winery was crowded for a Sunday night. Many of the revelers from the wedding party at the winery the night before had decided to stick around one more day, even though the weather had turned too nasty for golf. Lena was happy for the noisy, public scene. She didn't want this last meal of their week together to be intense and sappy.

"Is that why you wanted to come out tonight instead of eating in?" Kim asked, more quietly and calmly arranging his napkin on his lap and picking up his fork. "For prime rib?"

"Yup," she lied, slowly savoring the first, salty bite. "You know what? It has just occurred to me how I'm going to market myself to potential employers. I'm only going to apply to firms run by men and I'm going to put on the top of my resume: Eats red meat and plays golf." She waved her fork across in front of her as if tracing a big headline. "You think that will help?"

Kim apparently wasn't in the mood for silliness. He had picked up his fork, but didn't make a move to taste the pork tenderloin that lay propped up on a pile of mashed potatoes and bright green broccoli spears in front of him.

"Hmmm," he answered. He looked distracted, staring at a spot on the table between them.

Lena tried to set an example, diving into her food with relish. Still Kim picked at his plate and pouted. Lena kicked the table leg to jar him out of his trance. He jumped slightly and looked sheepish.

"Sorry, Lena."

"What's going on in that pea-brain of yours?" she teased him. "Day-dreaming of new code you're going back to writing tomorrow?"

But rather than lightening his mood, her teasing seemed to nudge him further into his dark thoughts.

Lena had hoped that the public setting would keep her from having to have a serious conversation about their future, but she knew that's where he was headed. She had felt it coming the past couple of days. Kim was pensive and had sulked as she gained interest in getting out of the condo and back into the world. He acted like he didn't want to share her.

What Kim had done for her over the past year – helping her get ready for the tournament, caddying her to victory, providing a sense of security after Kurt's attack – it was more than she could have expected from any friend, especially one who was still recovering from the loss of the love of his life. Certainly, it was more than she could expect from a friend who had no commitment from her for more of a relationship than the platonic, dispassionate one she wanted.

"I'd like to know if you'd consider re-starting our relationship," he said finally, putting down his fork and looking directly in her eyes. His blue-eyed stare made her weary, and she sat back in her chair.

Lena was surprised.

"We have a relationship. You're one of my best friends in the whole world. Tied with Terry for best, I'm thinking."

"You know that's not what I mean," he said, refusing to shift his eyes from hers.

"Kim, you know better than anyone that my commitments are always short term." Lena put down her fork to concentrate on making him see clearly what she felt.

He didn't answer. His eyes didn't blink.

"You saw that even my commitment to golf was short term," Lena continued, in part to try to end his intense stare. "Once I won that tournament, I had no desire to continue. My goals are always like that. One triumph at a time. I was never even committed to my career. Or my marriage for that matter."

"But it took a lot to win it. The senior tournament, I mean. That's commitment."

Lena looked at her plate. She'd eaten only half of the juicy rib meat, but now, she was losing interest. I'm not even committed enough to finish what is on my plate, she thought. How could I ever stick with a relationship?

She sighed.

"I'm not going to be able to give you the answer you want," she said, looking him in the eye. "I'm not going to be able to commit to a relationship with you. You are wonderful. You've literally saved me from crumbling into a heap of self-pity the past two weeks. I love you for it. But, I know I can't promise you any kind of a commitment as a partner."

"Is it bad sex?" he asked her point blank. No use beating around the bush. It made Lena laugh.

"No, it's not bad sex." Lack of passion, maybe, she admitted silently only to herself. But not bad sex. "Don't be silly. I don't know what it is. I just know I can't do it right now."

"You did get married once. Maybe now, given the right choice, you can stick with it."

The phrase "stick with it" stopped Lena cold. Stick with *what?* Or, stick with *whom?* Stick with an accomplice to murder? Did Kim think she should have "stuck with" Kurt?

Lena waited to let the flash of anger pass so that she focus on what Kim had meant to say. He probably meant: stick with a relationship – not stick with Kurt. But the implied criticism still stung. She took a deep breath and composed herself.

"I don't know if I can or can't 'stick with it,'" she finally started slowly. "I know you aren't suggesting that I should have stayed with Kurt. Of course, I committed myself in a way with Kurt, by marrying him. But I never considered what I wanted or what he wanted from it. I just went along with the ceremony, with the tradition. Next time, if there is one, I hope I'll be a lot wiser."

"Why did you get married to him?" Kim asked, warming to the story. Lena was relieved the discussion had veered away from the subject of their relationship.

"I have no idea." She paused. "No, that's too easy. I didn't really think it mattered, I guess. He wanted to get married, I didn't care much. He seemed like a fun guy to be around at the time, and didn't seem to require much in terms of an emotional commitment from me. I guess it was convenient. And, I guess it's just like me to do that: I've always kind of wandered around people and not really committed to them."

Kim waited. But, now Lena was immersed in her own thoughts. She'd realized some time ago that her parents were happier on the farm, by themselves, away from other people. They were more comfortable in isolation than they would have been in town, even if their commutes would have been safer, and they and their daughter would have been part of a more densely woven fabric of humanity. On top of that, they never really seemed committed to her. She had come along unexpectedly, and they put up with her, but whatever she was going to get out of life, she'd have to figure it out by herself. They left her alone. And by the time she was old enough to go to school, alone was her most comfortable state.

"A lot of families are like that," she mumbled to herself. "No excuse." Kim let the unintelligible mumble drift past him, unexplored.

Lena took a long swallow of her wine and pushed her stiff, cooling mashed potatoes into a pyramid.

"I think that I ended up with Kurt for two reasons – one his and one mine," she finally spoke to Kim directly. "On his part because he needed someone who would leave him and fulfill his awful expectations, and I needed someone who wouldn't expect much of anything but neglect from me. I could slide by looking 'normal' – that is, married – without him asking for much."

Then something occurred to her. Hadn't she been asking Ryne for a commitment the last time they saw each other? It wasn't a time commitment, sure. But it was a commitment to exclusivity. Maybe that indicated some progress. She smiled at the thought.

Kim continued to watch her intently. Seeing her smile, he put his fork down and reached across the table for her hand. She acquiesced and let him hold her fingers across the table, even though it made her slightly queasy.

"Okay," he said, as if he'd suddenly given up the fight to either understand her or to talk her into a new relationship with him. Lena realized he had been ready for her rejection all along – expected it even – but he had needed to make sure he hadn't given up without trying. His default mode was to acquiesce, which was both his best and worst characteristic, Lena thought. It meant she never felt in competition with him, but on the other hand, it made him winning him over less exciting, less of a challenge.

"I get it," Kim said, as if reading her thoughts. "I'm not your guy. Or maybe there just isn't ever going to be one guy for you." He paused, as if suddenly recognizing his own compensation in that. "I guess I like the second option better than the first. I am not looking forward to seeing you with someone else."

"Ha!" Lena laughed, relieved. "I just about forgot! This was about you and not about me all along!"

She dropped Kim's hand and reached for the dessert menu abandoned on the table next to them, where four of the wedding party had finished and left. "Let's order dessert before I'm too tired to enjoy it," she said. Then, changing the subject again, "What's waiting at work for you tomorrow?"

Kim went back to work the next morning, and Lena was happy to have her space back. She spent a couple of days with Terry, helping her clean the wine shop and print new winter menus featuring small plates of comfort food – meat loaf, pot roast and pork loin with sage dressing. Then, with nothing left to put off the inevitable, she started work on a new resume and prepared to return to her condo in the city and the next chapter in her life.

LENA SAT IN ONE OF THE MILLION or so Starbucks that provided Seattleites their daily drug of choice and listened to the four intense young men at the table finish their friendly chatter, assuming that sooner or later, they'd get around to the business of interviewing her. They obviously knew each other well – better than she thought they would, given that the only connection between them that she had been aware of was that they were all angel investors in a company that Sarah, her old friend from TrueWeb, had started up six months earlier.

Sarah's bad luck had finally run its course, and a year after her divorce from her second husband, she inherited a small fortune from her grandmother and fled TrueWeb with a wealth of experience in marketing internet companies. A few of her favorite software engineers and website designers went with her. She wanted to start a website that sold clothing that women couldn't find anywhere else, but Rue La La, My Habit and a hundred other websites had already captured the hard-to-find, hard-to-afford online market for women's clothing. It was Lena's golf success that turned Sarah's attention to women's golf clothing, and the possibility of providing online access to the variety and pricing that was hard to find anywhere but in a couple of retail shops in Palm Springs and Phoenix.

What attracted her investors was not so much the inventory or the market, but the excellent algorithm that Sarah and her small team of software engineers had been creating. It matched a woman's physical characteristics with the styles and brands of clothing that would look best on her and suggested those styles and brands to the customer. And to prove the adroitness of the algorithm's choices, all of the avatars wearing the clothing the algorithm chose were pictured wearing the same size as the woman doing the shopping – only they looked a little thinner and a little taller. She called her company The Perfect Tee.

Sarah didn't want to run the day-to-day operations of her brainchild, though. She wanted to spend more time with her children, maybe take them to Europe for a couple of years to get the overseas experience and cosmopolitan education she'd never had a chance to get herself. So, she'd asked Lena to come in as CEO. But the investors had to give Lena the final thumbs up or thumbs down.

It was Lena's introduction to the world of venture capital – a world where they might as well say to each other: "there are only 100 rich white men in America and we all know each other."

The weirdness of their nearly familial banter gave her some distance and helped put her at ease, and she found herself thinking she didn't like these guys. A couple of them had apparently attended the same Seattle prep school. Two others had "summered" in the Hamptons together as children of blue-blooded neighbors. Lena never used a season as a verb, and the more she listened, the less she cared about them. If they hired her to run Sarah's new company, she'd be very happy to get the job. But if they didn't, she wouldn't ever have to listen to them again.

"What's your vision?" was the bizarrely open-ended question finally thrown at Lena once the privileged white guys finished catching up on their fascinating lives.

"Twenty-forty," Lena responded, deadpan. They stared at her blankly, the joke too mundane and far below them to even register. Not a good start, Lena thought to herself. Despite their bourgeois prattle, she really did want this job. It was good pay, kept her involved in golf, probably would mean she could attend a bunch of great tournaments she'd never been to before, and Sarah had assured her that once things were up and going, she could probably run things from Suncadia, Palm Springs or wherever she chose.

"The business core competencies are solid," she started again. "We've got the data base of brands and styles, the agreements to work in advance with the manufacturers on next year's styles, and the engineers are improving the algorithm every day. But, what I think we need now to stay ahead is to increase the interactive and social aspects of the site."

The four white guys all sipped their coffee and nodded. Given every company's interest in greater interactivity and greater social networking, she hadn't given them much. They expected her to continue.

"Let me give you an example," she obliged them. "Right now, we dress models – standard, cartoon avatars – in the clothing the women are shopping for. But why not upload a photo of the real shoppers, enhance their look just a tad to make them feel better, and then put the clothing on their own personalized avatars?"

"Lands' End has been doing that for years," chimed in the oldest of the four investors. "How does that move the ball forward?"

"Kind of," Lena nodded, softening her voice so she didn't sound like she was correcting him. "What Lands' End does is create an avatar with the same color of hair and skin and show her wearing the same size clothing that the shopper claims she wears.

"What we can do is actually make the avatar look like the shopper – only a little better, of course – and rather than create a body that is the ideal shape for a particular size, we can actually create a body that mimics the shopper's real dimensions."

"Sure," said the youngest investor, as if he'd already thought of it.

Lena smiled at him and continued.

"It may not be this way for men, but for women, a size 10 in one brand is not a size 10 in another. And while the waistband in a size 10 Nike skort may fit a particular woman, her hips may not be exactly a Nike 10. They don't know this until they get the skort at home, and have to return it."

Lena looked around the table. It wasn't selling.

"Every time you have to handle a return, you lose 30% of the profit of that sale," said Lena, "even if you ask the customer to pay for the return shipping, which isn't cool these days, by the way. You have to change that too.

"The more you can make sure the shopper is going to get the right fit and the more she is certain that the style will look good on her, the fewer the returns you'll have and the more repeat buyers you'll have and the higher the profits will be."

While venture capitalists all loved the words "interactive" and "social" – especially when convincing their preppy peers they were on the leading edge of trends – they loved the word "profit" more. Now the older investor leaned in toward her.

"Tell me more," he said.

"Well, once we know a woman's actual measurements – at least those she'll share with us – we can steer her away from buying styles that don't really work on her body. But the other cool thing is this: women love to shop together, right? Do you know why?"

The men looked at her blankly. Then, slowly they all shook their heads, finally admitting there was something they didn't know a lot about.

"Well I do. It's so they can get a second opinion in the dressing room. Now, once we dress their look-alike avatar in their skort or shirt of choice, she can post it on Facebook and ask her friends what they think. That's the social part."

"That's it?" asked Ken.

"Oh, I have a lot more ideas, all based on the core competencies of the company, but I don't really want to share them all with you today. I'd like to be sure you're serious about me first, and then we can sit and brainstorm together."

The men liked that. They wanted to believe that as VCs, they would be integral to the success of the company – not just by providing capital, but by lending their brilliance to the venture. Lena had just assured them she'd make them part of her team.

They spent another two hours talking about her management style, marketing, finance and other skills that she'd need to have at the job. And then one of them asked her about her golf game and the senior women's tournament she'd won. Luckily, they were all golfers, so she could give them a blow-by-blow story of the final match without losing them. She wrapped up the interview by pulling out her smartphone and showing them pictures of her trophy on the mantle of her condo in Suncadia. They were finally impressed.

OCTOBER HAD TURNED INTO NOVEMBER, and the frost had done its job, ending the golf season and turning the aspens bright yellow. Now that she had moved back into her apartment in Seattle and started her job at The Perfect Tee, Lena was back to a routine of driving up to Suncadia on Saturday mornings and back to the city on Sunday evenings. Kim came up the Sunday before Thanksgiving for a mid-day dinner at Portals and a little football on TV on the couch of Lena's condo. After the Seahawks lost, they got bored with the other games, and set out for the steep, short hike down to the river behind the lodge.

Kim had brought along his mutt, Cali, for the day. She had a white stripe down the front of her nose and floppy border-collie ears. Her body was that of a lab, and her black hair was wiry and coarse. She was an excellent mutt, Lena thought.

Rising up out of the valley on their return from the river, they turned to walk down along the abandoned driving range and then back up a couple of the long golf holes toward the club house before returning to the Lodge. The wide fairways between the trees were green and lush from the fall rains. It seemed as if the golf course was relaxing, realizing it would endure no more whacks with brutal irons for at least five months.

It was a sunny, calm afternoon – the kind of day that would be perfect for golf, if it were only 20 degrees warmer. Elk had returned to the resort from their summer sojourn higher in the mountains, and their scat peppered the fairways and greens. The air smelled like the rotting leaves that cushioned the ground under their feet.

They walked behind Cali as she darted back and forth, chasing little black squirrels and chipmunks up trees. The rodents let her get close before darting up, apparently knowing that Cali could never catch them. As they turned up the final path through the tall firs between the golf course and the Lodge, Kim suddenly reached for Lena's hand and pulled her around to face him. Cali took advantage of the pause in their forward progress and chased off into the woods after a rabbit.

"How about one last night of friendly sex before we go back to Seattle?" Kim asked bluntly.

Lena stared into his kind face. She had begun to believe that he was okay with their future as platonic friends. Apparently she was wrong. But she had to admire his directness, his honesty. And, it seemed like such a nice way to end a pleasant day.

"Do you really want that? Just one last night? Or are you hoping to win me over with some new, irresistible moves?"

"They didn't work before, did they?" he laughed. He smiled and kissed her lightly on the lips.

Lena pulled away and looked into his eyes, darkening in the waning light. He seemed so harmless. And kissing was so nice.

"Oh, what the hell. One night."

Lena took his hand to lead the way back to her condo.

"Oh, by the way," she turned to wait for Cali to catch up with them. "I'm going to get a dog at the pound next week. Do you think Cali will mind?"

THANKS

I ignored a lot of things that I should have been doing while I wrote Putt for Show, which means there are people who had to put up with my slovenly housekeeping (my husband), my inattention (my dog), my narcissism (my family and friends) and my procrastination (everyone). Thanks to my sister Renee Erickson for her unbelievable faith in me and her early suggestions on the novel, to Kristine Kurey and Janet Day for having the ability to judge but refraining from doing so, and to Diane Larson for being the best friend a girl could ever have over the past 54 years. Thanks to Darin Dickson for his cover design, only the latest in great graphics he's done for my projects over the years. Thanks to my golf buddies Ben, Shelly, Laura, Joe, Brice, Laurie, Liz, Walt, Jim, Caroline, Terry and Tom for being the interesting people they are, making writing easier.

As I was researching this story, I spent a week at the Hershey Country Club in Pennsylvania as a volunteer at the USGA Senior Women's Amateur Tournament. A special thanks to the pro staff there for giving me that opportunity.

Thanks, especially, to Ben for his patient editing and unstinting support through this process. And I can't forget to thank the game of golf for giving me a focus for my own mid-life crisis.

ABOUT THE AUTHOR

Marj Charlier lives at Suncadia on the eastern slope of the Cascades in Washington state with her husband and an aging mutt. She grew up in the Midwest and worked as a journalist for 20 years, including a dozen years at the Wall Street Journal, and in corporate finance for another 18 years. She took up golf at 50, and after 10 years at it, she still plays to a 18.

Putt for Show is her first novel. The sequel, Drive for Dough, will be published later in 2013.